A CALIFORNIA
CLOSING

A CALIFORNIA CLOSING

A NOVEL

Robert Wintner

YUCCA

This is a work of fiction. Names, characters, businesses, places, events, and incidents are either the products of the author's imagination or used in a fictitious manner. Any resemblance to actual persons, living or dead, or actual events is purely coincidental.

Yucca Publishing books may be purchased in bulk at special discounts for sales promotion, corporate gifts, fund-raising, or educational purposes. Special editions can also be created to specifications. For details, contact the Special Sales Department, Yucca Publishing, 307 West 36th Street, 11th Floor, New York, NY 10018 or yucca@skyhorsepublishing.com.

Yucca Publishing® is an imprint of Skyhorse Publishing, Inc.®, a Delaware corporation.

Visit our website at www.yuccapub.com.

10 9 8 7 6 5 4 3 2 1

Library of Congress Cataloging-in-Publication Data is available on file.

Cover design by Zoran Opalic of iNews Design
Cover photo: Fotalia/Simon Coste and Fotalia/kittiyaporn1027

Print ISBN: 978-1-63158-087-1
Ebook ISBN: 978-1-63158-094-9

Printed in the United States of America

For Tom Plouffe, a man of means

A View from the Top

Michael Mulroney is insolvent.

Insolvent—|in ˈsälvənt| adjective, unable to pay debts owed: *the company became insolvent.*

• relating to insolvency: *insolvent liquidation.*

noun: an insolvent person.

He puts a fine point on the difference between insolvency and having no money. Who deals in money anymore? Make that cash, long green, the pocket wad, and the short answer is nobody. Any day, anytime, he can pluck a C-note or three or eight from his wallet as if from thin air. It's plain to see he's got money and can get plenty more where that came from. So he's not broke.

Broke means no money, busted, elephant ears, no checkbook or credit cards, no influence or associates or friends of means— broke means no presence in the free-market flow. Broke was for people in the Depression. *Brother, can you spare a dime?* Soup lines and 5¢ apples are for broke people—people without resources, without hope. But a guy with assets and a clean shirt and notably pricey shoes and a watch that went a few grand more than your average tick tock, a guy with apparently hygienic inclinations— good teeth, fair skin, a haircut and a pleasant scent—a guy with a smile on his face because he knows what the world can do for him in return for all he's done; that guy is not broke.

Broke |brōk|: adjective [predic.] informal: having completely run out of money: many farmers went broke.

Insolvent, on the other hand, means still part of the game as defined by the modern, mixed free-enterprise system, in which cash might be king, but real moolah is reflected in numbers on paper or in electronic synapses measuring scads o' dough that can't simply vaporize but will accrue sooner or later to the viable players in that system, of whom Michael Mulroney is one. That is, persons participating in the modern system live free to buy more, to enjoy life to the maximum and pay later because the money will come. What else can it do? Cash is not king but merely the Archduke of Down Payment in the realm ruled by Credit—by which the world can be leveraged. Leverage is magic, making each little greenback worth many times more than its face value, making those little greenbacks do the heavy lifting on the front end, allowing the player to go long on value, on the back end, so to speak. Leverage is like atomic fission, allowing a little bitty bang to go *KABOOM!* So? If a guy is short on cash, so what? He'll get more, and he'll know what to do with it. It's only a matter of time, given his viability and track record.

Insolvency is merely a word describing a certain phase of that mixed free-enterprise system that every player will experience sooner or later. It may be a phase that not every player will experience, but it can happen to the best of them—maybe not to the extremely wealthy or cautious players, but the self-made guys who get in there and mix it up, who land a few and take a few on the chin and who fall down but get up and dust off and go again. It can happen to them, and so it does, as naturally as left-right-left. It may be a brief phase if the player still knows the moves. Or it can take him out, if he's old and infirm, in nature's inevitable way.

In any event, insolvency is a reversal segment, but it by no means disqualifies those players with continuing vim, vigor, and forward thinking, who remain networked and attuned to the common rhythm, integral and part of the scheme of things. Although slightly underwater, or, as the imagery goes, upside down, belly up, wrung out, pinched, in a jam or shitting through the eye of a needle, the insolvent, intact player is still confident in the ephemeral nature of fortune. Insolvency begins with *in*, just like inclusion, in the world, and incredible.

Michael Mulroney lives at One Summit Nest in a single-family dwelling, which should not be confused with a dwelling of similar profile in, say, Shanghai or Tokyo. The dwelling at One Summit Nest is shaped to accommodate a family and all its stuff, along with its visions and continuing needs. It's big, a rambler with ostentatious generosity, grandiosity, and luminosity on finish materials, volume, and redundant luxuries. He bought it right, on the way up for two point four mil and spent another point two on a new roof, no big deal. What, you want leaks? And the hot tub was a pittance, to ease his aching joints. He'll have to pay the pesky six points on the commission, and he owes two point two because he leveraged a ninety percent loan. He had the cash to pay for the house, but he also had golden opportunities on four new lots in prime locations right at point five each, which seemed serendipitous and convenient. Oh, the smart player sees the down cycle for what it has to offer, what would otherwise be an arm and two legs in a healthy economy. Beyond the incredible bargain, the acquisition budget of point five times four new lots included inventory, because a seasoned player knows the diff between a real budget and a fool's paradise, so things can only go uphill from here. Or would that be down-hill? Fuck it; you fill four lots with inventory for seventy-five cents on the dollar because economic indicators first leveled car prices at the dealer auctions and then eased to a slight but none-theless further decline. That made for a bargain if a player had the cash, and the player had the cash, in a classic example of that ironic phase of economic fluctuation: the rich get richer, and the poor do what they do best. Naysayers predicted that the slight decline would steepen to a descent. But what? Californians were going to stop driving?

Not. And few people in the world could be more snug in the catbird seat on a wild ride than Michael Big M OK Used Cars Mulroney. Pre-owned? Get the fuck outta here with that pre-owned bullshit. You want smoke up your skivvies? Get down the road to certified pre-owned. The fuck is that? They prove to you that it's used? Besides, used is the new new: BMW, Mercedes, Jag—who knows the diff between an '09 and a '16? You get your fucking image and save your fucking dough.

Michael Mulroney has depended since forever on swear words to make a point or deliver a punch line. He read somewhere that people who swear are most often telling the truth. He liked that and, factoring the correlation into his credibility quotient, increased his blue-language frequency. These days his language is nearly azure blue, though some find it exasperatingly blue. But those people don't truly comprehend the nature of truth or the need for some to strive for greater truth, like, say, a used car mag-nate. Michael Mulroney is renowned for honest deals, what he calls your honest motherfucker—but never in print or on the air. People want to sense decency, and they do. So why press the point? Why not leave the Mulroney paradox as another unnatural pattern in nature, kind of? That would be nature as defined by Mulroney's uncanny ability to serve the car buying needs of Californians—and a few Nevadans who come over for the fair dealing and honest language.

Yet, alas, a brief interlude intercedes, wherein the decline column goes from slight to steep, until inventory and overhead outweigh revenue. He's out on a limb with the house, and he can raise cash only as fast as the cars move out. Or he could sell the house, which could happen any day, but he's sure as hell not taking a loss on it. He fire sales a few cars as necessary because taking a loss on a car is all part of retail. The loss leader is old as onions, 19¢ a pound. It fills the store and keeps things going. It generates excitement—are you kidding? An '07 550 SL for $18k? That's the auction price—and it's cherry! And it gets them talking, especially the lucky fuck who bagged it. And talking leads to thinking, to pondering acquisition and residual benefits, including enhanced image and more fun.

But the specter arises: what if car-buying habits don't come back to where they were? Of course, they will; they have to because they always have and always will. What, you can imagine a world without more cars? It'll never happen. But what if car-buying habits don't come back in six months? Because that's the extent of the means to keep this show going. Maybe seven months in a pinch on some pledges. It makes for pressure, and nonstop pressure is tough—if you're a pedestrian pussy and not the greatest living closer west of the Fertile Crescent. As it is, a downturn brings out the best of the private reserve. Are you kidding? Californians not drive? Californians oblivious to brand?

Allison plops onto the sofa much as a small bird lights on a big limb, to chirp her little song. She announces good news, sincerely, in her pretty, petite way: she's moving to Hawaii and hopes that Michael will join in the fun. Mulroney laughs so abruptly he nearly grunts. What's she going to do, go alone?

I

It's Not like I Didn't Tell You

"We got one of two things going on here. Either they can't afford it, and there's nothing we can do about that but wish them all the best because living at the top of the hill isn't for everybody, and if they don't have the resources this year, well, maybe they'll be able to step up in the next few years. We'll be pulling for them.

"Or it's a lowball. A lowball isn't just a low offer, over and out. A proper lowball follows a setup, like they're doing right now. Yeah, they found another place for only a million nine ninety; it's a shitbox levitation act, cantilevered out the cliff face and hanging in thin air on four-by-fours. If it doesn't slide down the hill, it's still a dump. That's efficient. Isn't it? It has what they call 'bang for the buck' in your economy-minded market. It's a three-bed, two-bath Cracker Jack that'll suit six adults with teenage kids about as well as Victoria's Secret would do for a hippopotamus. You ever see a hippo take a shit? I have. They had one on TV a few nights ago. Underwater. Jesus . . . For a weekend beach retreat? Get the fuck outta here. What happens when the prunes and bran kick in? That'll make for some great beach weekends. They can drive up here to sunshine country and have a lovely fucking time. When the toilet clogs they can just cut a hole in the

7

floor. Why not? Shit rolls downhill, Marylyn! Haven't you heard? Let 'um buy it for chrissakes. They'll only boost the market."

"We shouldn't have to worry about them much longer. Nick promised they'll do something in the next two days."

"Worry? Fuck 'um. You tell Nick to tell his clients that the seller *knows* they got the cash. Or the borrowing power or whatever. We are well within their budget. They're shaking me down on a desperation check, to see if they might steal some money the old-fashioned way and really have a great weekend. I saw it coming. I sense this shit in my bones. I know this stuff. It comes out my pores. I feel it on my skin. They'll come in around two point two."

"That would be nice."

"Nice? What would be nice about it? It won't fly!"

"Once they put an offer on the table, people are usually willing to come up a little bit. I always think it's nice to get them emotionally involved."

"Emotionally involved? Give me a fucking break. I know these guys. I grew up with these guys. You want to talk emotional involvement? Line up a couple three strippers, outcall, with some decent liquor, and a bag of buds. Make it a playoff weekend and leave the wives at home. Now you're into touchy-feely country. Emotional involvement? Fuck. These guys need to come up a whole lot more than a little bit to get me emotionally involved."

"You sound emotional to me."

"Yeah, well, I got this pounding sensation in my asshole. Okay? So I get emotional. Call it self-preservation instinct. You want me to get lovey-dovey on a so-called deal? We need fair market value instead of what we got, which is zip. This . . . Is . . . A lowball. I could take it in the ass, but I think I won't, if that's

okay with you. That leaves me to counter, and the deal will die
if I do because we're starting too low. You know what happens.
With too much gap between the ask and the offer, the negotiation goes on too long. It breaks down to personalities clashing. It
gets personal and it goes past money and value, and people take
it personally. They get pissed off. Too much friction. The deal
dies. They need to come in closer to two point seven five, or we're
looking at a long slog across a frozen fucking tundra. I know this
game. The deal will die."

"Let's just see what happens."

"Yeah, right."

II

We Have an Offer

"Two point two. Two point shmoo. I told you: it's no good. We have no alternative but to stonewall it or go high enough to blow it away. I see no reason to prolong the agony. We stand our ground or attack. We do not die in retreat."

"Die in retreat? It's a four hundred grand difference on an asking price of two point seven five million! What are you dying over? Finally, we have a place to start talking!"

"I'm dying over four hundred thousand dollars. I'm in it two point seven five. It's worth the price. Do you think I could go out today or tomorrow or all of next week or most of next month and make that money back? No. I can't. And I will not walk away from that money."

"Look. We have an offer. It's more than we had yesterday or last week or at any time in the last three months. We need to show good faith. You know what they say: as long as you're talking the deal is alive. Alive is different than dead. We need to counter. You said you knew these things. Besides that, Michael, you are not in it two point seven five. You're in it two point four."

"Oh yeah, Miss Smarty-pants. Take that two point four and stack another point two on top for the roof and the hot tub. Then ask yourself, 'Hmm, do I need to get paid on this?' Well, do ya, punk?' I don't mean you're a punk. You just set me up for that line. But do you want to get paid?"

"You bought at the top and you want to sell on the way down. That. Costs. Money. Michael. If you want to sell your house for more than it's worth, then you're wasting my time."

"Fine. Counter at two point seven four nine nine nine."

"You want to drop your price by a dollar?"

"Yeah. In good faith."

"That's not good faith. That's an insult."

"An insult to whom? Don't forget the party of which you represent here, after yourself of course. It's me and my interests. Two point two is a lowball. Some people would call a lowball an insult. Some people would take it personally. Me? I'm showing good faith. Why are we arguing here? You got two choices: you counter at two point seven four nine nine nine, or you ignore their offer. I won't discuss it further."

"You said before you'd go to two million seven hundred thousand. Let's counter with that."

"No. I'll go to two million seven *if they offer it*. I won't counter with it because you know as well as I do where things go from there. You want faith? Counter a dollar lower. Let's see how good their faith is."

•

"Okay. They got your counter and said thanks very much and want you to know that they really love the place, so they want to make a counter to your counter. They came back at two million two hundred thousand and one dollars."

"They came up a dollar? Beautiful. Now we're getting somewhere. You know: the seller wants to sell, and the buyer makes like he wants to buy. That sort of thing. Go back with . . . let's see, our very best good wishes, our, uh, fondest hopes that they do see the value here and our expressed intention to do everything we possibly can to come to terms on a deal. So, in the spirit of compromise, we'll drop to two million, seven hundred forty-nine thousand, nine hundred ninety-eight."

"You think I'm going to rewrite this contract in dollar bites a half million times?"

"Nah! Just ink in the numbers. I'll initial."

"That's stupid. Besides, why don't you just split the difference? Come down to two million five, around in there. You want to sell the place or get stuck in a . . . a . . ."

"A pissing contest?"

"Yes. You said it."

"We're pissing real dollars here. Not your dollars. My dollars. I want to sell. He who dribbles first loses the money. Let 'um come up to serious intention levels. Then we'll talk about splitting differences and closing deals. Okay? Is that okay?"

"It'll die. You said it first. Too much back and forth with no progress. It'll die, and you know it, and you'd rather let it die than give in."

"I don't know any such thing. What is this give-in bullshit? Who's not giving in? Your client or your client's adversary? Be very careful here, dear. You don't know where this will go. You can't very well call two counters a pattern and think the pattern will hold dollar for dollar to halfway on a five hundred, seventy-five thousand spread. I'd hold firm before it got anywhere near that low anyway. I think it works in my favor to get the paper inked up on another dollar drop."

"Fine. If the deal dies, it's because you killed it."

"Deal? What deal? We got a lowball. I never saw a deal."

"Oh! Dirkson's here! We're on the air! Please don't use foul language."

"On the air? We're not on the air. We're off the air. Can't you see that? Jesus Christ. Whatever happened to reality?"

III

We're on the Air!

"We *will* be on the air. If you think and behave like we're on the air now, then it'll seem more natural when the camera starts rolling."

"Is that what you've been doing? Fine. We're on the air. I don't have to be in this, do I?"

"It helps tremendously. We actually get a Nielson rating, you know. People want to see who you are. Let's face it, a house at this price level, at this position in the neighborhood, reflects substance and, in some cases, personality."

"They're not buying me. Are you always on the air?"

"Oh, but they are."

"Get Allison in here. They'll buy her."

"Yes. She is much nicer."

"And prettier," Michael Mulroney smirks at the retort. "Little bird! Get in here! We're on the air!"

"Why do you call her little bird?"

Mulroney shrugs. "Because she eats like a little bird? Better than calling her fish face, isn't it?"

"What? Hello. On the air? Us?" Allison Mulroney enters as regally as a hundred-pounder can, pausing in the doorway for framing, the fingers of her left hand lighting on the jamb gently as wren's toes on a twig. Of her total weight, two percent is hair in a bouffant to the mezzanine. "Hello," she says again to everyone in general, waving her free hand slowly as Miss America at the millions of viewers watching just behind one-eye. She emotes for the camera, rather for the cameraman, who at that point is removing the camera from its carrying case. As the lens cap comes off, she elaborates, "I'm Allison. Welcome to our home."

"Oh, fuck." Mulroney seems untenably dour and thinks he has cause.

"I asked you not to do that," the agent chides.

"She's sloshed," Mulroney points out.

"I am not sloshed," Allison denies.

"Look, Allison. Come over here. Stand next to me." Allison meanders over and leans on her husband, who turns to the cameraman. "How long till you get the camera ready? Let's get this over with. Allison's good for another two or three minutes."

"Then what happens?"

"Yeah. Then what happens?" Allison would also like to know and, in fact, won't budge until she's told. The wren's fingers now grip her husband's arm like raptor talons, securing her claim on stability and domestic bliss.

Mulroney fondly covers her hand with his own, informing Ms. Moutard on the issue of what happens next: "She assumes a horizontal position and goes to sleep, not necessarily in that order, and not necessarily without a fuss."

"Dirkson, are we ready?" Dirkson is the talent, on camera.

He says, "You bet we are. Scotty?" Scotty is the cameraman.

"Rolling." Scotty plants the viewing cup onto his eye socket and focally ranges in and out—close on Dirkson, long on Allison—freeze! "My God! Where have you been all my life?"

"We've been waiting on you," Marylyn erupts, regretting her impatience, but nonproductive banter with talent and tech and hot product on hand that should have sold but remains unsold just makes her want to scream—not that she would actually scream, but she might whine. Who wouldn't?

"Not you. Her." Scotty zooms on Allison, into macro intimacy, to pores, tiny hairs, and perfection. "What skin tone. What poise." Scotty pans the alabaster complexion. Could this be Norma Jean revisited, not past her prime but still in it, gracefully aged?

Allison invites the scrutiny with a smile and a writhe, though her attempt at seductive warmth suffers a slight wobble. "I'm here," she says. "I have always been here. But you have not been here. Now you better hurry. We're moving to the tropics."

"Keep moving," Scotty enjoins, getting the footage he's been after.

"Scotty. Please. Places," Dirkson directs.

Scotty turns to stage right and holds.

"Hello, there. I'm Dirkson Duquesne—looks like Du-kezney but it's not. It's actually *du-káne*—and I'm *not* a local anesthetic! Ha! Gotcha. Hey—we're back again with this week's episode of . . . *What They're Doing Today in Heaven*. Here we are at . . . Wait a minute. What's the address here?"

"One Summit Nest."

"What's the street number?"

"One. I said one."

"Nice address. Okay . . . Rolling . . . Here we are at . . . One Summit Next . . ."

"Summit Nest!"

"Try again. And . . . Okay. Here we are at . . . One Summit Nest, and believe you me, it is."

"What? It is? It is what?"

"Let me do my job, please. Scotty. Did you get it?"

"I got it."

"Okay. And . . . Marylyn Moutard is here today to show us her listing and introduce us to the sellers, Michael and Allison."

"We sure are, Dirkson. Hi, everybody. I'm Marylyn Moutard. This is Michael and Allison, and they're going to hate giving this place up. I can promise you they're really going to hate leaving that hot tub behind too. We'll go out to the fabulous sun deck in the rear of the home in just a minute. But first, I'd like for Michael to tell us what he loves most of all about this place."

"What do I love about the place?" Michael shrugs. "It's a nice place. What's not to like?"

Marylyn drops the microphone. "Michael. We need to effervesce here. Emote. Give. Convey. Don't worry. Nobody will think you're frilly. You need to sound enthusiastic. This is sales. A pitch. Do you know how to pitch?"

"Okay. I got it." Michael looks down, going to character. He looks up. The camera rolls. "What do I love? About the place? That's easy. For starters, I love the view. Who wouldn't? You got the whole ocean out front. You know, the Pacific Ocean is the biggest ocean in the world, and from here it's easy to see why."

"The view. That's so important. Tell us about living here."

"Well. It's nice. It's really nice. We get up in the morning. You know. I'm thinking of getting a new bicycle, you know. Yeah. It's terrific riding around here. Some of the best in the world. I see guys older than me out there humping it. So I figure . . ."

"That's fabulous. That's *sooo* healthy-lifestyle living. Come on. Let's take a look at the gourmet kitchen. Two sinks!"

"Three sinks, Marylyn," Michael corrects. "Don't forget the wet bar. It's smaller, for your ice and drinks, but it's still a sink."

"Three sinks! Even better! And a six-burner chef stove! I can't wait to see that fantastic master bath."

"Yeah. Me too. Allison. Wake up."

"Wha . . . Oh. Hi. We're moving. We're moving to Hawaii." Allison speaks to the camera, but it passes her on its way to the fantastic kitchen. "I can't wait," she calls, practically shuddering in anticipation of tropical warmth. "You can hear the wavesh. And palm treesh."

"Yeah," Michael chimes in. "Your shirt sticks to your skin. You got heat ripples everywhere and racism, gridlock, and water shortage and fucking insects that look like fucking dragons and humidity to bend your fucking knees. And ignorance. Did I mention the ignorance?"

"Why are you going then?" Marylyn asks, shooing the camera away.

But Scotty keeps it rolling, so Michael tells it: "Because Allison wants it. And what Allison wants long enough, Allison gets. She breaks you down. She gets her way. *Capiche?*"

"How lovely." With a dismissive flourish, Marylyn moves flamboyantly onward. She would like to ask why he keeps Allison around or allows her to get her way, but instead she sweeps a hand majestically yonder, beckoning the marvelous entertainments in store for you, your family, and friends in this dream kitchen come true. "Now this! Is a party house!"

"How'd . . . I do? Howdy Doody." Allison ponders silly wordplay and its deeper meaning, which isn't so deep, and so she shrugs.

But recalling her childhood TV pal, she also remembers simpler times. Nobody relates but Mulroney, who watched Buffalo Bob and the whole gang along with the rest of the peanut gallery. He pauses in a rare moment of reflection, wondering where all those kids are now. Dead, some of them must be.

He laughs. "Dilly Dally. Clarabell. Phineas T. Bluster. Too bad, we never got to watch together. We could get a DVD, but that never works out."

"What are you talking about, Michael?"

"Nothing. You doody fine, dear." With an arm around her for affection and balance, he leads the way down the few steps to the sunken atrium on the way to the bedroom. "Now go lie down, so we can get this done."

"I'm not sleepy."

"That's okay. Just lie there, close your eyes, and breathe slow. Give it a minute. I got this for now. Then in a while you can get up and join the living—I didn't mean that. I mean you can get up and we'll . . . have dinner and watch a movie."

"No. I'm not sleepy."

"Fine. You help Marylyn. Tell her what you love about living here. I'm going out. I'm not waiting to sell this place. I'm going to look for a bicycle. A bicycle is something to be excited about. I'm going to buy a bicycle that'll show what living on top looks like and means and . . . and anybody can have the very best if they'll step up and pay up. I think a new bicycle now should be the best promotion available to enhance prospects for a quick sale."

"Wha should I tell her? I don't love it. I'm cold. It's always cold here."

"You want to get out of here, don't you? Sell, Allison. Give it heart. Pretend you're entertaining an unwanted guest who might tell everyone how gracious you are. Remember: It doesn't matter what you say; it's how you say it."

"Okay. I'll try it that way." Allison shivers again with a quivering smile and a sprightly flutter, as if drying her wings in a drizzle.

IV

Freewheel

Michael Mulroney finds a bicycle on his first visit to the most amazing bike shop in town, maybe in Northern California, maybe anywhere. Or so they say. Mulroney asks the easy question, which he often does; it's so easy—the asking, that is. The answer can stall out. But the salesperson answers with a knowing smile, assuring him that several other shops in town and a few more in the region might approach amazing status, but only The Spokesperson achieves that status, with more blank frames in inventory than any other shop could possibly have the money or sense to carry. That's because the owner is a bicycle fanatic, a true wheelman who might never win a tour leg but wants to be all things to all spokespeople all the time. "If you can't find your perfect match here, you can't find it anywhere."

"I don't get it," Mulroney says. "I get the part about inventory, with all the brands and the models and sizes. I got the same problem, and in this economy it doesn't make you amazing; it makes you amazingly wrong. Big inventory can break the bank these days. But what I really don't get is the other part, about why you do it if it makes no sense. And frankly, it makes no sense."

The spokes consultant shows the full range of his good-natured grin and follows up with a shrug. "Good question. But you're amazing too. You do the same thing. You're ready. The economy shifts, and you're still ready—expanding into a down market, even though it doesn't look anything like it did. But I'll tell you what Mister M. Let's have this talk when we're done with your fitting. I think a few actions might provide you with a thousand words."

Mulroney laughs because he loves the presumption. "Now that's some bullshit. But I like it. You know: my kind o' bullshit. Hey, you know me?"

"I've seen your ads. Who hasn't? And your car lots. I mean, you are well known." Mulroney rolls his eyes and shrugs, not so secretly pleased and nonetheless surprised that he is known even in such a rarified place. Then again, what's your average fucking bicycle hustler going to buy when he needs a car? Will he buy a new car? No, he'll go used, so he'll go M—Big M, that is, and that's what makes the world go round, what with your economic reciprocation and that shit.

The spokes consultant nearly squints in assessing Mulroney as a potential rider, cogs seeking cohesion on body type, age, pocket depth, and the latest technology that might be wasted on such an old fart, but then who else can afford it? "Do you ride now?"

"No."

"And you last rode when? I mean, regularly."

"Not so long ago, maybe thirty-five, forty years. Nah! Not forty. Thirty-five is all."

Breaking a slow nod, the spokes consultant raises a forefinger and exits to the back room. He reappears in a minute, wheeling a unit likely to amuse. "This is Equinox, a C-1A frame from Olioglo. This is the frame I ride. It's considered an ultimate frame for many riders, and it could be considered a step too far for you.

Then again, why wait? Why not give the best chance to the most fun and best feeling you've had in thirty-five years?"

"Hey, you knockin' my wife?"

"Not at all! I meant . . . bicycling!"

"Yeah, yeah. I'm fucking with you. Sorry. You were saying, a step beyond."

"The bicycle I have in mind for you is not extravagant, yet. Believe me. You're getting a solid foundation. You won't want to go out there with anything less. It can get a bit more expensive for performance goodies. But the main thing to keep in mind is that it's a parts jungle out there. You'll love the upgrades if you know what to get, and I can show you how. Given your age and projected miles remaining, you may want to take full advantage of the new bike discount of 12% on all components added at the time of purchase, provided the component is the top model from that manufacturer." Franco hesitates and then cracks the half smile on both sides, "You're no different than my other riders. You'll see. You'll want the best. I know these things. You'll find the C-1A at the summit of comfort, ease, speed, and efficiency. I daresay you will love it. This particular bicycle is sixty-five ninety-five, so not every buyer can afford it. But if you can, you'll be glad you did. You probably need riding things too, shoes and shorts and jerseys?"

"Yeah, all that." Mulroney hefts the Equinox C-1A from Olioglo. He laughs up front to show that he's joking, maybe. "You don't mean seventy bucks, do you?" He gets a brief stretch on the fixed grin for his effort. "Seven fucking grand for a bicycle?"

"We've come a long way."

"Yeah. Gee."

"Actually, the Equinox frame runs only thirty-eight hun-dred—it utilizes trapezoidal tetrahedron technology with triangular cross-sectioning in the maximum torque frame segments. It uses the new split tail design with interchangeable cage brackets and blunt stubs up front, tipping in at one point nine pounds."

"Fucking weightless."

"Nearly. It gets up to eighteen pounds or so on the build out. We finished this unit with great components. You can get better stuff, but this will give you the feel. Whatever you feel with this will only feel better with better stuff."

Mulroney loves the action; it's so brazenly expensive in such whimsical detail. Yet he also senses the action, going into overdrive to see just how much he's willing to spend. Oh, Mulroney knows the game, so he slows the pace with a few lobs. He takes a minute to eyeball some of the finer details, laughing inside—as if he knows what he's looking at. But he does glean in no time that this bicycle-spending miasma is à la Carte. All the parts are different brands. And he asks, unafraid to sound uninformed: "The fuck? Doesn't anybody build a whole bicycle anymore? I mean the whole fucking enchilada, with the tires and handlebars and all this tweezer shit?"

"Yes, of course. Specialized does. But it gets boring."

"Yeah, I think so too, now that you mention it. This is more fun, mix and match, huh? Okay, so you call these parts great but then you say I can get better stuff. What do you call those parts?"

"Well, that depends on the brand. Most componentry comes in four quality grades. I do think the top grade would be overkill for you because the only difference is esoteric, with tiny screws and washers made of carbon graphite instead of stainless steel. You can spend a few thousand saving a dozen grams . . ."

"Or you could just pass on the second half o' your baked fuckin potato and keep the money in your pocket."

"Something like that."

Mulroney hefts the bicycle again. He rolls it back and forth. "What would you call this Oliogilleto rig here? I heard you call it ultimate, and that usually means the very best. Is it?"

"It is. I mean unless you count the bomb."

"And what, pray tell, is the bomb?"

"The CX-61. Also from Olioglo but different. It's purist. It's . . . art. I mean, not to sound too crazy, but it's like this. Every single carbon frame today is laid up in Taiwan—"

"Wha? Taiwan?"

The spokes consultant hangs his head and nods. "It's the way it is. Olioglo hand picks his lay-up guys and gets only the very best of the best. You'd think it would be a subtle difference, but Olioglo frames are immaculate. However! The CX-61 is the only carbon frame in the world not laid up in Taiwan. Mr. Olioglo has them built in his basement, in his home near Genoa. They run about eleven thousand, but I have to check on availability and colors."

"I would think for eleven grand you could get sky blue with monkeys out the ass."

"You might get sky blue with monkeys or anything, but not because you ordered it."

"You're saying they send what they want?"

"I'm saying they're Italian. We get what they send. And it's gorgeous, every time."

Michael Mulroney steps back, perhaps for perspective. He doesn't mind the dough; nay, he loves lavish spending for the sheer exhilaration of the thing and for what it might reflect in a man of incredible success. On the solvency issue and its converse, he's always adhered to faith, what he calls the cornerstone of religion. God and Mulroney will provide. On a more practical level, a man must spend money to make money, and if the top of the ridge is an image to die for, it can only dazzle more brilliantly with a seller on an unbelievable bicycle. You think for a California minute that Big M on a bicycle won't make news? Oh, Mulroney knows the game. But he wants to get it right, wants to actually ride this bicycle, and he believes he will ride it if he gets it right.

"Look at these." But the spokes consultant stops and offers his hand for a shake, sensing the changing direction of the discourse, toward a closing. "I'm Franco, by the way. Pleased to meet you."

"Yeah, yeah. Mulroney. You know. A real fucking pleasure."

Franco slides a brochure across the counter, an 8½ x 11 so thick and pliable it feels nearly plastic, showing the bare bones frames of the CX-61 from Olioglo in the six color schemes available, maybe. "I'll call Chicago to see what they have. I know the Chicago crew well."

"Does it matter that you know them?"

Franco smiles and dials. Mulroney scans the options and boils the choice down to two, which he shows to Franco, who's reached the Chicago office and waits on hold. "That frame color is for the disc brake model only. You do not want disc brakes."

"Disc brakes? On a bicycle?"

"Yes. They're relatively new on road bikes, but they really are a specialty item for going very fast—" Franco holds up a finger as he exchanges pleasantries with his great good friend at Olioglo U.S.A. in Chicago and asks what he can get shipped today. "Oh? Well, yes. I think so. But the catalog shows that color in the disc brake frame only . . . Yes . . . You're sure . . . ? Sizes . . . ? Grazie. I'll call you back."

Franco shrugs, underscoring his point, that what is shipped will be what they'll get. But he *thinks* they can get one of Mulroney's two choices, for the moment, in a size fifty-three. Franco assesses the candidate once more and nods. "We're in luck."

"The fuck, you *think* you can get it? You just talked to the guy. He had his eyes on it, didn't he?"

Franco shrugs. "We often think what turns out to be otherwise."

Mulroney smiles again, this time shaking his head. "That's good. I gotta chew on that one. Hey, Frankie. You ever sell cars?"

Allowing for maximum potential, maximum return and above all, maximum fun, Franco pencils in specialty upgrades on every screw, washer, nut, O-ring, link, cable, rod, axle, rim, lever, tape, sprig, and relish. The build-out begins on paper, on a form that becomes a set piece in supreme excellence at maximum level. The Big M senses his transformation into the laydown of every salesperson's dreams, and he says, "You understand, this is an exercise. We're going through the motions here."

"Of course. We need to see if we can even put together what you want."

"Ease off, Frankie. You got the sales basics dicked—that would be service and product knowledge. Smoke up the ass is not necessary and could be a deal killer."

"Sorry, Mr. M."

"Don't worry about it, but give me a break, for fuck sake. All I wanted was a fucking bicycle, and you're putting together a fucking Mach nine supersonic screamer. And shitcan the part about whether you can do it. You fill in the blanks. What can't you do?"

Franco blushes, perhaps humbled, perhaps insulted, perhaps wondering how his world-class bicycling potential got him building out extreme machines for rude, old guys. Mulroney sees. Mulroney knows. "You were a contender, huh?"

Franco thinks and jots components into each blank. He eases into grimace—make that a smile. "I had my day."

"Yeah, we all had our day. Some of us. Hey, Frankie, ain't it the shits, the only guys who ever buy these hotsy-totsy bicycles are fat old fucks with no chops?"

Franco looks up and stares, not quite assessing for the third time but rather reflecting on a poignant moment. "Que sera," he offers in sanguine resignation, covering well with: "But today should be a good day for both of us."

Mulroney thinks he made the right choice. Duly recognized and being serviced as a man of means, this process feels right. He won't say as much because he wants to see how it plays out, but he's already decided to go whole hog; fuck it, why not? It'll help with the big picture. With a time and purchase to every season, it's important to open the heart, mind, and wallet on occasion, where pleasure and joy may be at hand, or may be lost for want of a few measly shekels.

Mulroney feels game and wants to see where a bicycle might go if a buyer is willing and able to spend a few bucks on the best. Franco jots, murmuring pros and cons on one seat post or another, a particular stem and its dictate on certain bars. He smiles blithely at potential yet again—with purpose—and finally gets to a difficult series of blanks. "We're here to get you as far as you can go. Why not, with such a solid foundation?" He reviews his choices and logic so far, through brakes, seat, handlebars, wheels, hubs, tires, and the rest. He has chosen top tier excellence on each component, meaning all carbon graphite. "We know how to take care of you. All Shimano components."

"Sounds Japanese."

"It is. They're great."

"You think they're the greatest?"

"They're definitely up there. Some people prefer Campagnolo. Campagnolo is Italian. It's a matter of taste."

"Gimme the Italian. I don't like Japanese. Fuckers kill whales and call it research. They eat 'um. Whales. Blowfish. Jellyfish for chrissakes. Can you believe that? Eating whales and jellyfish?"

Franco strikes a pose: listening to political opinion in stillness. "It sounds like a touchy subject for you."

"Yes, it is. It's touchy for the whales and blowfish too. It's no big deal for you?"

But Franco is smart and quick, sticking the shiv and pulling it out with no twist. "I love the fish and the whales. Campagnolo it is then. If you want to know the truth, Campagnolo is my personal preference. You want to try on some riding pants?"

"Then why did you assume I'd want the Japanese stuff?"

Franco shrugs. "Sorry. Campagnolo runs a good deal more money. But it's important to get what you want. *Capiche*?"

"Yeah. Fuckin *capiche*." Well, every closer has his downside, and understanding seems softer than a few minutes ago. Squeezing him onto a fifty-three because they didn't have a fifty-four was easy enough, but they get so obtuse, assuming Japanese.

Mulroney asks if the good stuff that may not be the greatest but might cost a heap o' dough less might be good enough for a hacker like himself. Franco says, "Of course, you can save a few bucks. And you might be happy forever. Or you might wonder. Why not return to cycling as you would have cycling return to you? Besides that, you're getting all Italian."

"Yeah, yeah. Instead of Japanese."

"This build on a CX-61 is state of the art, so far, and will be for years. You carry through with EPS, and I think you're going to see more miles than you ever imagined. We have another hurdle to get over, but if we can clear it, you're going to be riding a frame that's stronger than steel, lighter than feathers, aerodynamic as a teardrop, nearly, and with more sheer, raw love than you thought a bicycle could give you. You will have no metal parts, except for cables, so you will be rust-free forever. Let's get done with the pain, quick and neat: top of line throughout, fifteen grand. Give or take."

Mulroney has fifteen grand to piss down the rat hole any day he chooses and plenty more because of who he is. But Frankie's presumption may be verging on arrogance. Why sell a bicycle for four grand when you might get fifteen on five minutes of rolling the ticket? Mulroney doesn't mind the best but wants to avoid foolish feelings later, what his own customers like to call buyer's remorse on what they realized as superfluous, after the sale. He doesn't mind being a lay-down but doesn't want to bend over, like the suckers who shell out another two grand on a piece o' shit car for the fucking undercoating and headlight insurance and seat cover extended warranty and all that happy horseshit. Mulroney knows this business with specific regard to the emotional minefield at this juncture of the process known to Californians as the acquisition, as it reflects the essence of self.

Then again, maybe a buyer resistant to this natural process is stubborn and stupid. Maybe this kid Frankie is a natural. He does know the product, and a would-be bicyclist with adequate mobility is lucky to have his guidance . . .

Nah. Not likely.

"Bear with me, Frankie. I'll keep that number in mind, but let's back up to this EPS thing. What, pardon me, the fuck is EPS?"

"Electronic power shifting. Come over here." Mulroney follows to a display rack holding a bicycle and watches Franco turn the pedals and work the shifter. It's electric.

Mulroney smiles—can't help it, offering his catchall assessment: "The fuck?"

"Once you've been, you won't go back. The EPS package is part of your system. You can save about four grand going back to manual shift."

"And what's the last hurdle."

"Do you have a minute?"

"I got three minutes. What do you got?"

Franco leads to another display case, from which he pulls a magazine folded back on a review of the new CX-61. Mulroney scans. The review says, "The new CX-61 is only one more version of the best bicycle in the world, until you add carbon graphite wheels. Then it smokes everything else."

Mulroney feels testier than he'd like to feel; sure, this Frankie kid is a sales manager's dream, but who'd a thunk the Big M, himself, could get so carved up on a mere toy?

Franco does not interrupt the personal reverie, does not assert authority or fact but eases softly inside with the practiced nuance of a surgeon—never mind the blood and gore. "I can explain the pros and cons of carbon wheels whenever you want. I'm going to recommend the Certitude 1111s. You will be amazed. They'll add three thousand to your total and will include spokes, hubs, bearings, and skewers. Wait a minute." Franco picks up a phone

and hits one button and says, "Certitude 1111 front and rear."
He hangs up and says, "I just knew it. We have them."

Mulroney murmurs a question on who's skewering whom.
He knew coming in that this bicycle outing could go to quibble and squabble like things usually do, like maybe he should
offer Frankie eight grand on the X-15 or whatever the fuck it's
called—put it right on the card and out the door: tax, tags, and
dealer prep. And skewers.

Except that would be a lowball on a bicycle shop. That is low
and negative. Bicycles are clean and simple. Kids ride bicycles.
Mulroney was a kid, and maybe that's the attraction here. These
days are dark, so much waiting and ass-kissing and trying to sell
a great house at a fair price. A bicycle seems honest and innocent—and young. It's why he's here, for a change of pace, and the
change of scenery already looks better. So why not pay the price
as stated and ride on out, for the first time in years self-propelled
instead of deeply driven?

The quintessential bicycle consultant seems acutely familiar with these mental gyrations as they process in the prospective buyer's mind, or rather in the prospective buyer's voluntary
removal of his right mind, the moment fondly referred to in
shop parlance as the moment of truth. Franco steps back, feet at
shoulder width, hands clasped below the waist. He neither bows
nor waits but returns to the paraphernalia set out for Mulroney's
review and puts the shop in order, as it was.

This closing technique might be called modern, what used
to be called soft or pussying out—failing to ask for the money.
At least Frankie gave the price. And this soft touch really offers
no quarter for resistance. It's not like he's saying take it or leave
it, except that seems to be the situation, which doesn't trigger

the knee jerk, so maybe Mulroney is getting tired, or tired of it. Maybe the inner Mulroney is finally realizing the essence of the situation, or the practical side of spirituality, or some shit. Fact is, Mulroney has more money than time, or he will have and he knows it. So he probes, to be sure, seeking a drop on the game of give and take. "So with the good wheels and all you're saying eighteen grand?"

"No. They're included in the fifteen, give or take. I just assumed . . . I'm sorry."

"Don't be sorry. Product knowledge is half the battle. I think you have it."

"I try to stay up on things."

Mulroney grants his own knowing smile and says, "Wrap it up."

Fuck it. It's not a toy; it's a tool. Besides, what good is a man of means who can't sling some means around every now and then? Just look: the seductive finish and two-finger weightlessness of the thing emote movement, not to mention its very shape, a hi-tech hint of velocity with no effort—and no exhaust, no fuel and none of the petty suburban bullshit smothering what's left of the world.

Besides, it's only fifteen grand complete—including the special wheels! He thought there for a minute it would go to eighteen! That would be crazy. He'll spend a few bucks more on spandex shorts, wicking shirts, clip-on shoes, a helmet, carbon fiber bottle brackets, carbon fiber pump, a patch kit and under-seat pouch no bigger than his scrotum with less sag and plenty of room for emergency needs: spare tube, tire levers, and a double sawbuck for snacks, phone calls, a couple brewskies, whatever. But later on that; let's get the bike built first.

Of course, *wrap it up* is a figure of speech. Just so, Franco wraps up the details while Mulroney reviews the parts list. Franco computes total weight at just over fifteen pounds, which seems like a pricey pour. Mulroney would prefer seventeen or twenty pounds for better value, but this is like golf, with a lower number of pounds representing greater value.

God, I hate golf.

He can call it a grand per pound, and that has a nice ring to it. Facilitating the amazingly light weight are carbon fiber handlebars and seatpost. "Four and a quarter for a plastic stick?" Mulroney asks aloud.

"Yes, and worth every penny. You'll agree when it absorbs residual road shock before it runs up your spine."

"Yeah, beginning with up my ass."

Tasteless humor is not appreciated, so Mulroney asks more appropriately, "How will I know that I'm not feeling the pain I could be feeling?"

"Trust me. Everybody knows. You will too."

The fuck is that? You will too? Condescension can hardly placate primitive doubt, and Mulroney experiences his first disappointment in Frankie, who had his day. Does an old guy really need this space-age stuff? That condescension is what's wrong with the neighborhood. Make that the town, this god-forsaken stretch of coast infested with airy-fairy mental cases who couldn't be more cocksure of what's up in *their* universe.

What Mulroney knows with equal certainty is that this Frankie kid doesn't know shit, not about life or pains in the ass or practicality. He's a good salesperson, no doubt about it, but something keeps niggling at the old whaddayacallit—the old stickler that'll bung up product knowledge and service every time. Ah, yeah, it's the arrogance. How else could he see Mulroney as money-bags ripe for the plucking instead of a guy who wants to go for a bicycle ride? And at such a punk age. Frankie isn't a punk, but Mulroney wants to set the record straight. "How old are you?"

Franco blushes, as if facing his personal poverty of podium appearances and so far past his prime. Working at the best bicycle shop in the world is hardly a job to scoff, but he's still selling bicycles, when a man could be so much more. "I'm thirty-seven."

"A little old to be hustling toys, isn't it?" Mulroney doesn't make anyone feel inadequate by choice, but as old guy out he can level a playing field any day, as necessary.

"Sir, these toys aren't for everyone. These toys are for the select few. You can't get one of these toys unless you're a world-class athlete with a sponsor to buy these toys for you, or you're a success in life and can pay for a custom-built, tailor-made bicycle for yourself. You're making an impulse buy on a toy and accessories of around eighteen thousand dollars. Do you want a test ride?"

"Hmm." Mulroney knew it! Knew it would go to eighteen. And he knows a test ride is in order, that only a fool buys a car or a bicycle without a test ride, but it doesn't feel right. He's not ready. So no, he doesn't want a test ride. Not yet—yet he sees the seasoned dexterity in a natural closer. Franco won't belabor his own personal status or that of his product but rather turns the dialogue on a dime, back to the buyer buying what the seller is selling. Oh, this Frankie kid is good—could have knocked down a hundred grand annual in pre-owned back in the day. Maybe more. What the fuck—he could be knocking down a buck and quarter right now. Eighteen large on a fricken' bicycle? Maybe the magical seat post is working already. *At least I get a bicycle to show for the dough instead of a butt fucking from some glad-hand assholes*

*trying to lowball the homestead so they can show their hot-flashing
wives what a bunch of slick operators they are.*

Fuckers.

"Tell me something," Mulroney says. "When do you draw the
line on this weight business? When do you step back and say,
'Hey, it's a fuckin bicycle.' I mean it weighs less than a fuckin
bag o' spuds. So what, I want to drop a few more grand to take a
couple spuds out of the bag?"

"That's a good question," Franco replies, sliding his business
card across the counter, as necessary, disclosing his status as
owner of The Spokesperson, and as such, "I'm the designated
personal guidance consultant to qualifying clients. You qualify,
Mister M." With that comes the half smile of certainty, also as
necessary.

Mulroney studiously scans the card. "The Spokesperson? Did
it used to be *The Spokesman?*"

Franco allows his mild chagrin to form a smile in a calculated
quarter inch to the right but not the left.

"I mean before the lefties got to you? Got to you? Fuck. Before
they threatened to burn your store down?"

Franco will not distinguish such a question, so he ignores it,
to make the world a more productive place. "It depends on you.
How much do you want to spend? On minimal grammage."

Mulroney squints. "I want the mostest for the leastest. You
musta heard o' that. I guess around here I mean the leastest for
the leastest."

Franco slides sideways again. "The common rule of expenditure on cost-benefit for years was a dollar a gram. I now have very
competitive clients willing to drop a dollar on a quarter gram and
carry that standard on many grams."

Mulroney can't help but admire a consummate salesperson on a roll, and it shows. Frankie more or less compared him to other riders, very competitive riders at that. So Mulroney throws a leg over the trial bicycle to see how it feels. Franco stoops to roll Mulroney's pant leg up and wrap it with a Velcro strap. He gives Mulroney a helmet and instructions to ride up the street and gentle hill there to get a feel for response, stiffness, torque, and general ride. He cautions Mulroney to turn wide because a narrow turning radius can bring a rider down. "I put primitive pedals on here. You'll be riding with clip pedals, but this is just a test ride, and we don't want your foot stuck in the clip at this point. Are you familiar with clips?"

"How tough could they be?"

"Not so tough at all. You twist your foot, inside or outside to release from the clip. But we'll review that later. It's easy. Okay?"

Mulroney knows what a bicycle feels like; he's ridden a few. And the twisty clip shit will be easy too, and he wonders how he took the bait, hook, line, and sinker so quick on this bicycle hustle; sure, nobody lays down like the consummate salesperson, but still, this could be embarrassing. Twenty large on a bicycle? Fuck. But then he feels what he could not have imagined, which is effortless propulsion on a weightless, rigid frame, with each turn of the pedals giving far more propulsion than he deserves. So the deal is closed yet again, just as a closer of global caliber will close a deal. Mulroney can't argue with a feeling. This one is like air with pedals—carbon graphite pedals with adjustments for lateral swing, camber, and friction modulation on release. "Yeah," he says, dismounting from once-around-the-block. "It does feel good."

Franco smiles, sanguine as a surgeon with no mortality since Tuesday. "This one isn't even your size. Yours will fit perfectly.

You're going to love it." He wheels the demo unit back to its place, still smiling over his shoulder. "Besides that, your frame is better."

"How much better could it be?"

"This is the C-1A. You're getting the CX-61. La Bamba!"

"Ah! CX-61 sounds better. Doesn't it?"

"It does, especially when you add Certitude 1111. You just rode on aluminum wheels—your wheels will be four hundred grams lighter. Four Hundred! And that's rotational weight! You won't believe it!"

•

Mulroney can't ride his new bike into the sunset without a fitting, to be sure. The trial bicycle is a fifty-six centimeter with a lowered seat, while he is a sure fifty-three, or rather a fifty-three will surely work out perfectly for all parties, given availability, adaptability and the amazing 12% off on all componentry at the juncture known in all walks of retail as point-of-sale. The made-to-measure machine will measure precisely for a precise reason; if wiggle room was allowed, it might as well be Sears. The trial ride was a stretch, and it felt great, and it will be corrected to perfection. Franco beckons Mulroney to mount the made-to-measure machine for the precision made famous here at *The Spokesperson*. He lengthens the handlebar stem, the rear triangle, and the top tube. "How does that feel? I notice you hold your tension in your back. These measurements should fit you much, much better than the test ride. Are you more comfortable?"

Mulroney shrugs. "Call me a Luddite. I can't feel a pinch o' shit worth of difference."

"That's great. This really does fit you better. We can have a fifty-three here overnight express and built out for you in three days. You want it set up like we talked about?"

Mulroney shrugs again. "Is that the way to go?"

"Yes, it is definitely the way to go. Now. Where were we? Ah. Yes. Riding pants."

And so it's on to accessories, nothing extraneous, only those must-have support items for unimpaired road glory. "You mean those ballerina stretch jobs to show off my hard body? What do I need with riding pants? I can just wear my shorts. Why not?"

"You'll chafe. You really don't want to chafe. Come on. This'll only hurt for a minute."

V

Accessories and Pain

Michael Mulroney was a teenager when the new Corvette Stingray had a hood scoop option over a 427 with enough horsepower to smoke the wheel wells with burning rubber before gaining traction and screaming Jesus for a quarter mile or the first curve. That 427 had kid Mulroney fuel injected with desire.

So did Connie Conklin, star of his wet dream for three years in a co-feature of desire. He didn't want to marry Connie Conklin any more than he could buy a Corvette. She was slutty with a trash mouth and genetically deficient social skills, though her legs, ass, and chest seemed naturally select. She invaded his dreams three to five nights a week, fresher and friendlier than she ever was in person. She complained that a nice girl must protect her reputation, then she slid into his Corvette and undressed in his dream to apply every skill he could dream of.

She was like a new Corvette in every way, with horsepower to spare, no subtlety or nuance, garish paint and no doubt what kind of fun could be had. The Vette was actually more merciful, another ache in his chest but far less complicated. Love was mysterious that way, and Mulroney wondered if a car could be his soul mate. A car doesn't have a place to stick it in—not a good place anyway. But still, all in all . . .

A new Vette was five grand back then, which was like fifty grand now, unless you were seventeen. Then it was like five mil; fucking forget it. Mulroney had an idea: the Chevrolet dealer was so agreeable and gregarious on TV; young Mulroney would offer to drive the car around town so people could see it and want one. It would be like free advertising. Wouldn't it?

Boy Mulroney got three steps onto the showroom floor before Big Don Hasbro of Big Don Hasbro Chevrolet shouted at his entire staff, who happened to be on a coffee break: "Why would I pay flooring on these units with the entire staff on a coffee break at the same time?" Don Hasbro turned around to the ogling kid, shook his head, and walked away. The moment showed the essence of power. Big Don Hasbro was a no-nonsense commander. Mulroney also turned and left.

He would never drive a Corvette, not sooner, when he was merely a boy with no money, or later, when the dough was incidental but Porsche seemed more fun and, truth be told, more aligned to neighborhood tastes. He could have opted for Mercedes, but Mercedes seemed so . . . sedentary. He would buy a Vette now on a whim if Connie Conklin were still around and still hot and still open to a ride in a Vette. But she's not. He might find out where she is, but then he figures where she is: sixtyish and overweight. Well, hell, maybe she got good manners and turned sweet as sugar. Or not.

Michael Mulroney liked to think of himself as insulated from material need, except of course when he really liked something. But that was different. Years in the OK Car trenches left him battle-scarred and tough on the inside and shiny and flush outside. He didn't need shit and let the world know it. He'd emerged with status and recognition, going along with the rest on pre-owned, prior to understanding just who (the fuck) Big M really was. On that note he jumped like Jack, clear of the box, and went to *used*.

Some people think him unpolished and abrasive, and calling his cars *used* is perfect. So what? Give those fuckers a chance; they'll think the worst every time, until they beat you. Then they think worse yet.

The carbon fiber frame and fork weigh in just under two pounds—or maybe just over. Who gives a fuck? Franco fills in blanks and uses his calculator frequently, prepping the order on the finest bicycle frame in the known universe—the only bicycle frame not laid up in Taiwan but actually laid up in Ernesto Olioglo's basement in Genoa. Franco freely rambles as he works, assuring Mulroney that a few grams really do mean nothing next to frame geometry—and don't forget your rotational minimals, because that's the ballgame right there. The variable cross section of the frame changes every few inches for optimal rigidity and spring-loaded power transfer at various stress and flex points for maximum torque conversion and stiffness at high speeds or in sharp turns or both. Shape shifting based on tetrahedral logarithms, or some such, sounds like twenty-four karat bullshit, which is good and bad.

Mulroney reads the same geometric profile in the highly produced brochure, practically as Franco recites it, and he nods in comprehension; this shit makes sense, kind of.

He heads to the dressing room with the riding pants that Franco calls the correct riding pants. He feels old, like the butt of his old expression: it's just like pulling the pants off a fat girl. Or pulling them back on, shimmying, twisting, pulling the stretch fabric up but failing to get the riding pants up, which resist all the way into place. Arranging the nut sack is a stickler, and he pulls on each leg and the crotch and finally gets things sorted and settled. The next moments are difficult in a series: *What the fuck am I doing here? Who the hell do I want to see me in a tutu squeezing my gut into overhang? The fuck? I'm not this fat.*

"Come on out."

"What for?"

"I can get a better measure if you need it."

Mulroney steps out and Franco stretches his tape hither and yon, taking notes like a New York tailor, then announcing, "Perfect! We'll have you ready to ride by noon Tuesday. You want to get your things now?"

Luck, as it were, holds on the things, because *The Spokesperson* happens to have all accessories to suit the non-buff rider in stock. The hi-tech shirt has many zippers, pockets, wicking capacities, and cooling vents for the precision machine that will soon be Mulroney. Yellow socks with hula dancers, a space-age headband with wicking technology actually developed at NASA—"Fuck me. You don't sweat in space"—and $400 shoes good for nothing but riding a ridiculously light and expensive bicycle round out the ensemble.

"It feels right," Franco assures.

"Can you feel it?"

Franco defaults to the quarter smile, which is a half smile on one side only. Mulroney knows how it feels, and he feels he's learning Franco's repertoire of smiles for all ironies. He was selling before this kid crawled. Yet he admires the articulation. This is retail therapy. And he's impressed with the commitment: Sure, Frankie's the owner and probably knocking down a forty point margin, but the middle digit of each finger on both hands is tattooed with a single letter to spell L O V E, twice, for a two-fisted sales tool that would be hard to beat. Or imagine.

Every real salesperson has tools. But who would tattoo L O V E on his fucking fingers if he didn't believe in his product? Maybe it helps him with the girls. But why would he tattoo the fingers of both hands? These kids.

Franco pushes paper—no less paper than if a transaction was underway for a high-end performance roadster. Of course, such a transaction is underway, but who'd a thunk it would come to be? Mulroney helps himself to a perfect espresso, but he is quickly interrupted by another helpful spokes consultant standing by to serve and to protect the espresso machine from idiots. Mulroney doesn't mind and doesn't need to point out that his espresso machine has two-gallon boilers and can pull a shot in a heartbeat that makes the most miserable fucking life in the world feel like it's worth living, at least for the next few minutes. Never mind. He doesn't need to win a pissing or espresso contest with these guys. They're not bad guys, not his type of guys but still. He thanks the friendly fellow who really does know how to get the most out of a cheap shit espresso machine, and he savors the moment, pondering quality, service, and product knowledge, along with closing skills. He contemplates relative desire in a man or a boy anticipating a new bicycle or Corvette. Can life end up so far afield of the early dream? Not that life is ending, or that distance is bad. But a man wonders what's left of the boy he used to be. Very little is the short answer, and he wouldn't call this full circle. He doesn't seek the inner-child or miss the outer child for that matter. These are the days, mobile and affluent with the spice of life at hand on any given issue. The boy had something that went away. And the man has something else, allowing him to ride a bicycle designed for the most successful.

Mulroney drifts to the far wall of accessories to browse riding trifles while sipping his espresso. He selects a few high-energy candy bars, some electrolyte replacement powders, two water bottles, more sox, another shirt, a rearview mirror, a Velcro windbreaker caddy, an ear warmer, and on and on but only to five hundred dollars, which ought to round out the package for now. He wonders if the candy bars actually deliver high energy or just keep you from dropping dead. Or are they another cog in the scam—candy bars at five bucks a pop for some peanut butter and chocolate in a wrapper that babbles immortality and world peace, in the end going to the mid-section?

He'll eat one to test the effects—this one that looks like shmushed dates and bat shit with sesame sprinkles, but no; he'll wait. Other cyclists coming and going seem so focused on the miles ahead or a difficult past or an awkward relationship with the moment at hand or compensation for something or other or a need for grueling pain or self-effacement. Mulroney tries to feel the challenge but can't. So he eats the fucking energy bar, tonguing his gum line for pesky sesame sprinkles and gooey detritus.

Just beyond the bibs, jerseys and shorts, a group is glued to the big screen TV showing a bicycle race that looks like any other race but isn't. This race stands out, because Cadell Evans would later say he knew he'd won this race—until Lance pulled out with uncanny acceleration to take the lead and the race, not by a nose but a furlong. All the boys mumble and moan over Lance. That would be Lance Armstrong, the best rider in the world until he got discovered for performance-enhancing drugs and blood transfusions.

"What a bummer."

"What a bum."

"What a terrible thing to do to what we love."

"He doesn't even care."

"What a goon."

"That guy." They lambast Lance round the bend. What was wrong with modern bicycling? Lance. Mulroney had heard it before, not in detail, but enough to know that Lance had become a villain, because of his drug habit. Then again, Big M has a drug habit, not as complex and purely recreational, but a case could be made for drug-enhanced car sales.

"I was in that race," Mulroney intervenes, turning heads. "Not really. But I did watch it on TV. And I was doping."

Everybody gets it, but only one guy laughs—short. The others grumble over Lance, inappropriate sarcasm and irrelevance, perhaps pondering another potential problem for bicycling.

Scanning gadgetry, Mulroney lets the mumble fade and turns from the race that changed history, or some such. He listens to these riders apparently convened, ready to ride, their cleats clicking the cement floor. Franco approaches with the all-clear confirmation but will not say Olioglo or CX-61 or even Certitude 1111 out loud to spare Mulroney the blazing glare-down of his betters—or would that be the bitter envy of the peasantry. Instead Franco blithely murmurs his update, in deference to those gathered, whom he softly calls "The Big Boys." The label is a joke, but it's not. None of them are big, rendering bigness relative. After all, would not Big M qualify as one of the Big Boys? He would, but he doesn't, and that's okay with the M, himself. He has the cash, or same as, at any rate, and that's enough in this rarefied crowd.

Some are thin, lumpy, and stooped as last week's string beans. These are the climbers, at the top of the food chain. With aggressive good cheer they deny pain, except for understated claims of suffering. Like counting steep sprints since sunrise. One climber got in eighteen steep sprints before cramping up, but not so bad as yesterday. Another climber got in thirty steeps before rounding out his ride with a casual twenty-five at fifteen.

Two other climbers ponder the Triple Double Century next week with a yawn—the Triple Double C is a three-day race at two hundred miles per.

Mulroney steps up to demonstrate no cramping, straining, or striving for personal best. Chest out, stomach in, he shows what a man with discretionary millions looks like.

Another faction looks like refugees from a Thigh Master concentration camp. Massive quadriceps and IT bands flex on each step. The sprinters are the front line, sacrificial drones used up one by one to advance the leader—invariably a climber—in the spirit of team strategy.

One sprinter says he's still off after cutting his Wednesday ride to a paltry fifty at nineteen five—fifty miles *averaging* nineteen and a half miles per hour. One of the skinny climbers with grapefruit calves and bowlegs, from scoliosis or rickets or too many miles at whatever the fuck, laughs aloud, advising the sprinter to ride with the climbers tomorrow if he can handle eighty at twenty-two, headed uphill at a four-percent grade *on average*.

"I'll try to keep up with you bad boys," the sprinter says humbly, winning the round for lower expectations, putting the burden on the climber to ride out front for a change. "Then we can relax with some more steep sprints down in the flats." Mulroney will learn about *steep sprints* as ultimate currency in the spandex hierarchy. Steep sprints and the sunrise ritual call for pumping full bore up a short hill—less than a mile—then rolling back down to *repeat as necessary*. A three-quarter mile steep sprint is a few blocks from Casa Mulroney, a fifteen percent grade, though the macho elite agree that Mulroney's hill really can't be steeper than thirteen. The Big Boys jostle and brag and demonstrate endurance as second nature. They moreover show up to show they're still in the game, keeping the old stats intact. Twenty to fifty steep sprints or lashes can prove a rider's grit, except that the steeps take longer and look more painful than a beating.

The brute push of steep sprints makes a cruise over to Mount Madonna or Enterprise Hill or Hazel Dell seem like a more pastoral Hammerfest. That is not to say relaxing because even out in the countryside and foothills your ten-mile splits can accelerate a half-mile an hour for sixty miles. Acceleration over the long haul seems excessive, joyless, tortuous, sadistic and, worst of all, competitive in the macho extreme. But the chronic compulsion sorts the pain maestros into a pecking order, while making sense of the world around them, in a self-serving process fulfilling personal needs, to be sure.

Below the Big Boys on the two-wheel totem are the Vaginas, a group of young, urban professional men who self-deprecate to one-up the Big Boys, again lowering expectations to set the stage for victory, for coming up when nobody is looking. Deprecation notwithstanding, the Vaginas are way too fast for the likes of Michael Mulroney, which he senses straightaway as a Vagina invites him to ride—nothing too tough, maybe thirty at fifteen.

Mulroney declines, at least till he gets the feel of the thing. "This bag of bones needs some shaping up first." He imagines these guys going all out and calling it casual, just to show what a young man with discretionary energy can do.

They size him up, briefly. He returns the assessment—better to get this over with than drag it out. Michael Mulroney could buy and sell these pussies, but he can't keep up with the Vaginas. So? So what? What else you got? Little fuckers. At least they put out the invitation. That was friendly. But fuck a bunch of splits and steeps and whozits at whatsits. *I want to ride my twenty-grand bike in the sun. Is that okay with you? Oh, don't you worry; it'll go twenty.*

The difference between two approaches to bicycling—joyful on the one hand and painful on the other—is more than meets the eye. Accepting the pain challenge on pace, ascent grade, distance or any combination thereof is a standard to live by, for which to strive and grow. The level of difficulty is a matter of choice, self-inflicted, because no matter how low the body fat, how sculpted the thighs or lumpy the calves, the miles will be too few and too slow for some guys. Personal best can always be better yet but can never be best enough. Denial of pain is a measure of machismo, unspoken and also denied. Farther faster is the Holy Grail here, with sparse dialogue among compatriots who know the self-internal, whose inner-connectedness is best expressed in performance stats on distance and pace, with special emphasis on searing potential in a sprint or a climb.

A few riders stare at the old guy in tights and cleats. The stretch material grabs Mulroney like someone else's hands. Riding shorts feel like support hose, with foam padding thick as the yellow pages between his nuts and his butthole. Among those who stare and wait is Franco, who senses discomfort but stays mum, till Mulroney shrugs. "A guy hung like a billy goat won't get far in this rig. You want to wedge a bicycle seat up there too and then get the legs to move?" He lifts a leg to demonstrate the difficulty.

Obviously, Franco went too far, standing by with chamois cream, as if Mulroney would grease his thighs up around the arch of the taint like one of the Big Boys. Setting the cream on the nearest shelf, Franco says, "Don't worry. Cyclists have worn stretch shorts for decades. We'll fit you up." And he goes to the non-performance rack for a pair of stretch shorts in XL with no yellow pages. Mulroney nods and puts them on. Fuck it. This is all he needs. A pair of fucking shorts. Fucking yellow pages. Fuck. He hefts his nuts in one hand like a heavy hitter, seeking a more nuanced adjustment, and nods again, with room enough for a bicycle seat now. He looks around to see who's still interested and if they're getting the picture: he's not so different, not as fast or durable or physically fit or young as he used to be. But he's still hung and still game—till he passes a mirror and sees the old guy in tight shorts, till he moves along. Nothing improves with staring.

The shoes are clip-ons. That is, first come the shoes, then the type of clips, then clip quality as a sub-set of type, though in this case the quality quotient is foregone: supreme excellence and nothing but. Waiting for the installation of clips onto shoes, Mulroney recalls installing a water pump on a '59 Dodge or a '65 Chevy with fair certainty he did it quicker and with fewer wrenches. He tries the shoes on and takes them off and waits in his socks, then changes his socks, saving the hula girls for special. Maybe he'll save them for Hawaii, once he offloads the mother-fucking barn at the top of the hill. He slips into more sedate blue sox with sharks circling the ankles but decides to save those in the tropical trousseau too. He slips into a pair in chartreuse with black bands on top showing Godzilla whacking a skyscraper. As he stares, a Big Boy eases over and says his five-year-old son would like those. Mulroney doesn't look up as he stipulates, "These are my sox."

And these are some nice sox. He can decide later which to wear and which to save, but fuck it; he can get more. So he checks out for now, grateful that Frankie glanced at the ticket without wincing or murmuring the first peep over so many thousands of dollars, passing it over the counter top for review, acceptance, and payment in full. That would be cash or, of course, credit. Mulroney reviews briefly and slides it back across with his plastic on top. "Let's see if we can fit that little devil right on here." Mulroney knows it will fit right on there. Then he hopes it will fit right on there. Then he fears it won't, and he'll be rendered lower than old and fat and in denial of a greater pain. But somehow, some way, the little devil fits, and the little machine hums its emotionless mantra, capturing another electronic draft for the betterment of all. Franco goes to the half smile, which is half on each side, reflecting neutrality in a trade of many thousands of dollars for equal value shaped as a bicycle. He is a consummate closer and more, a poker player protecting the best interests of the entire table. Not a single ripple on his entire countenance divulges the magnitude of the sale, which must surely be his biggest of the morning. That's tasteful, even if the Big Boys see and know.

VI

Mulroney on Wheels

Then it's the middle of the night, not that night but two nights down, bicycle eve. Mulroney can't sleep, but he often can't sleep for an hour or so around two or four, no big deal. The same shit wakes him up for sorting, but tonight some new shit takes the lead, pulling out like a drugged phenom on a fresh transfusion. Big M Michael Mulroney is excited about a new bicycle. Fuck, he thinks, but not in a bad way; he thinks this round of insomnia fresh and revitalizing, a youthful invigoration of the spirit, possibly already worth the twenty grand. He likes it and has only a few more hours till opening time. What will he look like a month down the road? Oh, baby.

•

Pressed to rate his bicycle purchasing experience to date, Mulroney would have scored Frankie eight out of ten on the front end; he was cocksure confident with laser focus on closing the deal. And he did wow the customer. But it was a tad slick, a bit over-confident, a smidge condescending and a whole heap of unhumble. Nobody should do that, but frankly, Mulroney must fess up to his own in flagrante on the woefully low humility issue. Whatever. Eight for ten is a score to be proud of.

Arriving at The Spokesperson at two minutes to nine, Mulroney finds the doors open and a steaming latte waiting—and a gleaming CX-61 by Olioglo sitting front and center on the showroom floor, glistening with life, veritably roaring its brilliance and seething with hunger for miles. A few of the Big Boys lean on a display case but don't glance at Mulroney. They stare, not speaking, but their thoughts seem nearly audible, so keen is their focus on the new rig. It's the rig of dreams, nay fantasy, verging on the face of Bicycle God. Keen and envious, they struggle internal, begging the question: Who more than each one of them could warrant such a righteous ride?

Franco lets the scene set like the maestro he has proven to be—the total bicycle purchasing experience surges to ten for ten, as Franco reaches for twelve, coming in a minute late, allowing the audience to murmur with restlessness as the caffeine, mechanical excellence, Italian beauty, perfection and lust course through the collective bloodstream before calling out, "Michael! Amico mio. Buon giorno. La bella, si?" Even the guinea horseshit seems right, and without stopping, Franco wheels the new rig out the front door.

Finally dressed with minimal but unavoidable self-consciousness and a modicum of blushing, mounting his high-end, high-tech, state-of-the-art, world-class, top-o'-the-line, featherweight Ferrari space-age rocket ship of a two-wheeler, Mulroney moves. Equally unavoidable is blending with the spirit of weightless propulsion, of excellence, in essence, of a storm surge in nuance and overtone. He presses the shifters—they buzz their faint whisper ever so briefly, shifting up or down, talking to each other until agreeing on the precise adjustment. He finds a resistance that feels mildly amusing and surges with low-end torque. Oh, it's an acceleration common to riders fresh from the bicycle shop but uncommon to a man recently renown for used car sales. He will ride the twelve miles home in an act of sheer rebellion. Twelve miles seems like a stretch his first day out, but what the hell. He can go slow—and should go slow in sight of the shop, where more eyes watch than not, to size up the old guy, see what he's got, if he's a ringer from way back or just another wad o' dough out to embarrass everyone, beginning with himself.

What can he do, twelve at eight? Ha!

He can call Allison or one of the service guys at any of nearly two dozen car lots for a ride if he gets tired. Well, he can call Allison. The service guys don't need to see him in a moment of weakness, and they don't need to see a bicycle that cost more than some terrific pre-owned cars with Mulroney dressed like a ballerina. If he makes it home, he'll be averaging seventeen hundred bucks a mile. Fuck it; he's not really wearing frills or chiffon. He'd draw the line on that shit.

And the average will improve. And it's like the Zen guy says: you gotta start somewhere.

Besides all that, he will make it all the way home on pedal power, because it feels simply amazing, everything coordinated in grace and movement, getting him flowing down the road with a spirit too long gone. Road? Whoever thought the access road could be a thing of beauty? Who would ever take a car down these tree-lined, empty byways?

And think of the fricken' MPGs!

Componentry is all Campagnolo as ordered, including the derailleurs, the bottom bracket and (carbon) brake levers, carbon bars and bar stem and carbon wheels with some space-age spokes for hardly four grand more and intricately complex hubs. In a steady rhythm he tracks stats on his digital instrument panel that shows him holding fifteen with a max of twenty-two seven minutes in at 9:19 a.m. Sure enough, just under twenty grand went a tad over with the extra sox, gloves, spare tube and nine-function speedo, wireless, with a heart rate function, which is great, Franco said. "You'll be able to tell how you're doing!" Fuck it—it only added eighty-two grams, and that's only three point fuck-all ounces. Mulroney could take a three-beer whiz and save enough for a down payment on an old Vette—or a new Vette if he could pedal this bitch back to 1965. It feels light and effortless enough to travel back in time. But it can't.

Fucking nuts, but the guy was good, maybe great, planting those little seeds at just the right places. *Why can't I get my guys to do that?*

Shit. Twenty grand could have got scratch in all four gears off the showroom floor with some money left over for a tank of gas, a case of beer, and a motel in '65. And a house. A little house, maybe, but fuck.

Did Connie Conklin hold up or decompose like everything else? Would she turn up on a Google search? What would we have done afterward? Watch TV, drink beer, fuck some more and take showers? Walk around the block? Hold hands? She would have smoked a carton of cigarettes to get through her poses. Fuck. She's got to be dead by now. Must be—or at least mostly decomposed. Corvette ain't what it was either—out of the box'll run eighty grand now, give or take. You can't get a 427 anymore, but who needs the guzzle? They still handle better than a Batmobile, slightly. Mulroney could walk in, pick a color, and write a check. But scratch seems as tedious as a manual transmission. Here he's got, what, twenty gears? Maybe more? And this is different—none of the old gear jamming here; he presses the shifter slightly and the chain slides into place like clockwork. Youth came and went, and here he is, getting his jollies on a bicycle. Sunny day, a little breeze, blue sky. He could do a whole heap worse. He could go quicker than youth, drop fucking dead in a heartbeat. Or a blink.

So?

It comes down to life and no alternative but to pedal up this fucking hill. Besides, Big M OK Cars might sound like a used car lot, but it's times two dozen lots across town and into the hills. And online, now with CARCHEX, Auto Corroboration, Moto History, and Pre-Owned Zone. Which is something, and he's still frequently soft spoken, reasonably fit, not a bad looker, and quick on the draw. So you got to ask yourself: is the Big M himself a fucking four-star, bona fide cash magnate Big Boy, or is he a buff motherfucker or both or what?

Damn.

It's all the same: Vettes, Connie Conklin, bicycles. It's the reach for something new. That's all it is, all it was and likely will be. The motherfucking world goes away on you unless you keep pedaling, find something new to hump and get it on. Fuckin' ay! Life is for the living. You never really want a Vette—you just want to feel it around you, make it lunge anytime you want, for a while, till everyfuckingbody has a chance to see you behind that wheel.

Same thing with Connie Conklin—proving the power. She would have been fun, but she wasn't nice. She was a rough, chain-smoking, foul-mouth bitch with the tightest little body ever seen. He could Google her. Nah. He can fantasize what slipped through the cracks, like he might go back for some sweet bye and bye, but he can't. No life is free of loss. Let's say he found her. Let's say she looks good and dresses well. She's an intellectual vegetarian with no moods, no demands, a magnanimous outlook, and no strings. Let's say they have an excellent romp. Then what? Snacks and a little late TV before bed? Maybe they'd go again next week?

Or maybe she's a fat chain smoker in a doublewide three months late on her payment with a fouler mouth than before, with dirty dishes and feet. And twelve grandchildren. On their way over.

You get down to it; the single, lasting loves are the dog and the wife. It's the home pack you most often share the three bonding behaviors with. That would be sleeping, eating, and playing—not sex. Sex occurs best between members of different clans, herds, flocks, and groups to fend off the retardation, sometimes.

The dog grew old too. That was tough, much tougher than this hill, which is nothing but physical, and that's the easiest thing to counter in a world that keeps coming at you with another toll to pay, as long as you show a pulse. Come on, hill. Is that all you got?

Things clear up at the crest, where gravity finally benefits the home team and warrants a higher gear. Downhill. Overdrive. It feels like the last day of school, ever. The only climb here is the speedo—to twelve, fifteen, nineteen—get it on, bitch! Speed is freedom, like closing the deal right now and real money . . . till Mulroney squeezes the brakes and pulls over, twisting his cleats free, desperately dodging his first dose of road rash as the little phone plays its sonata between the spandex and spare tire. Mulroney finds footing and plucks it free and slides his finger, and a little voice sings: "We have a *counter!*"

Mulroney says, "Hello."

"Yes!"

"Who is this?"

"It's your real estate professional! We have a *counter!*"

Sometimes practical advances seem most available by ignoring technical advances. For example, what would he have lost by leaving this thing at home? "I'm waiting."

"They came up! *All the way* up to your compromise price!"

"Pulleeze. I didn't have a compromise price. You have a compromise price. What is it?"

"Two million, four hundred sixty-nine thousand dollars! We did it! Congratulations, Michael. We really are a great team."

Question: If a man on a bicycle sighs into a cell phone, can the sales professional on the other end really hear the message? "Look, Marylyn . . . We could be a great team, but we're not yet there. A team divides the labor. So far, I'm the only one *working* this deal. You represent me, not the buyer and not the deal. Me. You have yet to ask for mo money. *Capiche?*"

"This is a good offer."

"It's not my price."

"You don't want to sell."

"That may well be. Deliver the message."

VII

Spandex Monkeys

Mikey's first bike had a girl's frame and came secondhand with training wheels, but who cared with mobility at last? The trainers got wrenched off halfway through day three. Mikey was six already and nobody's fool. By seven he made his case for a Schwinn English Racer, the most desired bicycle in the world, which was known as the world back then and not the planet. It was a place where nature and adventure still waited. The Schwinn English Racer had a Sturmey-Archer three-speed shifter on the handlebar near the right handbrake. The shift linkage was chain-pull, inside the rear hub. Twenty-eight-inch wheels on a twenty-six inch frame were too big for Mikey to reach the pedals from the seat for four years, presenting a difficult choice: he could coast in style while sitting on the seat with his feet dangling, or he could stand on the pedals to gain propulsion, rolling his little huevos over the top bar.

Juvenile billy goat huevos?

Oh, baby. If they could only see me now. The descent accelerates to forty, pulling a G-force grimace in high-speed youth recalled. Tears stream—of joy—though Mulroney wonders who will cry at the used-car magnate's funeral if he French kisses a eucalyptus doing holy screaming Jesus on his fricken' fucking fly-weight bicycle. Creamed Mulroney has a certain feel to it, but who'd show up? *I mean, besides Allison.*

At age twenty Michael paid eighty bucks for a Peugeot UO8, a ten-speed in modern format that got him through two more decades till he sold it for three bills, a margin he couldn't refuse, though he'd now pay triple to get that bike back. Quintuple would be better than what he ended up paying for this new rig, which was what? Fucking exponential is what, which is more than any kid's toy should cost.

Five years later the next Peugeot got cranberry spray paint over the chalky white frame and boring decals. Then came a thirty-mile race that a young fellow with a new paint job couldn't help pushing in high gears for twenty miles—into the wall. Fatigue made him look old, and he wondered why the older guys passing by kept staring. A veteran advised, "You can't push high gears like that. You slide side to side over your saddle to keep the power over the pedal. Too much pressure. You got DDS." That would be Dead Dick Syndrome; Mulroney stood by a tree, waiting for his pecker to do something. The veteran told him to tilt the seat down a notch forward to ease pressure on the anus/dingdong nerve. So he did and eased the numbness until grooved seats came along.

Ten years into the groove, the media interrupted this program for BREAKING NEWS! The tragic consequence of bicycling! DDS causes impotence!

Mother Mulroney called in a panic. "Do you have numbness in your shillelagh or trouble getting an erection?"

"Who needs to know?" She needed to know because she was his mother for chrissakes, and a bicycle will bring it on.

Several decades down the road but only a week into his new ride, Mulroney eases out of town. He is unafraid but aware that road familiarity goes out the window on a bicycle. In a car, two miles is three minutes. On two wheels with a square inch of rubber on the road, it's different. He rides the brakes. His neck cramps, with his head tilted up to see ahead at high speed.

Did Lance Armstrong's testicular cancer come from groin friction daily, just like Bob Marley's brain tumor stemmed from nonstop ganja? You can't abuse nature.

Bicycle machismo has no logic, no sense of self-preservation and is invisible to the untrained eye. What's made to seem casual, nonchalant, and ho-hum is actually an uphill push so painful that joints grind like failed bearings. Bicycle macho is complex, not obvious. It has no props—no loud pipes or fag dangling from a teeth clench or driving one-handed in tedious self-consciousness with leather, fringe, conchos, and chrome. A bicyclist wears shiny shoes with cleats, spandex, and a plastic shirt with three back pockets stuffed with candy bars. Bicycle machismo has no body fat. It's a lean and mean pain machine, pushing the heart into the throat as necessary for a move. Lance went wheel to wheel with the pack leaders on steep grades, veins popping on the collective brow. At red line, or maximum give, or the threshold of thrombosis—Lance broke out and pulled ahead decisively—make that crushingly. The Frogs claimed drug enhancement and less friction because Lance only has one nut. The frictional charge never stuck and no need; Lance was so drugged. Yet lost in the media melee was a truth, no matter what drugs or how many balls or what size: tougher than your average toothless tattooed wonder, Lance demonstrated the difference between a macho pose and laying it out.

Here it is, Lance: change your blood with this space-age blood so you can go faster. Okay?

Sure. Why not?

Because it's cheating! That's why not! Cheating the whole wide world is not the same as winning! Yet Mulroney demonstrates as he imagines it might have been, for the feeling. Amped up, gearing down, he accelerates, not to be confused with pulling away crushingly. Mulroney's move may also be invisible to the untrained eye, especially in traffic, except from the Big M point of view. Women might see it too, women down to forty, or forty-eight. Like that one there, in the Volkswagen. She checked him out. There she goes again, with the smile.

Mulroney rides with a rearview mirror too—came out and asked for it, drawing glances from the bike shop elite like a pedophile at day care. Rearview mirror? What's the old fucker up to? What's next, training wheels? Or one of those cute electric motors? The rearview clamps low on the handlebar. Hardly an ounce—make that twenty-eight grams—it shows the big picture at a glance: who's veering close or fast. Otherwise a look back pulls the bike into harm's way, or overcompensation takes it to the ditch. Mulroney knew these things years before these twerps were born. They see this rocket rig as an old-guy supplement. When they hone in on the Certitudes, they groan—on a surge of more envy. Fuck 'um. The old guy is out here doing it, is he not? The Certitudes were Frankie's idea because they keep an old guy going longer. So? No big deal. Old goes well with poise. Mulroney's been around the block on two wheels. He knows the drill, just as he checks the rearview to see two riders out of their saddles pushing top gears, coming uphill from behind casually as a jog in the park, gaining with embarrassing ease. He sets with aplomb—and indifference, as the younger set passes easily.

He flips the mirror up to see what she saw, the one in the VW. But an old guy with a puffy face looks back, Poppin' Fresh nearing apoplexy. He doesn't feel puffy or old. He feels like the same guy. So what?

The chinstrap bunches his chin to make his cheeks puff with acorns for starters. The crop-top helmet makes him look like Friar Tuck. But he needs the helmet. Doesn't he? Fucking helmets.

The puffy face amused her. That's all it was. Merely mordantly curious, she smirked, which is not a smile. What a rude kid.

He coasts to the light. What's the rush? A fat kid on a so-so mountain bike worth less than half of Mulroney's front wheel passes casually, breathing more from fat than effort. So what? Factor the potholes, pitfalls, knockdowns, drag outs, upper cuts, hooks, jabs, and body checks of the four decades Michael Mulroney has on the kid, the pace reckons about even. Or five decades—some of the kids won't even make his age, much less on a bicycle.

Past the last light in town, traffic thins. So do thoughts and clutter, as the busy thoroughfare becomes a country road, lushly green. Mottled light hides the bumps. Sunbeams jumble in the leafy tint; blinding brilliance breaks the shadows, so he squints to get it right because a steep shoulder spills forty feet to a rocky bottom. Mulroney eases in to speed.

With speed comes a mental process devoid of recollection. Fuck it; you got your memories, and then you got your modern technology. This is a carbon fiber speed machine for chrissakes. What's that worth? To be perfectly honest, it's hard to tell. You still got to pedal the sumbitch. It'll roll backward if you don't. Mulroney is breathing hard and sweating. His chest is pounding—but it doesn't hurt. That would be a kick in the head. So what's the diff between humping this high-ticket whore to the top of the hill and a department store model? He'll need to sort that later, at a lower heart rate. At the crest he coasts into the descent and gains speed to the bottom, where he stops to look back up at what he couldn't see coming down. He flips the mirror again. Still puffed and ruddy, he looks more alive, if not younger. Two boys in a passing pickup yell out the window, "Spandex monkeys!" Mulroney looks back again as another two riders descend in tight pants and gaudy accessories.

One yells back, "Inbreeds!" Mulroney laughs along, involved and invigorated, mounting up again for Watsonville, a California dream of Mexico with better weather and irrigation. And why not? It's only another twelve miles out.

VIII

A Beautiful Place to Be

Salinas is forty miles farther south and well known for its iconic place in literature . . . But it's grown more distant from Eden than it feels from Lodi. Strip malls, light industry, factory farms, and row mansions to the horizon fill what used to be wide open when John Steinbeck called it a long, golden swale. Like devil spawn— like Versailles mated with Levittown, yielding Doric columns, Roman parapets, swing sets and tricycles under a soft blanket of sound. Fights, farts, fucking, flushes, and forks clattering are a context for the muffled desperation of life passing with intermittent calls:

"What more do you want from me?"

"You cunt! You ruined my life!"

Watsonville, on the other hand, is what it was, yielding produce for sale roadside, like at the Corn Palace.

Chiles rellenos are made from scratch at *El Ateño*, where the cook *no habla Anglais* and builds *rellenos* with *pasilla chiles, no poblanos pero pasillas*. Exquisite *cucina* precedes Four Dollar Tuesdays at the restored Fox Theater across the street. These are the days, my friend, in blessed relief from the rest of California.

Allison—Ms. Mulroney—is a country girl at heart who once imagined life in California as a lovely stroll around the block, which it might have been if the build-out wasn't so rampant and the weather was a tad warmer. But it gets cold and wet, and the scene refracts with every fad, cliché, media trend, and lifestyle, predictable and chronic, spurred by a *go-for-it* mentality that feels oppressive. But it's home for the Mulroneys, at least for the time. Oh, Hawaii was her idea; not that he would mind, given a level playing field, but it's not level. Do twenty car lots count for nothing? Or twenty-two, or four, or whatever it is? At least the problem of location is physical and manageable, while the problem of compatibility is something else. Michael Mulroney often draws on old images to restoreth his soul. The inherent problem is also age-related, as the images get older and older. Only the wedding night still rings clear after so many years: "Oh," she cooed, with her feet in the air, "I really hope we can, you know, till death do us part." That was decades ago, when a babbling brook murmured sweetly as a bull trout surged upstream. What a woman, and he marveled that he'd thought as much for so many years.

Allison is a keeper, a certain sexual object, which women want to be once the sexual objectivity begins to wane. But a woman over fifty with a concise pooper and breasts residing above a reasonably flat stomach may not necessarily be married to a contented man. Sexual thrills fade after a few thousand rounds, but that's why God invented reefer, liquor, and low light—to compensate and enhance. That's what most women don't realize, that a bit of exotic lure makes a man want to come home. Women often resist the idea, until the tables turn, like when that kid with the camera drooled over Allison. Did Mulroney mind? Not a bit. Did she look better, after another man admired her? Let's just say it puts a gal in fresh perspective. At any rate a man shouldn't be horny all the time or proud of it, but he does feel blessed with fortitude—maybe that's why he still rides a bicycle at his age. He's grateful as well for a practical, easy wife. So? Maybe they'll move, if the price is right. A car lot can run without him easy as a dozen car lots, at least in the short run till he finds a buyer and opens a lot or two yonder.

Watsonville on approach is clearly a pleasurable place in a world of diminishing returns. Take the corner of Lakeview and 129, with a single mom, old-school—twenty-eight, give or take, with no tattoos, no body piercing or slovenly appearance—make that thirty-eight but still a package. Okay, showing some difficulties in her face and neck. Forty-eight seems more the mark, which isn't to say good from afar but far from good. She simply shows some age, which happens to the luckiest among us. Mulroney doesn't know her age, but can plainly see the regional mix of road wear and classic lines. She's well preserved, so she could have had a personal trainer and cosmetic surgery if she's from Mulroney's neighborhood. But she seems more original, physically fit as a function of work. She looks like the real McCoy, a woman of sustained curvature and facial beauty, despite the sun and dirt and challenges. Like original beauty, she seems seasoned with care and still a classic. She's got a little hook in her nose, but that too is like a rule successfully broken.

She sweats under a load of boxes, her print gingham moistened but hardly soiled. Laboring like salt of the earth, she seems soulful as Rose of Sharon and may be a descendent. The place smells like country. She and her young son make a modern fresco of olden times: Rosa y Panchito resigned to simple life. The little dog tags along behind. How cute. Manual labor and hard breathing seem cleaner in Watsonville and not so rare. Panchito works harder than most kids, steady and slow, getting it done.

It feels like a good place to stop, so Mulroney can blow his nose, reshuffle his nuts, rehydrate, and watch the boy and mom unload the car and U-Haul. The Oldsmobile is dinged and faded but seems good for a few more trips. Yeah, closer to forty-eight. How does a woman get here, single mom in a farm town—a woman past the age of realization, who looks like she always knew better?

The U-Haul is a set piece with the bungalow, a stone's throw from California 129. The boy will ponder direction out that window for the next few years, or maybe he'll go to the other side of the house, to watch the chard go crimson over a hundred acres, or he'll watch the big machine base-yard across the road. Maybe he'll develop tumors from pesticide over-spray while he fancies a future. Lakeview Drive runs north to the littorals of the Eureka Canyon Range at the edge of Corralitos. The yard on that side is flowers in hundreds of rows separated by gravel paths for golf carts, so suburban wives can ride and point at what they want and tell the driver how many.

A FOR RENT sign wobbles in the breeze till Rosa pulls it off the doorframe to claim dominion, just as California was claimed for Spain. Panchito hoists a folding chair under each arm. Rosa gets the other two. They carry the four-top table, the matching end tables, and coffee table, turning each upside down, so the particleboard and staples are facing up. The oak-grain laminate suffers from age, coming unglued. The strips flap with each step. Rosa shakes her head and mumbles.

Still in the truck are the rickety lamps, the toaster, radio, twenty-five inch TV, the bric-a-brac to make the place homey, and the odds and ends of daily lives that strive for more of the same.

These are the days the boy may treasure, when his poor, old, hard-working mom was hardly more than a girl, and they made a home in which to grow. You can't beat Watsonville for natural charm. And leave it to the Mexicans to live as they should, as life was once lived in America, with less of everything but hope.

Wait a minute. What? A buck-and-a-half, four-slot bagel toaster in designer white from Williams Sonoma? No dings or dents and the tags still on?

Hey. The fuck you staring at? Fucking second-story guy.

Mulroney throws a leg over and clicks in. Rosa knows the guy pulling up in the truck, but her greeting seems marginal, a half-nod. Rosa may be younger than she looks, because hard knocks look old at any age. She can obviously still get back up from down in the dirt, and it must be the motherhood thing that keeps her going here.

Juan Valdez could be Panchito's father or the latest stand-in. His self-esteem throbs like an artery, especially when he stands near his truck, a chopped and lowered unit with four back wheels and four doors, a very long bed, spotlights across the roof, little amber lights all over, and more chrome than he's got in his teeth. Why won't he help with the furniture? At least he brought a new blender—and it matches the toaster. He's got a load of blenders and toasters. And what? Bread warmers? Pasta machines? Must have knocked off a delivery truck—a big truck parked by a house in the upper burbs, where he got the artwork. It's a painting of a pregnant devil with a bull's eye on his stomach.

What?

She looks worked over with nothing to show but a kid and some top-drawer appliances from Juan Valdez. She could have a yard sale at fifty cents on the dollar and convert to a month or two of groceries. Take some of the pressure off. She's built well though. Probably what got her in trouble in the first place. Who knows? Maybe the kid'll take care of her in her old age.

Yeah, yeah. You see me. I see you. I'm riding my bicycle. You're a grit with a truck payment higher than your IQ and a load of stolen merchandise. Yeah, yeah. See you, chump.

So Mulroney eases out, keeping an eye on the swarthy boyfriend, because a man of experience naturally senses the rearview.

IX

View is Everything to Me

"Hello? Mr. Mulroney?"

"Yeah. What?"

"Hi. This is Judith Elizabeth Cranston Layne with Coldwell Banker Clifton Baines."

"Who?"

"I was wondering if I might be able to show your house in, say, ten or twenty minutes?"

Aw, Christ on a crutch. "Ten minutes? I don't know. I just walked in. Allison's not here. She'll throw a fit if you show the place like this."

"My client is very excited to see it. He's driven by three times. He says he didn't stop because he didn't want to see it, because he was afraid he'd fall in love with it, and he doesn't want to go over two point two, and your place is way, way over his budget."

"Do you honestly think it's way, way, or just way, or maybe it's only a few bucks over his target price? Who the hell doesn't go over budget? Nobody is your correct answer. So, you think he's a player? Or a dud?"

"Yes. Most definitely I do believe he'll play."

"Yeah, fine. Bring him by. Give me thirty minutes. I still got my tights on."

"Mm. Well. He has a plane to catch."

"Fine. Bring him by now."

"See you."

Mulroney hangs up. Then he dials, rethinking the exchange with Judith Elizabeth Crampton Pain. She said *him*. What does a single man want with four bedrooms and four baths? Who cares? Maybe his wife is passive, but he's got live-in in-laws. Or he's the money partner, and the other half will adapt as necessary.

"This is Marylyn Moutard."

"Michael Mulroney. Hey. We got one coming by in a few minutes. A single guy. Some woman from a Coldwell Banker office with a bunch of names."

"That would be Judy Layne."

"Yeah. I'll be here. Any word from the good-time boys?"

"Of course. They countered. They raised you a dollar. They think you're playing a game. They think you're strange. They're willing to play along."

"So where are they now?"

"Don't waste my time, Michael."

"Did you have a little chat with them, you know, about good faith and wasting your time?"

"All the appropriate dialogue was exchanged. They're at two million two hundred thousand and two dollars."

"Good. It feels like progress. Let's counter with two million seven hundred forty-nine thousand nine hundred ninety-seven." Marylyn sees no humor here. "Marylyn?"

"Yes."

"You'll follow up with this one coming over now?"

"Yes."

"You might want to tell the good-time boys we got another player."

"Are you done?"

"Mm . . . Yeah. I think so."

"Well, good."

"I'm glad you're pleased. Don't I need to initial the papers for the counter offer? I thought that was required by law."

But Marylyn's thoughts are rendered conjectural with the phone clicking dead. Was it a soft click? Or an emotional click? Who cares? That's the problem with selling a house. It's such a bother of emotions and strategy, none of it mattering until a legitimate player steps up with the money, and the deal closes. Then emotions and strategy matter even less. Who in their right mind would play footsies on two point two, or two point two oh two or whatever chickenshit lowball they came up with, thinking they can step up to the good life on a ninety percent loan? Because that's what they're banking on, sure as California is the leverage state.

Meanwhile, who can even develop a decent strategy for his own life with nonstop straightening the furniture, sweeping the decks, putting things away? And for what?

Well, for better prospects in case the eight-name woman coming over with the three-time drive-by might be the player in question. The next hour will likely suffer slow death on one more mind-numbing discourse by another halfwit wannabe kicking the tires and fingering the dents. But prospects defer to attitude, and if he's a stiff, the whole afternoon will still be left, in spite of this imposition. In the meantime, luck will favor the receptive mind in a well-swept and sorted house.

As a salesperson at heart, for whom the fundamentals are second nature, Mulroney knows these things yet feels foolish turning on the lights and elevator music. He feels stranger than when he had to stream strings of plastic banners on a car lot. Plastic banners are obviously plastic, but this is not obvious. People think it's real. They think that having lights on with elevator music is how it will be, with them firmly installed in their new lifestyle. No—they don't think it; they feel it.

Now why the hell is that?

"Mr. Mulroney!"

"Yeah. Come in. Come on up. I mean, take your time. Do whatever . . ." Fuck it. Do whatever you want.

So enters Judith Elizabeth Cranston Layne with Coldwell Banker Clifton Baines. "Hello," she says, huffing up the entry stairwell, which, you'll notice, reflects both the Lloyd Wright influence as well as the Donovon Hewitt imprimatur—"*They* are the architects. Can you be*lieve* it?" Offering her card: "I'm Judith Elizabeth Cranston Layne with Coldwell Banker Clifton Baines." The card says it yet again, as if such a moniker could ever be remembered by anyone but Judith Elizabeth Cranston Layne with Coldwell Banker Clifton Baines. "This is Roy."

"Hello, Roy," Michael Mulroney says, heaping scoops of warmth and hospitality as only a seller who wants to sell can do.

"Hi," Roy chirps, tucking his head more securely into his apparent shell. Roy is painfully shy, perhaps pathologically introversive; this is plain to see, clarifying the challenge to Judith Elizabeth Cranston Layne with Coldwell Banker Clifton Baines and Michael Mulroney. The buyer must be made to feel at home, like it's his home. Like he's okay, and the place is okay, and he in the place is equally okay.

Okay?

Roy's head is shaved, and . . . could it be? Nobody wants to stare, but apparently, his eyebrows are shaved too.

His skin is pale white—wait a minute!

No, his eyes are gray, not red, so he's not albino. He's only a shut-in. The timorous demeanor is thorough and makes the seller wonder where a so-called buyer with nuts like chickpeas will *get* two point seven five. Yet here again, the seasoned veteran defers to rudiments: *Never* prejudge a prospect. Some of your wealthiest people on Planet E look like schleppers, ragtag as bag people just off the boat in need of a bath and a job. So you just can't tell, though this one seems particularly unwealthy.

But enough assessment. Judith Elizabeth Cranston Layne with Coldwell Banker Clifton Baines takes the lead, pointing hither and yon, brandishing insight like the leader of a marching band. "I know this house! Come. The kitchen is a*maz*ing."

She must know something about the net worth of the party of the second part. Or she's a cold closer. Closers don't waste time on peasants—so either she's a closer or she didn't suss him out. But she seems on—on the trail, on a scent. She's toying with him, telling him what to think and when to think it. Is this Roy an idiot *and* a world-class pussy? Because the kitchen is not amazing or a*maz*ing. Fuck it. She leads; he follows. Let her sell the sumbitch.

Roy looks where he's told to look. Sometimes he touches what he's looking at, or what he looked at a minute ago.

"Just wait! Till you see this bathroom remodel. It's *fab*ulous. The *tiles* are fabulous, and I a-*dore* this use of glass block. Don't you?"

"Yes, I do," Roy says.

Mulroney explains, "The master bath wasn't a remodel, actually, but a rebuild, up from scratch, or from a hole in the wall at any rate, surrounding the ff . . . fricken' ruins of this cockamamie, sunken-floor tub that was . . ."

"What color was it?" Roy asks.

"Dark blue. Not a bad color. But the design was late seventies, Roman orgy, with the tub sunk about three feet deep, and backrests under the showerheads, in case you wanted to cover the drains and fill it. And sit in it. It was awful."

Roy reaches gently to touch a glass block. "So . . . No more Roman orgies?"

"Hey, it'd be your call, Roy," Mulroney assures. Judith Elizabeth Cranston Layne with Coldwell Banker Clifton Baines shifts uncomfortably. "You'll probably need some fresh Romans."

"Oh!" Roy gasps, blushing headlong to cherry on vanilla.

Judith Elizabeth Cranston Layne with Coldwell Banker Clifton Baines recaptures the lead that Michael Mulroney unwittingly stole. Displeased as a seasoned professional who's had her front-end T-boned, she smirks, suggesting that the deal is officially choked unless she can save it with charm and skill.

What she can do is give a seller a fucking break. Are they not headed for the same goal? If not on the same play, they're at least on the same team. Aren't they? Really?

Casting dourly over her shoulder, she guides the mark to the master. Turning to a new future on another flourish, she proclaims this bedroom . . . Is. *Absolutely*. *Fab*ulous. So are the views from the rear and front decks, fabulous, but then calling the two views equal could lose the unique, not unlike one-of-a-kind characteristic each of the views commands. From the rear deck, which, by the way, is the location of the hot tub, you look east, to the Eureka Canyon Hills in a panoramic vista to die for—"while you're soaking your bones, I might add."

"O'er the freeway," Roy murmurs.

She leads the way, away. "The front deck, on the other hand, is more succinct, which is not to say smaller, which it is, if your brainwaves process only mortar, tiles, boards, nails and such, which the sum of these parts surely surpasses by a long shot. This front deck overlooks the biggest ocean in the entire world with an unobstructed view for a hundred eighty degrees that will take your breath away. I mean it will literally . . . literally . . . It. Is. *Fab*ulous! And I think it goes without saying that if a place *ever* captured the claim of Views! Views! Views! Well, this *is* the place."

So the rapturous real estate rhapsody flows mellifluously from Judith Elizabeth Cranston Layne with Coldwell Banker Clifton Baines.

Michael Mulroney laughs short, stifling a request for a barf bag—nor will he pantomime the grunt and gag reflex, not even as a joke, because such could be misconstrued, miscued, potentially lewd and ultimately screwed. Rather he excuses himself for a beer, though he doesn't mention the beer. What if either one said yes, I think I *will* join you in a frosty quaff?

Please. A man draws the line.

Judy, the overflowing storm drain from Banker Baines, babbles on. A fly on the wall may sense that Roy is suffering just like Mulroney. But maybe not. Roy seems appreciative. Mulroney considers intervening, to assure Roy that the place is just as it is, as he sees it without the adjectives, and that he can design and build any kind of lifestyle he chooses under these rafters. But no. He senses a time in the future, where he may need to reference Judy Cuntish Baines' pitiful excuse for a front end, and any word here would subjugate his position. Might she sell it? Not a fuckin chance—not to Royboy anyway. Mulroney knows a chump when he sees one, which is not to judge by the cover but to sense the essence, of which your world-class closer has sensed a few.

Selling a house is a curse of sorts—that's what Sales Manager Mulroney would tell his team if any fucking one of them knew who they were dealing with and had the smarts to ask. They don't.

But Mulroney comes clear on two points of realization, which is not another California song and dance, but the situation revealing its truth and its needs. The first insight occurs in transit, on taking leave of Roy and Judith Banker Baines, proceeding to the fridge for a beer or two.

The second illumination is one week later, also in transit, bidding adieu to the odious Mrs. Mumford Milguard Munro, moving again to the fridge for a beer. Lining up side by side, as if the week between them didn't exist, Mulroney glimpses meaning—make that singular meaning among myriad potential meanings, this one with notable relevance. It comes down to possessions and the karmic debt of ownership, which comes down to drudgery. How blessedly seductive the aging Brahmin can make life seem, as he heads out to make his way in a compassionate world, alone with a beggar's bowl. Objects demand maintenance, lest they lose their dollar value. Bane Judith prattles on, restating the obvious on the views, the tiles, the furnishings and fabulously refurbished falderal festooned like fungus from rafters to foundation—so much stuff that a talking head must keep up to get it all in, or out. She can't shut up . . .

The time between the two moments was not dead time or gone time, though the house-selling task puts a tinge on all time. But a tinge also defers to process; nobody actually sells a house. A seller waits on chance and timing.

Sorting the rubble of the week in between, Mulroney seeks something to admire but comes up short, like a hobo late to the landfill on trash day—all the good bits are gone. That's what the house sale process feels like, bereft, like a dump in late afternoon. It's nonstop cleaning, turning on lights, and finding the goddamn elevator music. Fuck.

Several items from the gone-dead week could have value, even if only as amusement and/or entertainment. Like Roy's career—make that Dr. Roy. A timorous man to be sure, he is also a young surgeon specializing in lower gastro-intestinal maintenance, repair, and replacement as necessary—what Mulroney would call an asshole doctor, though only in a private moment, to himself. The good news, such as it is: Judith Baines did qualify the party of the second part, affirming as well his aspiration to greater affluence and appropriate imagery, mobility, superiority. After all, he was shopping the neighborhood at the top of the hill. Roy glittered on paper, but the bank said no, even though everyone knows doctors are rich, or soon will be. Alas, Roy had "suffered a reversal in his investment strategy"—JEC Layne's language. Roy *simply loved* the place but crapped out. The good news was her concession that she too suffered from her own mouth-hole effusions—"I don't do this for fun." In fact, prattling on and on and on gave her a ripping fucking headache every goddamn time. Roy wanted another visit, just to see if that lovey-dovey feeling would hold up. Judy Layne advised that another visit would be great, any time, after a visit to the lender, just to see.

She saw. Not to worry, said Judy Layne, though she didn't say it directly but rather through the agent of the first part, she who first acquired the listing, Ms. Marylyn Moutard.

Roy may be back, said Marylyn, according to Judy Crane, because he's a doctor after all, as in practicing physician, with Medicare, Medicaid, Medical and other sundry medi-mother lodes to mine, and anyway, she, Judy C, loves the place and will definitely be back.

The single item rising from the ashes of the-week-that-was was Judy C Layne's return, as promised. It's a vision, through a glass darkly. Mulroney smiles wanly as Mrs. Mumford Milguard Munro, in basso profundo, assures Judy Layne, "You know, view is everything to me. View is everything to my art. So, I mean, we must have view. We need view. View is our primary need." Mrs. Munro's harrumph is meant to underscore her and her art's need for view, in case anyone in hearing range didn't quite get the point or the first person plural required to include herself, her art, and her life.

"Then, too, we also need space, as well. You know, I teach art. I have up to twelve students on some days, and each and every one of my students needs space for a big canvas. I would estimate eight feet by eight feet. Each."

Mulroney calls from the fab kitchen: "Big canvas? That's a fricken' tent." Judy C turns purple, as her sensitivity dictates.

"That's the work space required, not the size of the canvas."

"Oh. I thought you meant that each one was . . ." He strolls back in with his cold brew.

"Yes. It's apparent, what you thought."

"Oh, I think you might be surprised."

"Oh, I think not."

"Well then. I'll leave you two ladies to . . . whatever's necessary."

Mulroney takes leave yet again, not exactly proud of restraining himself from telling this bitch to get the fuck out and pronto but feeling good in speaking truth to women. Fulfillment derives on yet another glimpse of the ineluctable: that life is but a series of leaves in taking, till the last curtain falls. He sincerely contemplates prospects for Judith Cramden opening wide for the Big M under special circumstances, say, like his expert facilitation on a double ender—make that six points on two point seven five—if it was late, and he could get a few drinks down her. Not that she's such a pussycat, but the principle of the thing might go a long way in alleviating the angst and the other, with the cleaning and low lights and fucked up music.

"Such a boor," Mrs. Munro enunciates clearly enough to be heard from twenty paces and around a corner. "The place is not right. It doesn't feel right. Maybe it's largely because of him. Maybe it's only because of him, but one supposes that the cause of the trouble is secondary to the trouble itself. Don't you agree? You know, the right atmosphere of a place is quintessential to my art. A place has to feel right. I don't speak for myself alone. You know?"

Yeah, right. That cow knows what Mulroney is thinking. If she knows anything, she's smarter than she lets on. Now there's a difference between last week and this; last week the dog and pony show came after a great bicycle ride, and this week the ride has yet to occur. They have a name for that, when the aftermath seems somehow less than the anticipation. Damn. What is it? Oh, yeah: life. On the other hand, Mulroney feels better when a ride is over, but that's because it's out of the way, and maybe that's life too. Then again, he feels better, looking forward to a ride rather than hanging around the house with that uppity, nasty woman.

So Mulroney finishes carb-packing and saddles up, as it were, wincing as the minimally padded crotch support in his spandex riding shorts sorts itself between the nuts and the seat, a *Sella Italia* minimalist dream with hardly skeletal carbon graphite bones and a gram and a half of *TechSkin* designed to wick the sweat right off your taint while sliding to and/or fro as necessary, smooth as a baby's buttocks, but not pressing the vital nerve, directly below which the seat does not exist. It's the finest seat that money can buy, imposing itself presumptuously as a stick up the nether vortex. Well, not up but under, with an equally egregious assertion, such as Mrs. Mumford Milguard Munro would like to make up Mulroney's sphincteroo—with her broomstick! Under and alongside, till the point pokes the backend of the nutsack . . . Mm!

Wait . . .

What about . . . What about a new seat for well-hung wheelmen? Call it the Eggcup, and instead of a leather-wrapped cattle prod pressing hell out of the gonads, the seat would stop at the front of the taint, short of the scrotal sac, allowing the thin and lovely air as nature intended for a more natural dangle. Support? Easy! At the front end of the seat, slightly lower, would be two eggcups, side by side, one for each nut.

The Nut Cup? Nah. Who ever heard of a nut cup? The Candy Dish, perhaps . . . No! The Jewel Caddy, and it could be like . . .

Nah. Maybe the Double Barrel . . . No. Who wants shotgun imagery so close to his nuts?

It's the Eggcup.

But why settle for half a market? What about fulsome female riders known to suffer the labia squeeze every bit as bad? Majora?

Majorum? Majori? Fuck it. The Eggcup. It's perfect. Equal opportunity too.

Something to think about anyway.

Labicaddy?

Hmm.

Gimme a minute.

X

Aging Gracefully

Michael Mulroney is a self-made man falling behind in a mad world, dashing headlong to entropy. With dynamic energy sustained, he wonders how fast he can actually go on his new bicycle and where.

He takes solace in movement, in the rhythmic circle of wheels and pedals and a chain and legs pumping to keep the show on pace. Muscles do the heavy work, as the temple of his soul becomes a refuge, in which to take in the lovely scenery. Pastoral images displace his dissatisfaction. It's nice, but some notions persist: *I think, therefore I doubt*—Mulroney's synthesis in life is not what he'd anticipated. He's not sure what, exactly, he'd expected or hoped for, except for the presumed more, more and more of the thing. Moving to someplace else rarely cures life's shortcomings. When all those Joads fled the dust bowl for California, they only got fooled in the end, like they could have stayed home and eaten more dust. But moving now could be different, a change of situation that could change a worldview. He has more stuff than the Joads, starting with a huge house at the top of the ridge and the market, and he wonders if it could all fit in a beat-up truck.

California factors again in the scheme of things, with the nut bowl replacing the dust bowl. Would the Egg Cup sell well in the nut bowl? He thinks it would. Agog on ethereal fads and intrapersonal workings, channeling spirits and irrigating colons, trends serve a collective libido. That is, this market could be ripe! Hawaii, on the other hand, is sensual and lusty, which seems different than chronic and strange.

Allison Mulroney is slight but sturdy, naturally proportioned in the chest and womanly built, with good hips for more feminine curvature than those with bigger endowments or enhancements. Besides, some of those could have been guys, as everyone knows by now. She feels constrained in making her mark, or maybe she has no mark to make, which is okay for her and maybe beyond okay. She measures success daily in simple tasks: filling the bird feeder, watering the garden, putting something out for the deer and skunks and raccoons. She imagines happiness in warmth, in the archipelago to the west, where color and scent can also abound in more spritely abundance, with her nose not so cold. She imagines less of the pesky pop culture. Everyone walking around in their underwear seems like fun, and why not, with trimming down and bulking up gaining momentum?

Long-distance ownership can be tricky, but Big M OK Cars is a precision machine that could cruise indefinitely. It's up and running; buy cars, sell cars with a name you can trust, and they do. Or, the whole show could sell in a jiff. What would Mulroney do without car lots? He doesn't need the money he makes, and so many millions in a lump sum would be another challenge. Nobody takes a payout in a lump sum. Still, oodles to spend might open new vistas. Maybe that's what's missing, a new vista or two. He could bankroll a project or a cause, maybe something worthy, something civic. Maybe he could be a hero on CNN.

Maybe he could sponsor a month sabbatical in Vegas, with everything staying in Vegas.

Allison understands new horizons, new stimulation, new challenges. She won't respond to her spouse's anxiety depression because he shuts her out, won't open up in confidence, can't say what's ailing him, and Michael's idle distraction doesn't help. She often says she wants him to be happy, which isn't to suggest a girlfriend. Oh, she knows the difference between a strapping young man and a dirty old man. It's their ages. But a young man is easier to accept for his raging hormones, and Michael Mulroney is difficult to accept on many levels. Allison tolerates these things, and she giggles or winces if pressed. She also knows that well-meaning women who press her for feelings actually think her silly, but then they go away, which feels good. Anyone who watches TV knows that the male of any species wants the alpha slot. Paramecium males are crazy for paramecium vagina, when you get down to it, unless they're zygotes or morphodites or osmotics. It doesn't even matter; the male of the species is overbearing. Michael is alpha, and it simply seems unlikely that the well-meaning women in the area will ever be comfortable with that.

Besides, sexual appetite is a symptom, not an objective. A man understands a time for every purpose under heaven, a time to be born and a time to die, a time to reap and a time to sow. Somewhere in there comes a time to live, and therein lies the Mulroney misunderstanding. Maybe he missed something, but that possibility merely affirms his uncertainty. Life is not so complex: with the material side dicked and a beautiful wife when she's sober, which is more often now, with the occasional meetings. He has what he always wanted, what he'd always worked for. He's made them secure and then some, affluent, mobile and discretionary—a bit reversed for the moment, but look at the numbers. He could liquidate quick on a fire sale and still land on his feet—well, if they wouldn't mind renting and didn't need much money for clothing. Because the numbers get so big that a quarter inch either way can mean the world. Or the basement.

Allison calls out from another room, complaining or explaining or asking, but he's reading, and the exhaust fan drowns her out, and he thinks the drowning feels nice, as merciful as silence used to be. He thinks she doesn't know how he feels.

It doesn't matter what she's saying because it's another fugue on the inconsequential, a monologue that will not become dialogue because he will not yell back up the hall, "What?" He lets it go. She quacks and forgets. Maybe she'll ask again later, or not.

A few minutes later he's in the garage, tinkering with something but he's not sure what, standing, listening, trying to remember the last few minutes since he sat on the crapper.

Opening the mind and shutting the mouth feels better these days. He suspects it's what success comes to. Like last week when this old gal pulled up right here in front of the garage in her aging faux roadster, a late eighties Pontiac Fireball, or was that a hairball? Big M OK bought six Fireballs at auction and offloaded the last one a year later at cost less twenty percent. People don't think about the cost associated with flooring a used car for a year, but they should.

She stopped in the road with a personal need. He'd been a few miles on his new bicycle by then, so he was degreasing the sprockets and chain with solvent and a toothbrush.

Aware of a car stopping in front of the garage, Mulroney stood up. "Oh! There you are!" she said.

She seemed pleased with life and her car, as if she didn't know any better. Early to mid-sixties, she beamed through thinning skin, its translucence highlighting the veins, as wrinkles underscored her smiling eyes. As a lively character, her platinum hair and easy demeanor said it all: *we might be dead in a minute or two, so for now let's live!* She'd stopped to say hello—no surprise, really, at the top of the hill in sunny California. Come to think of it, no surprise either when she appeared to be . . . coming on. A sensitive fellow can tell. It hadn't been so many years since a woman made ovations, but she stood out, a milestone on the long and winding road. Yes, a tad elderly, but opening up and staying open is a way of life that can feel ageless. So, what the fuck? And her fun factor felt contagious—okay, not contagious . . . uh . . . worth sharing. Okay.

It's only natural. As the years stack up, womenfolk seem more aligned to the game spirit. The older woman in the Fireball could be a classic example of game leg, next phase. She said she nearly ran him over on his bicycle the other day and couldn't help noticing that he looks like Billy Bob Thornton.

"Then I thought maybe you *were* Billy Bob Thornton. You know, like, you moved into the neighborhood. Or are! Are you? Billy Bob? Thornton?"

"No, I did move into the neighborhood, but that was a while ago. I'm not Billy Bob Thornton. I don't know if that's a compliment or not. But thanks for not running me over."

Her smile firmed up in a practiced flirt. She batted her eyes like a dame called Nora in black and white and murmured, "Ooooh . . . He's my favorite. I live just around the corner and down a block."

"Yes, well." Michael stood and stepped up to lean on the car door for a neighborly chat. "We're practically neighbors, with me here and you around the corner and down a ways. It's nice to know the neighbors." She glowed and let him look.

And so he did, ogling her cleavage as intended and thinking her well preserved. Writhing with pride, she eased out, waving like a screen goddess of yesteryear. "See you!"

Since then, Mulroney walked around the corner and down a block twice, just to see, to no avail. He laughed both times, striking out on someone's gramma. But he laughed short—ask not for whom the delusion tolls. It tolls for thee—oops, here she is again.

"Oh, there you are!" She'd been looking for him too.

"And you!" he replies.

"Yes. I saw your car and thought, you know . . ."

"Yes. Thanks for stopping. Say, come in the garage here. I want to show you something." She winces, like she knows what he wants to see. Or show.

"No. I've got to be getting home. Just wanted to say hi."

"Alright. I'll bring it down. I'd like to get your opinion."

She shrugs, "Suit yourself," casting the furtive adieu over her shoulder.

"I'm Michael."

"Betty. Betty Burnham."

"Yes." Head cocked querulously, he remembers.

She's Betty Burnham—Mrs. Alfred N. W. Burnham of the Highborough Burnhams, founding family of Burnham's Department Stores. Before that, back in the formative decades of American department store fortunes, the Burnhams were something else, a hard-scrabble clan climbing to the financial stratosphere, or gaining altitude at any rate, on Alfred N. W.'s temerity, courage, and deafness to the neighbors' complaints back in Cucamonga, where he first bought chicken wire and wood and built cages by hand for his minks. They shit and smelled like rodents in cages, before they squealed, when Alfred wrung their little necks.

Alfred had spent much of his youth as a paperboy—even as he hand-fed his stock to sexual maturity—theirs. Oh, the saga was part and parcel to the retail empire, with its myth and magic set in the timeless beauty of Burnham Abbey, where a fabulously wealthy man could best remember his heroic climb from poverty to this. He called the minks his "pets," dispatching them with no emotion but with practicality on the road to fortune. So began Burnham furs, specializing in mufflers and hand warmers. The little minks multiplied quick as rabbits. Rabbits tasted better but could not compare for softness and money. Then came stoles and coats.

The taciturn boy became the humorless man and stayed that way. Alfred N. W. Burnham visited the old Mink Rectory a few days before passing, to tickle some chins, scratch some heads, and snap a few necks. Among his final pearls: "I wish I could clear the pearly gates that quick."

Mulroney read the bio in the Sunday supplement not so long ago, with profiles on Alfred's personality, his uncanny mercantile instinct, his staggering wealth, his vision and timing. Betting the farm on department store format with furs on the mezzanine, Burnham diversified years before furs fell from favor. Burnham's proved that a department store can endure through diversification—even under duress the farm became the abbey. Briefly referenced in later years was the age difference between Alfred and his newest wife Ellspeth, who caught his eye in the Mink Rectory with her knack for dispatching the little critters. With her trademark-dimpled smile she helped the little fur balls in their ultimate sacrifice to human comfort. Free of squeamish sentiment, she told the department store magnate, "You should see me on a bushel of beans." Her gambit stole his heart; she seemed so refreshing. "A pound in three minutes. Try me sometime."

Talk about a game gal with spunk and verve; Betty Burnham proved adaptable to market variables. An initial public offering of the biggest closely held corporation in California was impressive in its own right, and then she sold her Burnham stock just in time. She lost a half billion but had a few billion left, meeting the regional standard for wizardry.

She said, "It was nothing, really. You pick up the phone, call your broker, and say, 'Sell.'"

Selling put four point three billion in the widow Burnham's mink purse. Post-Highborough, the mink purse became Betty's hip pocket in faded denim, in tribute to California's enduring dream.

Ellspeth Burnham's fortune went from seven point one in three years to four point three because Ellspeth wanted out. Betty wanted denim and a used car, wanted to go native in the suburbs like normal people do. Could she adapt to that? It was fun to think so. She began with blonde as a concept but demurred soon to azure platinum.

A few billion, *mas o menos*, made no difference to Michael Mulroney. In a pinch, she would later confide, she honestly felt she could get by on twenty million. "Easy," she would insist. Downsizing is in! The California scene is so dynamically adaptive, and really, visible wealth had become passé. Contentment and mobility are the new big things. Acquisition? Who needs it, when we can measure our burden in pounds?

Of course, that's easy to say with your nest egg secure. The Mulroney egg is hardly a few million, and that's on paper, given medium to long-term maturity, once we get past this minor climb out. At least he has peace of mind, because he has the skills required to endure. Sure, he'd take more, but he won't chase it. He's had fun and feels proud of what he's done. Michael Mulroney started with twenty bucks. They like to say Alfred N. W. Burnham came from the mean streets, but that would be the mean streets of Palo Alto, where his father was a mere millionaire—which was real money back then. Who couldn't get filthy on a thirty million line of credit from square one? Old Alfred's bio missed that little iota. Who cares? Mulroney got his, and it's plenty more than Al Burnham's got—he's dead. And look . . .

She's honking alongside the garage like a fast friend. He waves cheerfully, but this makes twice that she wouldn't slow down, much less get out of the car. Is she Highborough aloof? Why else would she be so lively and then dismiss him on a little wave? Maybe he should stroll over one more time in the early evening.

He takes along a dog-eared color chart, first wiping it with a rag. He'll ask her opinion on the right color for his bicycle. Engagement is the ultimate compliment for lonely old women. From there he can size her up. This could be productive and, moreover, a correct application of honing and developing his funding skills over many years.

Mulroney imagines intimacy between Betty and the late Mr. Burnham. She was no deb, but she was nearly young enough to be illegal. Alfred N. W. represented lifelong security, even if his billions were single digit. It's hard to tell how she finagled the prenup, and Mulroney can't help but surmise some lip-gloss skillfully applied. Oh, men are weak, and she surely had a leg up.

Hardly an optimist, Mulroney senses grace in the aging process as it is shared in the neighborhood. Would anybody think twice about a twenty-year-old kid walking down the block to visit a twenty-three-year-old girl? They would not. But that is what people do. Or they can do anyway. It's what Mulroney should do because he wants to, because he's a good guy, and she's rich enough to save his bacon. And she seems inclined to engage.

He anticipates a fine time no matter what, because attitude is important. Maybe he'll have a beer or two. Maybe she'll offer tequila, a fine sipping grade. It's only six, but both are old enough to prefer an early start.

He hopes she's not a Republican, but fat chance. Then again, card-carrying membership in the religious right might make her more fun on a volley. Let's see how she holds up to a nonbeliever. What if she's a born-again fundamentalist reactionary tea-bagger, sitting pretty on the heads of fuzzy little animals?

Highborough?

Old money?

Could be.

But a neo-fundamentalist, he will not enjoy. How could he, if she's a dyed-in-the-wool, hand-stamped, tax-dodging, war-mongering enemy of nature? How can they be friends?

Then again, it's not really friendship he's after, which sounds cold and calculating, which it isn't—well, it's not cold at any rate. Or at least it's not meant to be. So what exactly is he doing? So he turns around and heads back toward home, as if he only walked up the road for a better perspective on his color chart.

XI

Cadence

Michael Mulroney hasn't smoked marijuana in a long time, till tonight. Three days may not sound like a long time, but a man imbibing twice a day to help cut back on liquor intake feels like he's teasing demons on two sundowns running. He let himself run out, thinking that's what a doper must do. The last bag came last year at the auction in Portland—good cars, a great market, and good buds. Cocktail issue buds. Nice. Buds that let you pass for normal—California normal anyway.

This bag from Watsonville, though. Who smokes this shit? This is insane. These kids got no . . . no . . . What? Did I just think something? Fuck.

Watsonville buds are not unique but from seed stock found up and down the coast, San Diego to Seattle. Not that geography matters much because it's all grown indoors—on either side of Mendocino anyway, where old Humboldt County growers have their pride and don't give a rat's ass who says what about X2 subsonic hybridization and E2 Extreme Frequency grow lights. That's like saying the new Mitsubishi roadster is kind of like a Shelby Cobra. The Mits goes fast and can take a Mercedes off the line, but it's not a Shelby Cobra.

Michael M doesn't care about hydroponics or hybridization. He stared at the street hustler who mumbled ninety dollars for a quarter ounce. What? It was eight bucks a lid only forty years ago, Mexican laugh reefer. But eight bucks was a chunk of the rent money, and let's face it: value is not what it was. Which comes back to downsizing, with people who traded free spirits for stuff over the years and now want to trade back. Nobody trades back, and the modern pot dealer talked like a real estate maven on low voltage, stoned stupid, slurring half-baked claims of excellence.

Mulroney used to be hip, but hip changed somewhere along the line, leaving modern Mulroney marginally mellow. The kids murmured and shuffled, passing a few joints, checking out the old guy sideways and thinking him uncool or way too clean. Turning to a mumbling joint smoker ripe as room-temp Brie, he asked, "What?"

The kid mumbled, "Pot, crack, ice . . ."

Mulroney said, "Pot. What do you have?"

"Fucker wants to know what I have. I told you. I got pot. You want to get fucked up? What's a old fucker doing getting fucked up? You heard me. So what do you want?"

The socio/political/hydroponic/cosmic diatribe droned on, till Mulroney interrupted. "Yes. One of those. A quarter. Ninety bucks?" He felt dumb for bringing twenties, only twenties and a few Cs, because tipping was not cool. He felt dumber still for bringing an inch of twenties. So he said, "Fuck it. Gimme two." He peeled a C off the bottom and four twenties from the top. Downsize this.

He could have got burned—oregano in rubber glue, Kentucky blue, whatever. But what could he do? And who cared? He didn't want a hit from the common joint but didn't say, *Nah, I'm not wearing a condom.* They would have stared, wondering why he talked so strange, because humor is not funny to street people. So he stuck his nose in the bag and said, "Smells like a skunk's butthole." The kids laughed. The old guy said skunk's butthole.

The kid laughed again. "Watsonville bud, man. Your lucky night." Mulroney shrugged and moved on, because frankly, the kids looked filthy. Did they fuck each other without rubbers and share needles? Who knew? Did he need to get high four minutes sooner? No. He did not. He would amble casually around the block and back to the car and attribute the delay to practical hygiene. Make that twelve minutes till he got the thing rolled, sealed, lit, inhaled and . . . we have ignition and . . .

Mulroney lifted off, melting down. Watsonville. Farm country. What? He didn't get burned, unless you count brain cells, which he tried to do, watching the thoughts come and go. What?

So the old guy sat out in his car on a side street, stoned, pondering his bicycle, a man at peace at last feeling good at last, acquiring nothing at last, blessed with recollection. He didn't get burned after all, unless you count brain cells—wait a minute; did he already think that? What extraordinary bud it seemed to be, so freely allowing life to pass smoothly with no purchase necessary, except for the bud. But then time could pass nonproductively, one hour to the next. Maybe that's why it's illegal.

Before he knew it, the hours passed pleasantly through the evening and sweet slumber to a beautiful dawn and that which compels a man to movement, bowels and bicycle—and another bowl, a small one in the spirit of moderation and bringing all the best to the top o' the mornin'. And a latte, for the spirit of the thing.

An early ride serves two purposes: cardiovascular stimulation and mindful wakening. Mulroney rides in affirmation of self. It's tough to get it up and get going, but then it's easier without so much pesky awareness of aches and pains, with consciousness all comfy cozy in its goose down comforter. So he takes it easy, feeling the essence of ease on his way to the peak. The bike shop kids assured him that climbing a hill is easier the next day and more fun.

But they're not kids. Thirty, thirty-five years old and working in a bicycle shop seems like a kid thing. But so does huffing up a hill first thing. So an old dumpling in spandex grunts up Hazel Dell. Never touching foot to pavement, he gears down, sweating already like a split tomato in July. But it feels good—more like his money's worth than he's felt in a long time.

Onto the summit for new heights in personal perspective, Mulroney knows he should *not* try this again tomorrow. But on a single rotation of Earth, perspective gains momentum on a climb up the backside to the same summit, a half-mile shorter to the top but steeper, grinding joints to bare metal at anaerobic levels, where an old rider can exceed recommended pressure and blow a gasket—where a weak blood vessel in the brain or the heart can pop, sending a rider over the top to seizure in a purple gasp. The great thing about a little puff or two is that these climbs become one in a process unending, as it too becomes easier by way of familiarity. Or is the old guy actually bulking up?

Scratch that. Pain transfer is facilitated by an agile mind— make that a mind free of muscular flex, a mind that can change a wall of agony to a mere nuisance, like a gnat flitting past. Then comes mile two of the long climb to the ridge, where the mind buckles like a dam near bursting. What now Mr. Miracle Mindset, whistle Dixie?

Oh, it's not all hearts and flowers, this heavy dope and rocket bicycle routine. Worse yet, if a guy pulls over to rest or decompress he'll play hell remounting on a steep slope, coasting downhill to get his feet clipped in five seconds or twenty yards, setting him up to brake at twenty mph for the turn back up to regrind what was already ground once. So what's gained? A bummer mood is what. This shit can kill a guy.

Better to hold ground, slow down, and distract the mind one more time. Give it something other than pain displacement to chew on. Maybe time a split from the start of mile two to the tippy top. That's what a split is. Isn't it? What else could be split but a segment from the whole? The speedo/odo/trip meter/cadence/split timer/elapsed timer/clock unit's split function is a subset of the elapsed time function, accessed on the function dial between odo/trip meter and . . . It's like a checkbook ledger, with numbers changing at random. Functions are reviewed in detail on pages 93-105 of the instruction manual, and Mulroney can get it. He can re-time this segment every time and shoot for personal best next time, though reaching the top with no coronary ought to count for something no matter what the time.

Fifty yards to go . . . Mulroney counts, projecting revs to the summit, ignoring the quadriceps clench and sides cramping, focusing on reassurance of self. Surely a man huffing up Hazel Dell is better off than puffing and guzzling on a sofa watching Breaking News of mayhem around the world and box office gross from Hollywood. Hurt gets magnified on a stronger pulse. Hurt lets a rider know where he's weak. Then it's life at the top—the real top, the not-for-sale top, which is not a house, but a hill. Then again, he did buy in. You can't get away from it, really.

A rider streams tears on the descent, outracing joy and sorrow into the stretch. Mulroney of America—no, Mulroney of Ireland riding point for the Guinness Team—wait, make that the Bass Ale team. Guinness is too dark and strong at this speed. A Guinness might be good later, but for now Bass Ale makes more sense into the curves and straightaways, letting the graphite go, easing the brakes and watching the little speedo climb to thirty-two, thirty-five, thirty-seven, eight, eight and a half—now pump the fucker! Suck it up! Go low—to forty-three and win by a nose!

Riding Hazel Dell the front way the next day is a push but the approach is through Watsonville, heading out San Andreas Road past strawberry fields forever, cutting up Beach Road to the bridge and across to more fields and under the freeway to a highway through town and out to 129 and Lakeview. The idyllic route may turn a page on Panchito's walk from rags to riches, or his hirsute father whose truck cost more than his kid's house or Rosa's struggle to provide.

Or Rosa's pooper. What harm in a look? Besides, a bicycle ride-by is random, infusing potential with karmic beauty, like drawing an ace to a royal spread if you're lucky, or a five if you're not. It was a good pooper, honest and true, perhaps a low-mileage pooper. But who is Mulroney to ponder mileage and gravity *vis à vis* poopers? And who cares? Stoned stupid under azure skies to outer fucking space, where the fucking planets and asteroids are, flying around and back, over billions of miles for light years. Oh, bicycling is better than ever—and she's not there.

Then it's day three in a row. Ignoring sore muscles is easy with puffy clouds overhead and a cardio chest strap signaling pay dirt at eighty-five beats per minute standing still. That's up from the usual seventy-two—but the usual seventy-two is rare, because it only comes down from the overbearing ninety if nobody's on the phone trying to fuck Mulroney from the hindside and asking him to bend a little farther and back up just a tad—please; don't get him started, and don't sweat eighty-five up from seventy-two; it's the reefer. The rig and the brisk aspect of nature at this time of year will absorb aberration and then some, to target HR optimal range at one twenty-eight to one thirty-eight, with one forty-five to one fifty okay in spurts, like the last mile up the Dell. Meanwhile, it's miles of golden afternoon and country road out front, room to move, to pump and feel good. So it's a leg over, down the drive, look left and right for the rubberneckers, drunks, and crazies and out.

It's sixty-nine degrees at a hundred ten ppi front and rear with two water bottles of electrolyte juice, the tropical fruit yellow kind, not that nasty pink shit, a peanut butter and honey energy bar and a feel for thirty-five miles of it, so let's get it on. Throw in a good ass shot on the clubhouse turn, and it's like it used to be. Who's complaining?

Or would it be ppcm? Tire size is in cm. How many cubic cm in a cubic inch? If it's two point five centimeters to the inch, it would be two and a half times two and a half, which is five plus one and a quarter. Six and a quarter times two and a half is twelve and a half times . . . three and an eighth?

Complaining? What a way to spend a day. What a way to meet the world, with a smile and a wave instead of a slosh and a slur, with some exercise instead of reaching for the sauce, like another slug o' sloppy joy could make you want to remember instead of forget. This is high. The buds are good too, and Mulroney makes a mental note to get more, lest he run out.

He pedals happily into the distance and feels happily distant from whence he came. Thirty-five miles is a step up from thirty, a leap from twenty, and a different level from twelve. Thirty-five miles is the longest route to date, taking in strawberries, cauliflower, chard, cukes, and berries to many horizons. It's a heads-up jaunt through Watsonville and out the backside, but people give an old guy more leeway, then it's a cakewalk up 129, two miles downwind with cars and semis speeding past at seventy-five with only mild buffeting in the wide bike lane.

The cut onto Lakeview turns the corner where Rosa and Panchito live, but she's at work and he's at school. Where else? Never mind. With pace and surge into more fields of greens, brussels sprouts and squash, past the vast nurseries, into the hills, up Hazel Dell and down, time doesn't matter. The world turns with life. Only the top two percentile of chunky white businessmen past the middle of middle age will feel this moment. Victory? Ring the bell! This is attitude and fortitude coming and going.

So a day resolves on fulfilling fatigue, another hit of Watsonville bud, two beers, a two-star movie, and deep sleep to sunrise. Hardly a balance of your seven basic food groups, it feels full and rich, which seems beneficial to the life issue. Why wouldn't it? Mulroney went overboard on a bicycle but already senses return on investment. Hazel Dell four times in four days? Get out.

Get on. Get going.

What?

But then why? The fuck? Not?

A couple three ibuprofen ease things into a familiar pace, with enough juice saved for the climb—like life, kind of. Franco advised seventy pedal turns to the minute, because the seasoned rider learns his best cadence and shifts up or down to maintain it. But labored breathing uphill warrants lower cadence, maybe, in the elderly.

Seventy cadence is an imprint, a muscle memory in which the legs take over. Pushing ninety downhill or fifty uphill, or coasting at zero to ease the muscles and memories or to stabilize on a steep descent with a cliff nearby is one and the same, kinda sorta, factoring frictional resistance. It's nine miles of flats to Beach Road, past the end of San Andreas, toward the first bridge, and another seven to Lakeview, also flat, with a light breeze and all pressures manageable. So the cardio holds admirably at one twenty-seven bpm over twenty-two mph.

Average speed is only twelve point eight, but fuck; one little hill cuts you back to eight or ten mph for a quarter mile or a half, and it's time to tip the first bottle. Who'd a thunk fat ass Mulroney would become a precision racing machine? Well, a machine anyway, one that still runs all the way to home.

A cadence check shows seventy, right on the money. Just for fun, a check on maximum cadence shows a hundred seven— where the hell? Oh, the long descent to Beach Road at thirty-three mph sustained. So why the average cadence of only sixty-three?

Mulroney knows why: because those superior macho nimrods at the shop held him back on seventy. Fuck seventy. Lance averaged ninety-five most of the time—about five gears up. He was on drugs and hot blood, but fuck those guys. Mulroney has borrowing power and will push seventy-five, when he can.

Okay, heads up; loose slag in the bike lane can take a wheel out from under in a blink. Then it's a pile up like road kill and road rash, pumping one sixty-five into thrombosis and going nowhere. You got to slow down anyway to make the turn. Asshole kids in the truck coming up from behind way too close—just for fun, give it a goose and . . . bingo, safe on the side road heading for the first bridge. Look at this: a hundred acres of strawberries on the right, a hundred acres of cauliflower on the left—and look at those guys with the machetes, top dogs for sure, cutting a head with one little push of the blade at the base of the neck, flipping the head up like magic and getting a hand under it and keeping it airborne like it's hot, so the machete can trim the leafy stalk from the sides and bottom in mid-air. It's a thing of beauty and skill, maybe the lowest-paid example in the world. Those guys make what, seven bucks an hour? Eight?

Then comes the beautiful curvature, rich on the senses all the way to the freeway and under the commuters speeding urgently to nowhere overhead. Finishing the first bottle at the Lakeview turnoff will avoid dehydration and cramping.

And there she is, carrying things in from the car—but not furniture. It looks like paintings and sculpture. Or chachkas. She looks tired or maybe tired of it. But fifty-plus is okay if she hangs on to that smile, so the unlikely bicyclist approaches.

She stops, her breath short on vigorous activity interrupted. With a large painting in hand she waits impatiently to see what he wants. Mulroney calls. "Hi. How's it going? Can you believe this weather? Hey, what happened to the kid?"

"What happened? What do you mean what happened? Nothing happened. Did something happen?"

"I guess he's in school." She waits for meaning. "I guess you're busy, still moving in."

"Yes. I'm busy. Still moving in." She nods abruptly. "My old place was too big. What does anybody need with so much room? I reached the point, you know, where I realized just how many things in my life were weighing me down. You know? Like baggage. And I don't mean the kind with those little wheels on the bottom. Ha! You know? I'm downsizing, and it feels fabulous. And I can use the extra money, you know?"

"Yes. I've heard that." Mulroney smiles as well, and the scene shapes up as friendly. With his water bottle poised for the quench, he says, "It's none of my business, but how much money can you save, living like this? Seems to me that the down payment on that Gonzales you're holding there would damn near cover the down payment and first six months on a farm around here. I mean unless it's a print." He shrugs. "It doesn't look like a print."

"It's not a print!" she barks, checking herself and turning to Camera 3, as it were, to a different angle on the countryside, where spaces are calmer, generally speaking, then turning back to this . . . this . . . man, who might be nosey but who knows art, who knows Gonzales—who knows real estate and comparative value. "I know. He's expensive. But I got it from the artist—uh . . . a long time ago. You know. Down in . . . uh . . . Oaxaca, where he lives. I went there. And got it. I've always loved him. I mean his work. I went there for the art. And I found his house. Can you believe it? He's such a doll, and I honestly think he gave me a great deal because I speak Spanish so well. You know, it just shows them that you care, and you're not just another tourist looking for a steal."

Such a doll? How Spanish could she sound with a nasal Noo Yawk overlay? But look at this stuff: it's a post-Neolithic modern fucking Aztec art museum. Oh, she's *got* the dough. Or . . .

Wait a minute . . .

Mulroney falters in mid-inventory as Juan Valdez pulls in too fast, hits the skids and steps boldly into his own dust cloud. He reaches the woman in two strides, turns his back to her so he faces Mulroney and stops as if to defend her from attack, or defend her honor, or attack Mulroney—or make Mulroney's eyes water.

"Whatchou want?"

Some clean air to breathe might be nice.

"Juan Valdez!" she chides, intervening awkwardly, handing him the painting and inhaling deeply as if gathering her wits or straining for more of that incredible man smell that can drive a woman nuts. Some women anyway, or at least one we know of. She offers her hand to Mulroney. "I'm Rosa, by the way."

He shakes it. "Good to know you. I'm Michael."

"And this is Juan Valdez."

"What he want?"

"His name *is* Juan Valdez?"

"That's what I said. What of it?"

"Nothing. Lucky guess."

"Guess what?"

"Nothing. I guessed his name was Juan Valdez."

"You guessed his name was Juan Valdez?"

"That's what I said. It's not a big deal, is it?"

"It might not be a big deal to you. To me it's stereotypical and racist."

"You mean because it's Mexican."

"You know what I mean."

"I don't know what you mean, actually. I know what I mean. I mean Juan Valdez isn't Mexican. It's Bolivian. Everyone knows that—except you."

"Except you—it's not Bolivian. It's Columbian."

"Columbian, Peruvian, Whateverthefuckuvian; who cares? Juan Valdez is the coffee bean guy, a Mexican with a Colombian name. Besides that, his name is what I guessed it was. What's racist? I wouldn't ever have guessed your name was Heather or Ashley—or Rosa. Does that make me an ageist?"

"No. It doesn't. I'm sorry. I'm from the city."

"Not to worry," Mulroney assures. "By the way, if it's not a print, it's obscenely valuable."

"I know," she blushes. "I love it. I got a terrific deal."

"Did the Cisco Kid here deliver it for you?"

She blushes. "He was in on the—he knows the artist. You'd be amazed how many people here have family in Oaxaca."

"Yes, it's amazing. Hey, Rosa. I don't want to cool off, okay. Welcome to the neighborhood."

"Thanks. I think I'm going to love it here. See you." So she turns away but turns back. "Do you live nearby?"

"Closer to Canna Screws." She looks puzzled. "Santa Cruz."

"Oh, yeah," she laughs. "Perfect. Say hello next time."

"I will. See you."

He rolls out, his eyes seeking focus ahead, his cleats seeking clips on pedals.

Juan Valdez asks again, "What he want?"

"Do you mind?" she slogs the artwork toward the house.

On the roll again, Mulroney checks the rearview to assess the situation, but it wobbles. He stretches his neck, but with a produce semi coming on, the situation seems adequately assessed. Once through the wobble and recovery, he checks the rearview again to see if she saw his bonehead play.

Nah, she wanted to get the hot art inside.

And he settles in to cadence revisited.

Juan Valdez. Stinky Le Pew would be more like it. But that's French. Stinky Valdez?

He drains the second bottle and rises to re-sort the nuts, then settles back in to blow the nose one side at a time with a finger press and thumb wipe. He peels open the energy bar with his teeth and checks the cardio: looking good at one-twelve bpm over sixty rpm.

So it's official, past the clubhouse turn to the home stretch.

Did the boyfriend give her that name along with a few toasters? When was a princess ever named Rosa?

Maybe Juan Valdez got a steal on the art. Brought it up, and she's fencing it. But where do the kid and dog fit in? You know? You don't put a hundred thousand dollar piece of art in a field-hand bungalow to make ends meet. Do you? No, you don't.

What you do is, you spread your legs for the guy who brought it up, because you got this sick craving for macho greasers, most likely because you wasted your first fifty years on overtly sensitive men in the urban core.

Then you agree to take care of his ex-girlfriend's kid because the ex is strung out and besides, the kid helps secure the arrangement and keeps the back door open. Rosa didn't seem seasoned enough for such a tight-knit setup. But then she did shut down the macho asshole in a blink, so she might know more than she lets on. Tough looking fucker. No accounting for taste. Nice painting though. No accounting for taste.

So ends the refreshment interlude of the thirty-five-miler, rounding a curve three point eight miles past California 129 and just past the Casserly Store into a headwind, which wouldn't be so bad, but the high-energy bar isn't coming on, and it's sixteen miles to go with the final seven fairly uphill. And the headwind is gusty.

Hazel Dell coming right up, and the next two miles may well pump the cardio past the anaerobic redline, where all systems will remain on go till the peddler throws a rod or seizes a piston or blows a gasket or scorches some rings and pits some cylinders, till an old, worn-out man gets off and walks.

Not really. This is cake. Fourth time in four days, and it's charming.

Cadence drops to thirty-one. The sweat pours, and seeking a rhythm in his strained effort, Mulroney feels the pressure rise, head and heart and skin. Sweat goes from pouring to oozing.

Well, you're gonna feel pressure. He sure as hell won't get off and walk. He's reasonably sure. He couldn't walk in these three hundred dollar shoes anyway. Or was it four hundred? You get off and walk; next thing you know it's the bike shop guys passing casually and seeing the old guy walking. What a revolting development that would be. Fuck it; they don't have a clue who Chester A. Riley is. But they got Mulroney pegged. Or think they do. But would it really be worse to be seen walking instead of straining like a bogged engine on a steep grade? Or flopping on the side of the road with the blue tinge?

Nah, just push—and pull. Control the breathing. Keep it steady, and there, it levels already. This is only the false summit a half-mile up, a mile and a half to go. But that's a good thing. The pressure can ease some on this level part. Mulroney can decompress a bit before digging deep for the long climb out.

XII

Free of the Material Plane

Rose Berry had been around the block on the investment, equity, and creative financing thing. She viewed the game board in terms of inevitable victory if she could keep energizing the positive as only a spirit-based, urban woman can do. That is, a winner among women will know in her gut how to move the pieces to rise above the mundane, workaday world. Not that she was poor or downtrodden, but a gal wants to exhale sooner or later—wants to ease into something more, something better, something fuzzy or frilly, something plush or flamboyant—something to show for her effort. Because a game gal is on, every day.

Youthful energy wasn't what it used to be, but Rose could still compete in a society ruled by corrupt, white men.

She would not see this messy relationship with Juan Valdez as two horny people deferring to convenience. Yes, he was a subsistence Mexican enamored by a classy gringa; and yes, she was a classy gringa with a taste for salsa *picànte*. But it was more than mutual infatuation and sex, much, much more. For one thing, the sex represented deeper meaning than mere friction of an intimate nature, much more, considering her recent issues of self-esteem. In fact, the sex proved she still has what it takes to attract a man and keep him in the home *cucina* at mealtime. Anyone dismissing Juan Valdez as a greaser would only be jealous of his incredible virility, his Latino machismo, his cut, his scent, his leer, swagger, threat, and truck. Only a heterosexual man would write him off, or a lesbian.

For another thing, getting involved with Juan Valdez confirmed her wits, still the most proven fundamentals of her survival to date. Maybe she dismissed him at the outset as well, but that wasn't racism; the guy was just so obviously on the make for white pussy. She did not appreciate that phrase one bit, but in the context of the misery, hardship, and deprivation his people had been through, white pussy took on new meaning, less heinous and sexist than when hatefully used by the general population. Juan brought a different value set to bear on the overall context—more compensatory, a balance in nature, a just reward—reparation, as it were. Or his usage could be simply idiomatic and phonetic: pu̇-sē. To him the potentially vile word was merely English.

After the fact it hardly matters. A guy that macho, that virile, that oppressed and exploited, a guy who rings the bell and keeps it ringing, can call it white pussy or sideways sloppy Joe, cooter, snapper, hairy taco or whatever he wants to call it . . .

But God, she hates that language, and he's white too, in the racial sense, unless the Mestizo influence makes him . . . Who cares? He's more man than she's ever had, and she only points out the importance of perception relative to preconceived prejudice in the socio-racial matrix because, in this case, she was right!

A guy comes on staring at your breasts, your crotch, your eyes. What does he want, approval? You size him up for violence and write him off as a no-count scum who's bound for friction with a woman or his hand before midnight. The streets are crawling with those guys.

Or maybe he's bound for a swift kick to the gonads, if he insists.

Then you play what you might think is a smarter angle—or at least a safer one—than the one you played with what's-his-name, the stuffed shirt, the prissy-priss-paper-pusher, Professor Smoke 'n Mirrors, who taught the accelerated course in hocus pocus, with a bang on the head and again in the shorts. You get swept off your feet and left for dead. You try to stand up from down, and short of that, you just crawl out of the mess. Then you get back in stride a bit smarter, a bit tougher, which is maybe all you ever need to do.

Anyone who ever played Monopoly can learn about money: She who finagles the most properties rules the world. It's easy if you get the ivories to lay down right.

Rose Berry never wanted to rule the world, and she would likely decline the opportunity if offered. She merely wanted to improve her position and maybe her love life and place of residence. Is it so unreasonable for a woman to have the same opportunities as a man, to expect a nice place to live with above-average-to-excellent accessories, professional and artistic neighbors who have dinner parties, and a heterosexual male mate with a six-figure income closer to seven figures than five, whose manners and apparent love for his woman are envied by all other women, whose body fat does not exceed eighteen percent, and whose stamina and appetite for romance are impressive and from time to time exhaustive?

No, that is not unreasonable, which is to say it is reasonable. She was, however, sick and (excuse me) fucking tired of lonely nights after tedious days of nothing to show but chump change for eight hours' work—by the clock! My God, where's that at?

Nowhere is the short answer. And nowhere was where she felt stuck, watching the world wallow in prosperity, while she worked away the endless, awful hours in one menial job after another. America got richer and richer, and she got the rest. Hostess in a medium chic restaurant, manicurist, dog walker, exercise class for fat women leader, temp, substitute teacher, fashion clerk in a massive department store, telephone solicitor, shampoo station girl, and on and on and on . . .

Bo-ring.

Every day the news lamented gas, groceries, tuition and real estate, all up, up and up. But who kept coming up with the cash to make those markets? Does not supply reflect demand? Wouldn't prices fall if nobody could pay? And who got the higher prices?

Let's face it: America is filthy (excuse me) fucking rich. So how could a smart woman get her share of the plunder?

That was the question.

Here, too, the obvious answer was so simple that very few could see it: she would borrow. What better time to jump off the high board than into a pool full of money? No better time was the answer, which just so happened to be the time she'd had her eye (and her heart set, somehow, some way) on possibly *the* most fabulous Victorian house in San Francisco. Sure it was in Noe Valley, which is thick as it gets with hip, chic, radical, political, artistic, and prohibitively expensive essence. But the place was so quintessentially delicious, scrumptious, perfect and then some. Talk about classy digs and hot and cold running hetero men.

I mean, those 1930s classic kitchen cabinets with the white frames and antique glass were perfect, and the huge deco bathrooms, which isn't Victorian, I know, but still, make the place more perfect.

It was a tantalizing, exasperatingly exquisite example of the hip-prosperity movement that fueled the run on Noe Valley. Imagining life in such a house felt warm and fuzzy and perfect—and stimulating without end. How could anybody get tired of that stuff? It reeked of attention to detail, and if ever a thing existed that had to be possessed, and a person simply had to have it, this was that, the match made in Heaven—or Noe Valley, a little lower than the angels, maybe, but not by much and so much easier to relate to, if you knew what was up.

Prospects tingled on her skin, signaling the receptive mind that maybe, perhaps, if the goddess within was willing, it was meant to be. And maybe it would be, but you can't make a down payment with a tingle. Well, you can put the tingles out there, meaning that you can visualize a thing to facilitate its evolution, and that's an important step, and if you think it's not, then you're the (pardon me) fucking fool.

And don't think for a minute that a material item does not evolve into ownership by a particular person, because it does. It's the same as spontaneous generation, like when they made flies happen on that meat. That was flies for chrissakes, and this was a Noe Valley Victorian. It was a wish upon a star either way, but different; this was grown-up and really real. Besides, at two point six million, what difference could it make? She couldn't afford the point six, much less the two. So putting it out there and having a little fantasy fun didn't hurt anybody. Did it?

Till she had a date with Rommel Dunbar—his real name, he insisted, and so she challenged, "Swear to God?" He sneered but would not swear, and she later learned his real name: Randy Davis, and that he'd upgraded on the name issue to enhance compatibility with the high-end, dominance-based real-estate market, focusing on your better blocks in Pacific Heights, Russian Hill, the Upper Haight, and so on. He *said* he wouldn't trifle with Noe Valley; "It's so, well, we won't go there."

"We could at least talk about it."

Rose and Rommel met by chance, though both shopped at the Marina Safeway for better odds on the random payout of the relationship-based society they lived in. They lingered in produce for the freshness and fertility most ambient and suggestive there.

Dairy could also be productive but remained second to produce with all variables factored, because of your lactose intolerants, which, let's face it, are more prevalent in the mix than you might imagine. Would you hate to miss a fabulous catch because of that?

Gluten is another matter altogether, and you simply can't know till it's too late.

Meanwhile, in produce, they browsed broccoli heads, on sale, with subtle touching and peripheral observing leading to brief eye contact confirming common knowledge of life and its organic niceties, cruciferous vegetables not the least among them. She agreed to meet him for wine in spite of the obvious age difference. He couldn't be more than thirty. Maybe thirty-five. But he was cute, peevish, and foppish with his studied lexicon referencing debentures, take-out paper, underwriting and, of course, IPOs relative to maturity or pre-maturity.

Pre-maturity? Isn't that a sexual problem?

She didn't ask, immersed in the initial phase of romance, where discretion and good taste rule, speaking of which, this guy knew how to present. Overall was his cashmere topcoat with the tag hanging out the collar, maybe to show that it cost four grand on its initial offering. She read it aloud, apparently pleasing him.

"Oh, that," he reached back and plucked it off. "I didn't really want it, but it got cold and I was passing by Wilkes Bashford and Harold, my main man there, was standing in the doorway hugging himself and he called out that I looked chilled, and you know, he was right, and I could just, you know, put it on my running charge there. So, what the hey?"

She took his meaning to heart. This casual declaration of vast expenditure en passant to effectively marginalize a surface discomfort, on the fly, as it were, literally defined him as impulsive, playful, tasteful, appreciative, and warm—and he had no charge limit at Wilkes Bashford, which meant all his drawers were top drawers, just off Union Square. How could anybody not admire such an up-and-comer who transcended the discretionary with the supremely, casually convenient?

She smiled playfully, surmising that this pup was a cutie, and she just might go All. The. Way. He would at least be more durable than the men she usually met. Or should be, anyway, given his tender age. And a woman likes a bit of, you know, staying power, if only in the short term.

Rommel mentioned the Victorian in Noe Valley also en passant, which seemed to be his preferred mode of reference. It was their first really meaningful talk of lifelong dreams: retiring at thirty-five for him, allowing forty if the money was good enough to keep him on the job—and the job could keep him stimulated. Owning a Victorian was her passion, her dream, her lifelong wish and desire, as soon as possible. She loved the idea of a single house costing two point six, but it might as well be eleven point twelve for her.

He scoffed at the notion of anyone's life on hold, with so much money at hand, with so much to be enjoyed right now for a measly three mil, which would be more the case with closing costs, remodeling and furniture, realistically. But what's the diff, two-six, three-oh? It wasn't chump change, that was for sure, but it was hardly an amount to retire on or lose sleep over, not in this arena, not with the vision and the daring and the . . .

He paused to catch her, eye to eye. The . . . let's face it, the balls to call yourself a player in the Bold Economy.

In a week Rose would consent to sexual relations with Rommel in gratitude for his help and to silence his plea. Rommel lamented that he'd never known love and couldn't be sure what it was or when he would feel it, but he felt something; he was sure of that, and he thought, maybe, this was it. God knew: this was something.

He sent a dozen long-stemmed roses, with scent, the hundred-fifty dollar variety. She sniffed and blushed. He blushed too. She imagined a romance starring him and her, beginning with her showing him the nature of gratitude and a thing or two about true, lasting love. She felt light as gossamer and as delicately lovely. Sensations warmed her heart from within, like tequila can do.

His thought bubble was a single, boyish scene of pornographic sex over the caption: *So what? You work. You go to school? What?*

At least Rommel Dunbar's mannerly good taste made him more tolerable, once she swallowed his high-finance affectation. And he must have been smart; he'd done so well. That is, the roses seemed heartfelt but in their way also casual. And he'd secured the Noe Valley Victorian with such easy facility, on two phone calls.

What? That's all there was to it? Well, he was admittedly loose with the term "secure" but a verbal on a rate lock was nearly money in the bank. Just you watch. He'd get it closed, which would be a great favor for him to do for her, though the transaction was of such, shall we say, small proportion.

"Small? Three million dollars?"

"Well, it's not like . . . real money, you know."

"It's not like real money?"

"No. It's a number. That's all it is. A relatively small number."

"Yeah. A number of dollars."

"No. It's not dollars. That's where most people fail—in their perception of danger. You know I'm a Kaidofu master, but I don't want to go there, except to tell you that we train with wooden knives, so that we can see a wooden knife, even if the attack is with steel. You see? It's not real dollars. It's ink on paper. Or a blip in the ether, if you will. It's not the same as cash. It's a simple measure of faith, or, more accurately, it's a measure of the faith no longer necessary in our mixed free enterprise system, because we have more money than faith requires. Listen, dear: America is swollen fat with money. The money is pouring over the flood banks. This economy has more money than Niagara Falls has water—and the difference is that Niagara Falls keeps a fairly constant flow where we, America, are flowing stronger every day. You think you can dam it up? You can't. So you jump in and ride the current. Get it?"

"You mean like over the falls?"

"Now you sound like one of the workadays who can't see the forest for the trees. Let me ask you something: Do you like cashmere? Do you like caviar? Do you like Noe Valley?"

"Well . . . yes."

Just like that, the very next evening materialized with Rose dining at Rommel's to sign docs on the deal that was going more secure all the time. Sho'nuff, he wooed her, answering the door in silk briefs and a cashmere sport jacket. Allowing no time for reaction, he led her to his computer and sat her in his plush, doeskin throne with twenty-two ergonomic adjustments including lumbar support, a moveable ottoman, and a subtle massage function that rolled the sides of the lower back. "I call it Dunbar lumbar. What do you think?" He didn't wait for her thoughts but told her she was in the driver's seat. She liked it.

She recalled the first time her daddy let her steer the DeSoto and how the two experiences were remarkably similar in causing a giddy titillation to rise on her skin.

Reaching over her shoulder, her new daddy punched up his website. "Look at this." He'd initially called it urbanfox.com, for his namesake the Desert Fox, who wasn't a bad Nazi, really. "I mean, they all were, but he was cool, you know." Urbanfox.com also scintillated with double entendre, hinting that he was dumb like a fox, or that he was foxy, though *that* one could be troubling, taken the wrong way, you know. At any rate, it didn't catch on and needed more focus on the object at hand, which was strategic maneuvering in a minefield laced with gold, or a goldfield laced with mines, depending on, well, you know.

So he changed it to winwinwin.com, what it should have been in the first place because that's what it was, a devilishly clever extension of the old win-win situation, with one more win, as you can see. "Now it's catching on. Let me show you how it works."

Just like that, Rommel Dunbar let his jacket fall to the floor—it was so unseasonably hot—as he created before her eyes the most creative form of creative financing yet created in your creative segment of California commerce. The bank allowed for the down payment to be loaned by the bank and secured by a second mortgage, held by the bank, behind the first mortgage, also theirs. That would have made you blink in the past, since no lender wants to be in second position, especially not to themselves. But that thinking was flawed, because second position *is* first position, if it's second to yourself. Don't you see?

Not to worry; by holding the first mortgage, the bank secured the property, so it made no difference, really, who held the second mortgage, and the bank was happy to hold it because it charged out at five points higher than the first. So they'd make even more money by separating a small portion of the loan and calling it a second. Risk? In this market? If prices went any higher, we'd need to leave town just to find more stuff to buy!

The beauty of this arrangement was that Rose would need to make no payments, not on the first or second mortgages, not with property values rising quicker'n Jack's beanstalk—a subtle flourish of excitement at this juncture included brief contact between his own beanstalk and her shoulder, the operative word here being brief, which went along with natural, and not exactly stiff but in the semi-ready phase that was so amusing and cute in the young ones.

Anyway, he wouldn't go there either, just yet, with momentum gaining on the simple success so available to those who could wake up and smell the gardenias. "Are those gardenias?"

"Yes. Good nose. I have them flown in. Don't you love them?"

"Yes. They make me . . . They make me. . ."

"I know. Me too."

Anyway, the bank, ultimately happy to serve, just like it said on TV, would simply reappraise the house upward every other month, increasing Rose's debt on the technical side, but who gives a flying fuck (Rommel's rhetorical question) on the practical side, since she could sell the place anytime and *make a profit(!)*?

Don't you see? Everybody wins, including the bank, the buyer, and the house! That's why I call it winwinwin.com.

In the meantime, she could live there for free, just riding the note a month late like a big wave surfer hanging ten till the odd month reappraisal, and boom, she's in there clean again on a sixty day cycle. "Now, I don't mean you just live there," Rommel said.

"Oh, boy," she murmured. "Here comes the catch."

His silk-clad nub rested on her shoulder at this juncture, perhaps more obtrusive than natural, though casual contact was the attempted effect. His dingdong on her shoulder was meant to be incidental, unthinking, perched there by chance in the soft flurry of excitement. "You're not just living there, if you're living your dream," he crooned. This last sentiment rang true and then some; it echoed from the figurative hills and bounced off the walls of her heart. It numbed her shoulder to the swelling bratwurst resting on it. It shut her up and opened her mouth on a whimper as her eyes virtually beheld all the crazy wonderful images of herself living in Noe Valley in the most fabulous Victorian ever. Such a montage was indeed enough to counterbalance and make sense of the red knob that somehow, someway, effortlessly if not magically had slipped around the corner while unveiling itself to fill the gap in her expression of delight and proceeded to tap her tonsils.

It wasn't so bad. Rommel Dunbar, or Randy Davis as she came to call him in the end, had the romantic sensitivity of a pneumatic dildo. But he would not tire, even as he loped headlong to tiresome durability. "Yeah, yeah, you're the cock o' the block," she would moan assuredly three times over the next six months, once after each reappraisal upward, till, alas, reality in California, like all trips eventually will, adjusted downward yet again.

Rommel's next appeal was for a small, short-term advance, not even thirty days, much less ninety, on a few bucks to get him through a closing next week that would set things straight again. He'd pay back two points over, which, if you cared to punch the numbers with a twelve-month amortization extrapolated on the back end just for fun, would come out to over a hundred percent return on investment, and besides, it was the least she could do, given the dire straits little Miss Smarty Pants Rose had got him into.

"Sounds like junk bonds, unsecured," she said, because she'd learned a thing or two in her days of money meditation.

"Secured? You want security? I'll give you security. How about you make me this friendly little loan, and I'll keep the roof over your head." His bleak attempt at civility left them both with the shakes, but downside potential is present in every scenario, and it waited in the wings for this one. She should also make arrangements to make a few payments, he said. It wouldn't be that many payments, but a few to keep the shit from hitting the fan. Not to worry, those few payments would be interest only. Of course, payments on three point three are higher than on two point six, but that difference was also technical since the appraised values were still greater one month to the next, and anyway, payments on neither value would be practical or possible.

"I have a better idea." She attempted nonchalance but couldn't quite quell the shakes. "How about you make payments up your ass. Then take that stupid, overblown house and stick it up your ass. Then take your little loan and stick it up your ass too." She was bailing out, as they say in the business.

"You can't bail! You own that house! And you owe me!"

"Fuck you, Randy. Fuck you. Fuck the bank and fuck you. You can use that for your new website: fuckfuckfuck.com. Get it?"

That language didn't come easily to Rose Berry, or at least it didn't use to, before her exposure to unscrupulous moral standards.

Is that an oxymoron? I mean, if you have standards, aren't you scrupulous, I mean, by nature?

Oh, fuck it: the awful ring of truth hung in the air like roach spray, causing a wince but ridding the kitchen of varmints too. So she felt well rid of Rommel Randy dumbass, or whatever his name was. What a buffoon. What a blowhard. That guy couldn't tell which end was up, who was who, what was money, and the difference between owned and owed? Or a debit and a credit? Boy, what a debit. No, wait . . . Never mind; he was a liability, not an asset, so goodbye, good riddance, so long, adios—like the song says.

So a woman walked away in the most spiritual sense, letting go of her heartfelt desires, or their vestige remnants at any rate.

Walking away from the material plane felt good and was a known remedy for life's problems, though few people manage to find the simple solutions most available. Walking away wasn't the same solution to life's tedium as borrowing two point six million by signing a fax document. It was different. It was letting go. It was casting fate to the wind. *Que sera, sera, whatever will be will be* . . . What a great song that was, and oh, how true.

And who would be waiting right outside, idling at the curb in the getaway car to take off with the loot for a new life of romance and luxury? None other than Mr. Reality himself, who was just as surprised as she was, because that's how the fates play it, by chance, just when you thought you were down—and don't forget destiny, karma, the cards and, of course, the goddess within.

Under any other circumstance, she would have sounded the alarm: pervert, stalker, rapist. His tit-scan was trumped, however, by what, in actuality, was meant to be. Yes, he appraised her, chest included, before murmuring as only he could, "¡*Hola, Señora!*"

Of course, a lady doesn't ride off in a truck with a strange man. But a woman of spiritual and material means could sense synchronicity when it came her way. She knew when things were taken care of. So, yes, she would take a ride with him. Because a gal who could ask the tough questions would be open to good fortune. Where did she need to be? Out of town, the farther the better. How could she get there? With a ride, and there it was, bringing up the closing question at last: Why the fuck not?

Besides, there was a kid in the back. How bad could the guy be? I mean, I'd have gotten in if it was a dog back there, because you know a man with a dog is okay. But it was a kid. How much better was that?

Besides, how weird could he be, with fine art, along with the kid? I mean, if that was weird, then I was too. I mean, really. The kid was staring, but still . . .

"What is your name?"

"Rose."

He nodded once. "Rosa."

She loved that—Rosa. "What's your name?"

"Call me Juan Valdez."

"Oh, God. You're kidding!"

"No. I kid you nada. I am him."

"Jesus. I mean, you know?"

"I go south. You go south?"

"Yes. South will do."

So she blinked out of a dream gone bad into a dream of adventure, to the soulful side, far from urban dandies, fops, buffoons, and banks. As if for safe measure, the karmic goddess had sent her a ride down the road in the vehicle of her redemption to Santa Cruz, everybody's lifestyle Mecca, where a shoebox bungalow in a surf slum could run three million, or four if you hesitated. Then you could stare at waves rolling under young dudes going agro day after day till next year when you could ask five million or seven. It was so real, so elite, and refreshingly unique from that superficial Noe Valley scene.

"I am Panchito." This from the kid, at last, his bugging, blinking eyes seeking approbation of something or other, like maybe his thick, Mexican accent. But he was a cute kid and, better yet, he had a cute dog. "*Esto es mi perro*, Cisco."

*¿Que? ¿*Panchito *y* Cisco? *Ustedes esta mas* . . . uh . . . young. You're too young to remember Pancho and Cisco."

The kid didn't comprehend, but give a girl a break.

Her Spanish wasn't that bad. Well, whatever. It just felt right; an old beater truck with a kid and a dog. What could be wrong? Headed south at that. A woman had to trust her instincts, and right then she felt nothing but relieved. Ugh, when she thought of that guy and his fake names and cashmere coats, laying his dingdong on her shoulder and calling it romantic. Ugh. Good riddance. And a good lesson too: you can't get blood from a turnip, though she did try.

And a woman's most merciful critic should be herself. It was okay to mess things up—it was bound to happen now and then—as long as she came out a little bit smarter. Sure, it seemed like life's critical juncture, in which a gal needed a new place and still does. But buy? Are you kidding? She'll rent, thank you very much. That whole down payment, leverage on paper, no worries, and odd-month-reappraisal routine was a fool's paradise. Better to let the vehicle of your destiny hit the pastoral landscape of America resurrected and be free! She nearly trembled at the prospect of downsizing to ten cents on the dollar—and updating the décor and furnishings next year. Or the year after. Maybe. Now there was an alternate reality to Noe Valley. They ought to call that place unreal estate. Ha! Give a country girl the outskirts any day. And a country girl is just exactly what this gal had decided to be.

Next stop: Watsonville, a farm town with sidewalks thinly populated by thickset people in overalls and flowered gingham, where outdoor work was daily and most workers spoke Spanish first. It felt better, even as a concept, what might be called a lifestyle model: a little town in the country where real estate meant fulfillment of the dream and not a hotshot promising blue sky and a killing—make that a regular fucking massacre. And it was not Latino, not East LA or Watts. It was Mexican, like it has been and is and would be, rural for chrissakes, so it would change slowly instead of by urban reclamation, gentrification, and reactive anger.

Watsonville felt like the end of the line and farther from delusional turmoil than mere miles can measure. Beyond the peninsula and sprawling suburbs and way yonder of the hip, chic, avant-bankrupt delusion, the place felt clean and simple. And so she arrived at where a woman can live free and breathe easy.

How blessedly it began, with the most fabulous enchilada plate and a quiet night in a hotel so cheap they'd never believe it a hundred miles up in *el Norte*. Juan Valdez's harmless flirtation and playful *abrazo* only made a girl feel good, if anybody wanted to know. Then he went home like such a gentleman, kind and sincere, maybe because he still had the kid in tow, but that only proved his decency, because kids usually do.

He picked her up in the morning for a passable latte but rancheros to die for, again with his charm, saying the kid was in school, and so they enjoyed their breakfast like none she could remember in the city; he was so simple and honest and straightforward and . . . masculine. He didn't even mention fleshy favors for another hour or insist for ten minutes after that. She wasn't ready, but then what woman is ever ready to be swept off her feet? It wasn't that she didn't mind by then. She did, but she gave it up in a process she thought of as adaptation, and she was frankly ready for a different go than what she'd recently endured—not so swanky-panky and a whole heap more man. Some guys understand the meaning of no and oh, oh, oh.

In farm country she could live simply, loving the basic beauty of the place and the lifestyle it had to offer: a little rain, a little sun, some dirt under the nails, and light perspiration across the brow and upper lip. It felt like a hundred years ago or something, like when Miss Kitty took Marshal Dillon up to the second floor of the Long Branch Saloon. Miss Kitty owned that place, because a woman could make something of herself even then if she'd a mind to. This place did seem a tad over the top on the deferred maintenance issue. The lace curtains could have been original. But it could all be updated! Moreover . . .

It was a lovely patina on him too, across his chest and incredible arms. It looked more like that stuff they spray on in the movies to accentuate muscle definition—not that this guy needed accentuation; God, the way his pants hung off his hips with that bulge and those eyes. What girl wouldn't be curious? And a truly mature woman will prefer more mature guys every time.

Soon she wished he would put his shirt back on, like in twenty or thirty minutes, she wished. That's the thing about Mexican guys: they know how to look at a woman, like, with romance instead of sizing her up for sex. Sure, he already knew her size, and could likely assess her inclination, or maybe he only assumed as much, but still. Those trucks always seemed so silly, but in a working farm town they seemed to fit. After all, those guys are Mexican and everything. It felt more real than the charade up north. Warmer too. So a woman let her defense internal ease up for a while with thoughts that maybe this was it, or could be it or . . . Never mind: this was the moment, and in no time it would be another moment, and there you go. It was so cute, the way he had to park right in front and kept looking out the window at it, like he loved that truck just as he would if it was his horse.

Things felt honest, so different than that goofy guy with his frilly things and endless name-dropping and unspeakable greed and god-awful smell of Right Guard and cologne. And, truth be told, all the stamina of a city boy. Ha! This was different; this was salt o' the earth, which was who she'd become, just that quick, because puzzle parts fitting neatly together make the big picture clear. The third world, cutting-edge art made it even better, more of an overlay than a synthesis, or maybe it was juxtaposition, but maybe that was just her, lingering for a while in the intellectual wallow so popular with urbanites. He smelled better too, more like a goat—a living goat, a muscular goat who lived hard and . . .

Whatever, it all . . . felt . . . or . . . ganic . . . Oh, oh, God! Oh . . .

It was like all of life before Juan was a fogbank of amorphous, vague images and inconsequential recollection and then came a truck bound for Watsonville, as life stretched onward with clarity and meaning in the most beautiful way. And it happened by chance! Which proves the adage that magic happens, and so it did.

Sure, a change that big meant a few growing pains. For one thing, a gal needed to make a living, but that should be easy. Nobody could starve to death in farm country. And this wasn't just any farm country. This was the Fertile Crescent West. You couldn't walk a quarter mile in any direction without coming onto one crop or another. She wouldn't want to steal produce long-term. But she could always do massage, maybe not in Watsonville, because salt o' the earth folk don't get massage, and besides, why hoe this hardpan with such premium topsoil just up the road? Big bucks, that is, and it's still an up-charge for outcall.

XIII

Big M OK Cars

Betty Smith changed her name to Ellspeth Smythe and swore it made all the difference in her life, her future, and her fate.

Perhaps. But events led to another name change a young woman could not have anticipated, marking the greatest difference a wayward girl could achieve. Becoming Mrs. Alfred N. Whitehead Burnham of the Highborough Burnhams, she woke up daily to her wildest dreams, as she would continue to do for the next fifty years.

But even billions get tedious in time. What can a girl do, spend it? Not ever—not even going at it two-fisted 24/7. Not double time or triple. Never, ever is how soon she could spend it.

But harking back on the unwed teen seven months gone with nowhere to turn, she gained perspective on money and its management—and appreciation thereof. She realized that the nature of tedium in the wealth/poverty continuum is far more easily remedied with money than it is with none. Wealth is better, and the good thing about fifty years is the total removal of doubt that time and massive, whimsical spending can allow.

A few odd events took place a long time ago. Most of the principals are gone. The details are fuzzy. A female child may be out there somewhere in a random universe. Time had reduced the filial connection to an accident of birth resulting from capricious sexual contact, resulting in a baby person of parallel DNA but with no more social connection than a ship passing in the night—or on the sidewalk in broad daylight.

But please, Ellspeth Burnham was not the first female to incur experience of a dire, personal nature and move on, and she would not be the last. Life is for the living, for those who can find joy in adaptation, and so she did. Her actions were not cold but practical. She achieved optimal potential for all parties concerned— and she did so with the best interests of all parties in mind.

She wondered from time to time, after coming into wealth so vast that money had no meaning, how a devil-may-care life could be, if cash-on-hand got down to a few million. She could downsize down to teensy-weensy with less than anybody and live simply in blue jeans and a used car, in a modest ridge-top bungalow with her pets, her knitting, and her garden. But what could she do in the meantime, give the billions away? That would free her from the constant demands of management and defense, but it seemed so . . . foolish.

Alfred died at ninety-two, young by the claim of those mourners lamenting the loudest; he had so many good years left. Such a pity, they cried and carried on. It was those same people who'd raised the wry eyebrow when, at fifty, he married a girl of fifteen. Detractors called it statutory, but Alfred called it technical, inconsequential with mutual consent, and legally defensible, as rendered by the in-house legal staff. After all, fifty and fifteen don't seem so far apart, staring down from ninety-two and fifty-seven. Besides, she knew enough to manage a house and grounds and kitchen staff. Nearly fifty years of it was proof.

The widow Burnham moved from mourning her dear departed husband to the southland of her idle fantasy—her idea of living a little closer to the earth. She longed for a change of scenery and a lifestyle that might recapture the old vitality. Who needs twelve thousand square feet and servants when the pesky laws of physics allow a person to be only in one room at a time? She could entertain in several rooms at once, but then the guests seemed so similar to the guests at the last entertainment, or the same entertainment, with the same questions and chitchat on who did what to whom and the degree to which it should be deemed *faux pas* or *de rigueur*, no matter what room you turn to. Worse yet was the endless speculation on money, its gain, loss or movement sideways. The guests seemed to agree in principle that it was a rough and tumble world out there. They found comfort in like company, oddly blind to the hazards of the overly insulated.

The media could be amusing at times, sniffing the Smythe/Burnham trail for bombastic effusions on nothing. It's what they do. Who doesn't make a mess, sooner or later?

She lived that life and had more life yet to live, so she went south, where less could be more of everything.

Feeling free and light again, she took up where she'd left off—suddenly, with a few billion smackeroos instead of being a single mother with a baby busting her chops and coming up goose eggs every time. Once again mobile and nearly anonymous on the ridge overlooking Monterey Bay, she felt snug, far from the society page but not from the world she craved. She couldn't have a boyfriend in Highborough, though normal urges arose.

Was she done with that sort of thing? She didn't think so.

She felt equivocal but optimistic, self-counseling that the correct man had yet to come along. A girl could have a fling or a regular man friend. What could it hurt? Her prospects? Ha! The odd man up the road might do, briefly. He looks hungry and feels vulgar. That seems refreshing.

Alfred N.W. Burnham's stroke had rendered him a man of few words for years prior to passing. His morose condition suited those around him, who agreed that the stoic mood likely suited him too. Nobody called him taciturn and cold, but he was. The shriveled old man in a vegetative state remained in the news, a moneyed celebrity and dry goods icon kept alive by the God-fearing insistence of the United States Congress, which stellar assemblage threatened federal intervention if the old man was unplugged. Alfred N.W. was still a pillar of capitalism who could return on God's will to glory in a grateful society, representing humanity, goodwill, convenience to church, schools and shopping and those values we hold dear.

A nation could pray.

Military incursion, earthquake, tsunami, flooding banks, and congressional scandal deferred to the Burnham context. Alfred N.W. and the hope of millions gave meaning to motivation and movement. The camera scanned for a blink, a sigh, a nod, a twitch. Was that a wink? What could he be thinking? Ratings remained solid, as the Burnham billions expanded and contracted with the Burnham respirator . . . until the Burnham saga went to breaking news: Death Just In.

The airwaves buzzed with bio, follow-up bio of associates, friends, fans, and family in their grief and devastation at the loss of the iconic giant. He'd been vegetative for years, and the nay-sayers had called it good-as-dead. It became official with death. Gone was the husband, the father, the son, the grandson—the great grandson! A hospital statement put the cause of death as *complications.* Two congresspersons demanded autopsy, so the media stayed on it. Heirs, assigns, beneficiaries, fiduciaries, and spouses declined to comment, even those with apparent claim to the bulk of the billions. The story moved when offspring older than herself promised litigation if bequeathals went in any direction other than the appropriate line. Cameras followed the body and went to split-screen to show the incredible man in his final days, when he breathed, kind of.

Why would she smoke a ninety-two-year-old vegetable? Then again, why wait? With Alfred dead the money got frozen in place. Viewers called for action now—for justice! Speculation swung like a pendulum. Alfred would have needed only hydration to generate a beep on the life machine; he could have made it to a hundred five if only someone had cared or had a heart. Or a hundred ten—vegetables can sit on a shelf for years and still be alive, with a pulse and social security number. So yeah, maybe she did it!

But that theory was cynical, and the grieving widow was the picture of innocence, a self-made woman living on a hilltop over a bay, all alone. Down from Olympus and into the suburbs, she'd downsized her lifestyle to the basics: a view, a used car, and a garden. She loved it. She loved the quiet, easy neighborhood, the convenient grocery store, the people saying hello and suggesting that she have a nice day.

"Twelve thousand square feet? Nobody needs more than three."

The tale of her climb down and march south lulls Mulroney, who nods and catches himself. Her cleavage is powdered. Does she sweat there?

She says her family history is deep and rich and a very important thing to share, so it's not lost, ever, and she appreciates his willingness to hear it, and . . .

He cuts her off: "You know. . ."

She leans forward. "No, I don't know. Why don't you tell me?"

She's coy, possibly receptive, but to what? To ovations of . . . not romance, but what? A romp? But two people at the age of better sense, beyond hormonal vicissitudes, can be so easily embarrassed and equally prone to gaffe. For example, what if she's not receptive? What if Mulroney presents something uncouth—something illegal? This flirtatious manner may be a ruse—or a misperception. Did she not recently migrate from the land of the socially misbegotten?

Then again, why would a man of a certain age and indelicate situation stroll up the street with a gift to call on a woman of even greater years, if not to achieve an objective? She appears to be a nice woman, and the plan is conceived, and it germinates. And a man has to do what he doesn't want to do.

She lingers furtively, but how can a man be sure? Of course, he can't be any surer than any man has ever been, except maybe for those who were sure. Mulroney was always certain, when it came to money and business, and he may as well see this as that. But what is he supposed to do, ask for a loan? But she's flirting. Should he whisper sweet nothings on a ninety-day note? Or maybe call it a grant to help a less fortunate used car salesperson? She murmurs over the past and the filthy rich people she's known. Oh, she used to hate that phrase, but then she came to hate more that crowd's obsession with spending and one-upping, her friends and neighbors watching each other and elbowing as they clambered up the rungs . . .

He glazes again, grateful for her renewed oration on one thing and another. He hesitates cutting her off again for fear of where things might go, though she does seem to be working up to something. He decides to stand up as if to leave—or maybe he should just plainly share his need, however humbling it may be. In either event, a true salesperson must ask for the money because a deal was never closed without asking for the money, and failure to ask dooms a salesperson to wonder what might have been.

She drones on that the latest phenom for richies is the good-works social circle. That is, persons of wealth let their magnitude be known, in order to make the A-lists of the nonprofit organizations working diligently to feed the children, clothe the needy, inoculate the poor—oh! Save the whales! "That one is ripe. My God! But you see everyone who's anyone showing up at these things, and the food and liquor are over-the-top, and the entertainment could not possibly be paid for because it's actually the guest list! The catch is, these people must contribute once a year somewhere, or fall off the lists. Well, there aren't nearly so many wealthy people anymore—I mean, of course there are, but not so many who let on. I mean, most of the magnitude people don't utter a syllable, and those who hint at magnitude don't exist. Not really. They think value on paper is the same as mountains of moolah. Ha! Paupers! Presenting as patricians. It's . . . deplorable, don't you think?"

"Hmm. Well. . ."

"Well, yes. I do believe that imposters to wealth are an odious bunch and, quite frankly, *our* cross to bear. It's not right, and it gets worse: the truly wealthy have so many burdens in maintaining social order. Really, it's why I'm so glad to be here. Everyone seems so . . . real. You know?" Yes, Mulroney knows. So she drones over cronies and confidants and the stressful life of the upper class, who must tirelessly defend the ramparts from the ever-clawing upper middle—and from the lower too, if you can believe it. The nerve of some people! "Animal rights my behind. I snap their necks! They serve society, and so do I!"

She made a deal with the devil a long time ago, and she honest to goodness has shared that little secret with nobody—nobody—until this very moment. "I mean right now this moment, with you, Mister Bicycle Man."

He rolls his eyes over a half nod to indicate something—maybe she'll take it as an avowal of trust, or the trust between them, or the beauty of meeting someone new and feeling like old friends—of his own love for the little fuzzy ones. He wants to say something but holds back.

She waits. "What? What were you going to say?"

What's to risk? What's to lose? She's human. She's been around the block. She knows about wealthy people and the merely rich who aspire to true greatness yet fall behind and hang on by the hair of their chinny chin chins; oh, she knows. He needs to state his case, which is nothing more nor less than an honest step forward, which is not a lunge into the precipice. Her hand has slid as if incidentally over to within touching distance of his, so he sets a fingertip on her wrist. She smiles. Is that a purr? Or is her stomach grumbling. "Betty. I have this . . . I have this . . . This. . ."

That feels like a swing and a miss with the bases loaded, bottom of the ninth. It's late in the game, but a guy has two more swings. Maybe better to save the last two for a new inning . . .

Loser! Life is not baseball, and sports analogy means you're out of your league, so forget the squeeze play and swing away for a stand-up double. At least. All men and women arrive at the age of realization, that in the end is solitude, and until then we must find true friends and help each other as we can. She knows this. She said as much. Moreover, underscoring the game- and series-winning potential of the situation, she removes her hand from under his fingertip and rests it on the back of the sofa, and fondles his ear lobe. It's a setup, to be sure, a warranted advance and much, much more, indicating that intimate contact may consummate approval of the loan application. Well, it could.

So they sit and ponder life and the world. The stage is set for success, the nature of which may well be symbiotic, in a way. A homespun billionairess in denim wouldn't dally frivolously, unless she would, but the potential reverberates in Mulroney's head like Tom the cat's head inside the garbage can lid when it got banged with a sledgehammer. DONNNNGGGG!!! All he has to do is ask, or perhaps fondle or diddle in kind to best fill the communication gap. The only thing for certain is that the move is up to him and pronto, lest the game be called.

Yet he hesitates. She's not too far from seventy, but he has liquor and the shadows are pleasant. She has a decent rack, though it looks firmly harnessed. But what if . . . What if he can't . . . Well, let her come and get it, if it's the getting she wants. Big M Mulroney could fuck a snake when the chips are down, especially if it'll get the chips back up. So he eases back to let her fondle his ear. She does, chattering anew over friendship and its amazing changes in form over the years. He listens, paying attention as an act of giving that feels selfless and grateful, nodding but not nodding off. The scene feels reasonable and civilized. And safe, which never led to a payout, but the game is still on, with no errors.

This is not romance. This is friendship. He's married, after all, and a woman should respect that. Besides, in the more reasonable light of rational thinking, he realizes that she won't want to take her pants off till dark, two hours out, call it modesty or another excuse in a series.

She giggles at the very idea of a neighbor being snooty—to *her*!

He giggles back, "I can't imagine anyone being snooty to you. You're too friendly." Mulroney recalls the salad days, when he would show a date what she'd caused to happen, and she would scream bloody murder or respond more cordially. It was just the same as asking for the money and seemed like a real savings in time, but that was long ago, when Mighty Joe Young was an upstanding youth, a figure to admire, an endearing character to those who got to know him.

This was not that. Betty B would hardly make a stink, and the Mulroneys are headed out of town anyway. Still, he's not a stalker or a flasher; Michael Mulroney is simply an aging man in a jam seeking help from a friend and willing to return service, which he senses she is seeking and he can provide if he closes his eyes on some co-ed ass from the salad days. Betty is good company, and he gives her a whirl in the mind movies, not exactly honking his horn but maybe . . . *getting to know you, getting to know all about you* . . . And he says into the lull, "What a crazy world it would be if everybody was, you know, making love to everybody else."

"Yes, it would," she coos. "And that's what's wrong with the world, people don't even know each other and they're willing to get intimate. But . . . What's this?" She sets a hand on his crotch.

What's this? She's discussing his dingdong in the third person as she rolls on about the difficult people she's had to deal with and their presumptuous behaviors regarding intimacy, when they obviously knew nothing of friendship or trust. He realizes her social skill; she's been talking away to make time for the move. *Mulroney! You loser!* Never mind. But wait: she's retrieving it, toying with it . . . *talking to it* . . . calling it Peter. His name isn't Peter. Where did she get Peter?

"Such a bold little Peter. Can you say please?"

"He has several names, actually, besides Peter. I used to call him Mighty Joe Young. Or Lord Jim. Or The Little Colonel. Gargantua. Jack in the Box—but Peter is fine."

Mulroney is rarely speechless but is rendered a man of fewer words. She's in control and knows it and seems to savor it, seeking his comfort level at the same time. He wishes he'd known it would go this way. How nice it would have been to relax with confidence rather than anticipate disaster, worrying over the mess and fuss of a terrible misunderstanding. Beyond his wildest dreams, he ups the ante on the loan app—make that the grant application that will not require a few hundred grand to get the job done, but a simpler, cleaner, more precise and truly regal one point five. Between friends? Chump change!

But it has been decades since Mulroney romped on a sofa with a date, and the exchange seems off. Maybe it's the yard work that makes her hands rough. At any rate, she's apparently convinced that a piston enjoys a dry cylinder. He seeks to change the scene by mumbling, "Fungo. I mean sometimes I would call him— it—Fungo. Like a fungo bat. You know?"

"I think Fungo wants to finagle a tonsil exam. Don't you?"

"Betty, I . . . uh. . ."

The sofa looks like high-end chintz. Why wouldn't it be? It's a leaf and twigs print, and surely she wouldn't want to disturb the lovely pattern with a load o' tapioca. Wait a minute—what are those yellow clouds?

Okay, it's her sofa and this does not appear to be the first time she's risked a few stains, but they'll never get the goo to go away under these conditions. But he can't very well ask that she get on with the tonsil exam, or if she knows how a Jewish princess eats a banana. Perhaps sensing his dilemma, she stops anyway in the worst way of stopping, to ask the most disappointing question in the world of Michael Mulroney: "Would you buy a used car from this man?"

Is Mulroney supposed to laugh? How does she know about the used cars? He never told her. Okay, so Miss Moneypants knows what he does. He has signs all over town. Still, he hates it when they ask the old, tired question about used cars and this man and would you buy one from him, like they thought of it first, like it's funny, like a little intermission here to laugh at a lame joke at his expense might be a good idea instead of an insult. Now look what you've done. The Little Colonel is standing down, taking it personal and getting depressed while somebody insensitive takes her leisurely time. And for what? An answer? Is that what they call hospitality in Highborough?

Actually, a little break might relieve the chafing. "Many people do. Um . . . buy cars from me. But tell me something. Why do you drive a Pontiac Fireball?"

She's thinking, not a good sign, but the interlude might work out—she can stare at it and get excited over finishing what she started. Maybe she can go freshen her Poligrip to keep things in place. Man. Did Michael Mulroney ever think it would come to this? Did he ever in life apply for a menial job because he simply had to have the money and feel so degraded?

"Don't you just love it?" She sits up. "It was my son's—my stepson, actually. But he can't use it anymore with four kids and all that stuff he's always carrying around, so I got him one of those, you know, really big ones he could actually use in combat." She giggles at the imagery. "I think of it as an urban assault vehicle. Perfect for him. But I like the little red car, the Fireball, so I kept it. It's all I need, and so much fun . . ." She drifts whimsically, perhaps on a vision of step-grandchildren in Hummers. And she sighs, knowing those little ingrates will never give her the time or respect she deserves—unless it's a birthday or Christmas or another needy occasion, and she mumbles about how much she loves the self-centered little mutts just the same. Mulroney waits in thin air, such as it is, and soon she turns, suddenly struck. "Isn't it strange, what we're doing?"

"Strange and full of grace."

"You know, I love the way you talk. I think I love the way you see things."

"You do? Betty, I need to. . ." Oh, she knows and pumps the jam in deference to his need. Mulroney smiles with no bliss, hoping for another discourse to spare the chafing that could kill the star of the show, just like the poor dead husband suffered.

"My mother, God rest her soul, couldn't come out and actually talk about, you know, this sort of thing." Now she wants to talk about her mother and this sort of thing? "But she warned me that it's unnatural, disgusting, a perversion. I think it's a shame, really; but she and I were so different. And I blame her for—no. I shouldn't say blame. I thank her when I realize the life I would have had if I'd listened."

"You think what is a shame?"

"That some people can't . . ." She stares away, nearly tearful, mercifully slowing.

"Do you mean that your mother . . ."

She turns back. "I've often wondered if my late husband would have been so good as to help me up and out of my predicament without my special skill. Do you know what I'm talking about?"

Well, he thinks he knows what she's talking about, and he may well be better off asking for it, but he won't ask for anything, lest he blow the one chance to ask for the money. She doesn't seem in the least shaky in the bridgework, and he wants to assure her that there's no shame in dentures, and removing them for a minute or two might be a perfectly acceptable idea. But no—best reserve initiative for she who will take it or not, in order to keep this pond placid, which is not the same as flaccid but could be soon. "Well, I can . . ."

"Shh . . ." She admonishes like a nurse, pressing his chest with one hand till he eases back onto the couch in surrender. How could such gentle ministrations indicate anything less than charity? Yes? So? Is anybody there?

But his eyes open on something less than Topo Gigio, as she grasps his personal self by the neck and leans in to give it a good scolding. She stares, as if waiting for a verbal response? People process personal issues in personal ways, and while Betty Burnham's gyrations seem strange, they should come as no surprise. Why not? Because. So Mulroney's lids lower again on a downsizing that seems inevitable.

Boy oh boy. A nutter, but he opens the eye internal on insight, causing yet another round of self-castigation, with silent yet caustic questions on the why and wherefore and how he could be such a dolt, stuck once again in the macho matrix. *How could you be so blind? Are not friendship and trust herein secured, by which a grant may still be funded!* Who cares if old Betty B is off her rocker? She said it herself: she's a natural. Always was—it's her natural skill that delivered her salvation from poverty. And here he is, her friend.

Mulroney peeks—she's playing patty cakes with a tube steak, mumbling a childish rhyme. He looks up when she asks, "What's wrong with it?"

"I don't know, Betty. You may have to eat me?"

"I may have to eat you? Oh, dear!" They share a crimson flush at the mere mention of the deed, till yes, she says yes, again yes, "but not now. Oh, not now. We must wait. We must wait for . . ."

"Yes?"

"Oh, so delicious." She moans. She stares.

Mulroney glances at peripheral movement, a stirring in the ether and the bushes. A passing sparkle could be eyes just out the window, beady under a wrinkled forehead, glimmering with intensity. Mulroney recognizes Phillip, the old guy from across the freeway who rides with Steffen. Phillip is self-inflated with bicycle glory from long ago, when he rode professionally in Italy. He never got over it and harks repeatedly about his glory days, when he's not bemoaning his Catholic struggle and his frigid wife. Phillip is lonely and horny. Steffen admires Phillip.

Mulroney wishes he was nineteen and glimpsing the future— seeing himself in his seventh decade and poised to pump the skull of a notable socialite while a man of pedantically parochial tastes peeps through the bay window.

He could have avoided this, even as many in the neighborhood would call it the good life, after all.

Betty Burnham sits up to ask what is making him so pleased with himself. Mulroney is at a loss. "Look, I would never impose on a neighbor's hospitality. I agree. Let's wait."

Fully apprised of the male character, she says, "Okay. Wait here," as she's up and down the hall, giggling like a girl.

The eyes duck below the windowsill.

A Louis XIV grandfather chops the heads off seconds as a draft chills the Majordomo. She returns wearing mink gloves and says she's like that man with scissors for hands in that movie—or maybe it's that other movie where the man has knives for fingers, and a woman dies but comes back as an angel to check out her husband's sexual adventures or . . .

Scissors? Knives? Goliath ducks for cover.

The mink gloves have fingernails—except that they're not fingernails but teeth in tiny heads, one head on each fingertip, each face showing stoic surprise. Mulroney doubts these gloves will help the situation, even as the left-hand litter surrounds the Little Colonel, who now feels dazed and confused. She seems encouraged, but he wants the silly gloves to go away, and he mutters, "You're chafing me."

"Oh! I forgot!" She has lotion and douses down like a kid with a squeeze bottle of mustard on a hotdog.

"You'll ruin your gloves."

"I can clean them! I've been waiting for this. I've been waiting for you! I *knew* you would come through!"

He will not beg the question: Come through what? Yet alas, sadly, she may wait longer because this cannot be. The star of the show cannot work under these conditions. She grasps harder in delusional defiance. He deflates.

"Don't worry!" She plants a wet, furry hand on his stomach, the other on his nuts, speaking of which, she appears to be *bona fide*, but assessment is set aside to get this one into the record books. And so, finally, at long last, hallelujah and hosanna, she sets to granting that most personal of favors with gourmet savoring and, since love will conquer all, deliberation and purpose.

Mulroney likes to watch, but this is over the top, just like the eyes rising again over the sill. A man must exhale sooner or later, and so he does.

A playful spirit could count the afternoon a great amusement, yet he surges into the most difficult questions, challenging his fundamental objective. The scene is unique, to say the least, strange and awful at most. Betty Burnham of the Highborough billions appears to have set one identity aside in search of another, or to make room for the other that's always been around, because she was always this way, which seems a certainty, because everyone is, or was. What that other self may be is conjectural every time—but this is no time for analysis. It's a time to move onward.

She gasps and hoarsely whispers, "My God, I haven't done that in a long time." She rubs stray effluvia into Mulroney's chest hair. "I read that this stuff is the best healing agent for your skin." Her smile is cherubic, heightened like a clown's with lotion smeared around it.

Yes, nuts.

The forehead above the windowsill bunches tightly in witness of neighbor relations on this segment of the ridge. Mulroney stares at the ceiling.

He anticipated remorse, but this is worse: covered in Nivea, spit and pecker snot, and she's whacko and nothing feels right, and now he'll ask for the money—no. Not now. Give it a breather. Definitely not now. Maybe tomorrow, or later in the week . . .

"You're so cute, all sleepy. I love that. Do you think I'm good?"

"Good at what?"

"You silly. You know. Making that little fellow go kablooey."

Kablooey? "I'd say . . . yes. Frankly, if you don't mind, I'd say . . . I'd say you're the best."

She loves affirmation of womanly skills. "If I don't mind? My husband says I'm the best. Used to say. He died. Some people think it's why he married me. They don't know. Do you realize the amino acid content?"

"You're a health nut. But your husband was ninety-two."

"Yes, and he loved me till the end."

Mulroney wonders how often she'll need a protein smoothie. "Well, we're none of us as young as we used to be. That's okay, if we go slow enough."

"I'm sorry you didn't like my gloves," she says.

"It's something I'm not used to."

"Look. I had to work each one, so small and just the right size. See? I slit their tiny bodies and scooped out the stuff and stitched them up with their fuzzy little faces at the fingertips."

"You're amazing all right."

She stares sweetly as a fairy godmother. He lies back and closes his eyes, drifting from life's strange need and payout, or potential payout that may be no payout, because a blowjob from the neighbor seems heavily weighted to the downside of dark potential, including embarrassment and hurtful disclosure to family members and no grant or loan . . . But that's negative, and once again he has only to muster the positive view on friendship and trust in order to count his little minks gamboling light and fluffy o'er the . . .

Waking up, he checks coordinates—after dark, but where and when, and what? Oh, Betty Burnham's sofa after a mink-fisted wank and a . . . Oh, man. Mulroney groans, up from the love seat. She's waiting patiently, understanding the needs of a man in late prime. She hints that a nice screw would be lovely, but she won't press the issue. They'll be friends and maybe have some fun again soon.

How perfect. This is the kind of generosity and understanding that bind a woman to a neighborhood and could well pave the way to understanding. Mulroney affirms the negative: no, a screw will not occur this evening. But next time! Of this a man doth pledge. Maybe, no matter what. "Betty. I'm curious. Are you a Republican?"

"Of course, silly. What else would I be? A druid? Gee, whiz. You are a kick, Michael." She touches him. "It's good to have a man around with some life left in him."

"Yes. It's good to be here." He moves for the door. Why press politics at this juncture? Though it is an election cycle, and donations may be a good topic. Moving like senior citizens down the hallway, she says, "That was lovely, Michael."

Lovely?

"Well, it wasn't tea and crumpets but it can be a great way to pass the time." She murmurs, slipping her hand into his, like making woo. Oh, brother. Taking her hand will mean another go, and another, in a vicious circle of remorse and restraint, until he can muster the mustard to toe the line, as he's shouted down to thousands of salesmen over the years, and ask for the money. He stops near another door and turns to her. But a tiny racket of whirring, chirping, clicking, and rustling preempts his speech.

"Come." She pulls him in. "Meet my pets."

The room is low lit in soft pastels. A bank of cages goes silent, as dozens of tiny eyes watch the intruders.

"Rodents," he says.

"These are my minks. Don't you love them?"

"Not like you do, I'm sure."

"It's my little hobby, for fun, for Christmas and special occasions. You have your bicycle. I have my babies."

"Your pets? Your babies? You skin them."

"Not exactly. It's not like tanning hides. They make furs, not skins. It's different, you know. Furs are lovely."

"Not so lovely for them."

"Oh, they don't mind! It lets them last forever in a way."

"You mean like you could be eternal as a lampshade?"

"Oh, you," she swats playfully. "I don't do big things. Certainly no coats. Not even a stole in the last few years. I did a muffler last year. But I'll stick to collars and trim now. I do gloves for very special people. Look at them. How could you not love them?"

"Yeah, that would be a hell of a thing, not loving them."

Some of her babies have babies of their own, who romp and frolic, carefree with needs met and none of the anxiety of the elderly babies. "Aren't they adorable?" She awaits affirmation, confident as a proud mother.

Mulroney mumbles, "Yes. Adorable."

She plucks a juvenile from a cage and cuddles it to her cheek. "And sooo soft. It's softness to die for?" She hands the baby mink to Mulroney, in whose hand it curls and stares up.

"Yes, well, they die for it, don't they?"

"Oh, you." This playful swat is more forceful, since a nerve has been touched, suggesting that her babies are actually dead rather than immortalized in—gloves. *Can you imagine?*

With an imagination more supple than most, Mulroney strains. "Why gloves?"

"It came to me. You could fit your finger in there, couldn't you? So soft and warm. The forefinger and little-finger babies are nearly ready. The pinky and pointer come before the others, and the thumb comes last. But they grow to the next size in a day or two."

"So we're looking at three more weeks for a pecker cozy?"

"Oh, you!" My, but she does love the earthy humor. "Guess who this pair is for?"

Mulroney senses bile on the rise. Who in the neighborhood could imagine what's happening here? He fears that his name is on the next pair.

She beams.

He shrugs, "Not a clue."

"Hold your hand up."

"Betty. No, no. Really."

"But I want to."

"I don't want you to."

"But I want to."

"Please. Betty. I don't want you to."

"You wanted me to a little while ago."

"That was different. Nobody had to die."

"It wasn't so different. A little bit of me dies when I have to do that. I mean, not that, that, but the other, what you wanted me to do, what you made me promise to do. You men are all alike. I want to do it for you. And I want to do something else for you. But oh, no."

"Honestly, the one thing was enough."

"But what if I want to do more?"

Perfect! It's a closing question no less than asking for color options.

"I can't wear mink gloves. But I have an idea."

"Why not? They're soft, warm, water repellant. You'll *love* them!"

"I can't. I mean I already love them."

"So? Minks breed like crazy, and it doesn't hurt them. Watch." She plucks the little beast from his hand with a practiced grasp around the chest, her thumb on its head, and . . .

"No!" bellows Mulroney, grabbing her wrist.

"Michael! You're hurting me!" She whimpers, dropping the little mink into Mulroney's hand. He sets it back in the cage.

"Sorry. Look: what you do is your own business, obviously. I just can't . . ."

"Psh . . . And here I thought you were different. You're . . . You're not . . . You're a tree hugger!"

"I'm not. I hate trees. I am unique in some ways, but I just can't stand animal torture."

"It's not torture. Michael, I don't want us to have our first tiff over this. You asked me to eat you. Then you asked if I was a Republican. What's a girl to think?" She waits, batting lashes, an opening for romantic truce.

Our first tiff? Oh, brother. "You leave the legs and feet on. You put the heads on the ends. It's . . . grotesque."

"The legs and feet are stitched very nicely, if I do say so, along the length of the finger, and the head is over the fingernail. It's animate. It speaks to me. You prefer bleeding heart morality? You try sticking a big fat penis in *your* mouth sometime. Now that's grotesque."

"You said you . . . had natural skill. It was mutual consent—wait! You're right. Let's not squabble. Dead animal faces on fingertips are . . . difficult for me. Okay? But we can do something together."

"Oh, God!" She laughs at his tactful caution and loves him after all. She can't help it. They will survive this silly impasse. She takes his arm to resume their dreamy drift to a sweet fare thee well in the sumptuous bye and bye, till we meet again, *mon ami*.

She said *ami*, friend, and not *amour*, love, and that seems good, what fleshy friction so potentially complex should come to, not beyond the realm of friendship and playfulness, but firmly within that realm. On pace with the playful aspect, she says, "By the way, I know your real estate agent, that Judith Elizabeth Cranston Layne woman. I don't know how you picked her. Or why. She drives a white BMW sedan, and when I asked her why, she said they loaned her a white one when her silver BMW was in for a service. She said all these years she's thought white was stark and chalky. She got it right. But then a friend called out, 'Nice car!' So she traded her silver one on a white one. Her silver car was six months old, but she didn't want it anymore, because BMW makes a statement, and nobody called out for silver, and white is perfect for what it doesn't say. She said that. She says, 'if you get my meaning.' I haven't the foggiest what she's talking about, but I do get her gall."

"I don't follow her too well either. And I agree there isn't much there, under the accessories. Except the teeth—for the quick close. But I didn't choose her, and she's not there for small talk. She's there to sell."

They come to the door. He steps out. "I hope we can . . ."

"You mean you didn't choose her for the same reason you chose me?"

Mulroney stares at the two answers available in the brisk night air. The first: that he didn't choose anybody—never has. He merely deferred to need, and she came along, perchance, with needs of her own. He wonders briefly if the moment is nigh, but alas, it is not.

He chooses the second potential answer: "Yes, choosing you was different than choosing her."

She waits for elaboration and finally says, "It's late. We came a long way in a short time. I didn't want to wake you. You looked so restful. You could stay here, but . . ."

Mulroney steps off. "Thanks. You are a great hostess."

"I should hope to say so." She moves in for the cuddle and a throaty moan. "That was easy. I know you men—you real men."

"Come. Hugs."

She nuzzles in the commingled scent of sperm and flowers. Mulroney imagines it at the fragrance counter at Burnham's: *Honey Suckle Mayo.* He laughs, amazed at his wit, wondering if he might have done better at merchandizing.

She joins his soft chortle, satisfied that a cuddle sums them up.

For his part, Mulroney is sensitive to her needs and feels the urgency of closing the deal prior to other necessities. He must keep hope alive, because a woman is still a woman at any age. "Maybe we can . . ."

"Maybe we can. Go now. Your wife must be worried sick."

"No. She's into cocktails by now."

"Now, now. Give a woman her due."

"Fair enough."

So it's farewell, so long, *au revoire, auf viedersehen*—till next time, with a peck on the cheek, since they only just met.

Mulroney strolls two blocks home, not feeling good or relieved but rather anxious, hoping the exchange will prove productive. If he's truly honest with his inner satyr, he must ask himself the ever-present question on every man's mind regarding the quality/satisfaction merit of the blowjob. So he asks, and he thinks, Yeah, that was terrific. Next time would be even better with the warm and fuzzies. Make that warm and cuddlies. The fuzzy thing could be a deal killer. Snapping the necks of baby animals? It's not the best of images to keep old Betty looking good, so he hopes she has the sense to close the torture room door.

Entering quietly, Mulroney listens. Allison is sleeping on the sofa in front of the news—*this just in*. She calls it keeping up to date, her habit of fading away with the news on. A TV woman is reporting on the anguish etched so clearly in the face of another woman, an extraordinary woman who travels with a small harp, playing to random listeners on a busy city street, bringing joy to their otherwise hectic lives. Then comes a brief history of harps and some well-known harpists.

The story is wrapping up when it breaks for Breaking News and another woman telling the world that a car just ran into a fruit stand in India or Indiana and killed a man.

Mulroney checks his machine. Marylyn Moutard barks that she will not say no to the offer on the table without a good faith counter. Mulroney regrets her use of mood to compensate limited perspective.

Allison sits up, groggy. "You don't even know who the harpies were! *Do* you?"

"Let me see . . . Weren't they the original cunts?"

"That's so negative!"

"Yes. I'm trying to change, but it takes time, along with the help of a patient community."

She plops back and surfs the news line up, complaining of the sameness in all the news and the giant corporations with corporate family values that own the news channels, which is *so* fucked. Allison won't use that language unless she's loosened up with sauce.

"Don't watch."

"I really shouldn't. It's sick. It's like that old guy in a coma like a cauliflower all those years, and they kept him plugged in because he was a billionaire. They spent millions keeping a pulse in the guy. Who in their right mind would want that? Then that bitch killed him. Oh, she killed him and everybody knows it. And she's a slut too, an old one. And the news people pumped it up like a sporting event. Like that was good news, and they were in these people's faces every time they smiled or cried. It got ratings. The guy died. So they made this TV movie about this family with all this money who kept the old guy alive. They should be shot." The liquor also reveals her hostility. "She lives up the street, you know. Probably up there fucking a hobo right now. Fucking Republicans."

"You never were so anti-news. Or political."

"I'm not!"

"Maybe I misunderstood you."

"You usually do."

Mulroney rummages the fridge and finds potato salad on the far side of shelf life. He sprinkles it liberally with salt and pepper, shags a beer, and sits at his wife's feet.

She asks, "Want to see if a movie's on?"

"Sure." So they settle in to two hours of thought deferment on a painless amusement they'll forget by tomorrow. They turn in. Mulroney could use a shower, but that's a chore and would wake him up again. Besides, Allison is snoring. Fuck it. Plenty of time in the morning. But he's got all this scented lotion and spit on his dingdong, so he gets in and gets stuck, thinking into not thinking, then getting out and quickly toweling and turning in before things revert, as they usually do.

Maybe he feels a loss of traction in his tentative connection to polite society. He's a salesperson, a used-car salesperson at that, a proven producer in a most competitive arena, where jugular instincts prevail. The years brought him a customer or two who walked in, pointed to the car of choice, and plunked down the dough, but the massive hoards needed to be sold—wanted to be sold—demanded that Mulroney convince them that purchasing a particular car would be the wisest decision of the day. Mulroney was the best. He could never actually train a staff to be so good, but they came close. So what happened? Did he squander margins on creeping overhead? Did sales slump? Did some lots shift inventory to steal profitability from other lots? Did Californians begin to think that pre-owned sounds better than used, and new sounds best of all? Or was it the lenders, hell-bent on ruining a used-car magnate with reduced value factors on anything not fresh from the factory? Fuckers. You can't devalue a car on a whim. A used-car guy only makes a go of it because a car cost thirty grand new but then devalues to fifteen in no time, even with low mileage. There's your value, your bang for the buck, no matter how much happy horseshit is loose in the ether. It's the year of manufacture that determines value. Yes, it's skewed and wrong, and nobody wants a nearly new car with high miles. But low miles in cream puff condition, nobody gives a flat flying fuck what the little digits on the title say. So why do they bust his balls on the greatest OK deals around, on what they call market fluctuation?

It's Mulroney's cross to bear, and so is the solution, which is actually no solution at all. What would he do with a measly hundred grand? He'd buy time, and if time ran out, he'd worry about getting more. Or not, if he moves to Hawaii and opens a used surfboard lot. Or a used golf cart lot.

Hey, has time ever not run out?

What if they had a drug to make a man more romantic—or crave foreplay? That would make this easier. They do, kind of, but a boner pill that drives a man into the nearest hole is not exactly a joy to anticipate. He can't feel good about wooing Betty Burnham. She's so odd—make that bizarre, with her Republican values and animal cruelty. Still, the solution to what ails Mulroney's World appears to be as easy as low-hanging fruit. That would be him, Mulroney, the original low hanger. And to think, a guy had only to walk up the road to get a hummer and a loan—make that a grant, most likely.

Mulroney drifts. One day he'll be stooped, old, and unable to mount, much less ride, much less uphill. Then what?

In the morning Casa Mulroney wakens to birdsong and garden titter, with Allison urging everyone to breathe the morning air and eat birdseed and be happy—that would be her friends, the birds, including Victoria, the chicken who showed up last month, out of the blue. Allison calls her a harbinger of things to come and tells her to be nice and share with the other birdies. She doesn't drink in the morning and, as usual, is free of the sundown demons and their day-after consequence. With childish innocence she feeds and waters, encouraging the birds and flowers to express themselves in song, color, and scent. "Or why be?" And if they have other concerns, they can speak, in their way. She asks that the birds, please, drop no dukey on the flowers. She assures them she's not mad at them—but it would be best if they dropped it, you know, near the flowers and not on them. Okay?

•

What a woman. She's nuts like the old bag up the road, but it's different. Mulroney could embrace her right then on sheer affection—make that love, most of the time, and a familiarity of years and so many things between them that he values, especially her thin body, but she's in the garden. He rolls to one side and feels his age and determines the morning might be good for massage. Hey—how can you tell if you're getting old? You get stiff in the back more often than the front. Ha! Mulroney just made that up. But that's another great thing about bicycling: anyone can get a massage, but after a thirty-five miler, a massage means so much more.

Mulroney moans, imagining the ration of grief Suzette will give him for getting so tight. That's okay. It'll be a tune-up, with Mulroney coming back together to run smooth for a few more miles. So he dials the number he knows by heart. Suzette is six one and a hundred pounds and reads books on correct eating, stretching, cleansing, sleeping, meditating, chakra adjusting, aura alignment and so on. She's too thin, at times painfully, like when her chest looks bony. Her bookshelves read like Fellini's library: *Integrative Karma*, *The Tao of Gallbladders*, *Your Spleen & You*.

Her hands are magic—the first time he thought her amazingly in tune, as she lifted his nutsack casual as squeezing his ear lobe and pressed underneath to relieve tension in the lower back. "You're making tension in my lower front."

"Yes, it's all connected," she explained.

Mulroney didn't think Suzette so old as himself, maybe because she doesn't drink, smoke or use negative language. She's three months younger actually, with a mystique. That would make her a few years younger than Betty Burnham. Suzette tolerated his humor too, laughing him off, which was different than jacking him off, which he thought at the time she was bound for. He didn't mind. What the hell. Suzette has great hands and might need a few bucks extra, and there he was on the table, all lathered up.

But she only wanted to ease the tension in his back, in her odd way. Besides that, she laughed at some of his jokes and ignored his reaction to treatment—roustabouts never got the tent up quicker on fewer moves. Then she was on to thighs and calves in her magical, soothing way.

"Hello, there. It's me, Suzette. I'll be gone till the twenty-eighth. Please leave me a message, and have a most wonderful day."

Gone. He could check the Happy Daze listings for massage therapy. But on his last try he waited twenty minutes past his scheduled time. The Big M—twenty minutes. Then she came out eating parrot shit on a rice cracker—spirulina, actually, smeared all over her face as if to look disgusting by design—her design. That's how the kids taunt and make a point.

They call it political, but it has no point, as in pointless. Mulroney asked if that was parrot shit on that cracker. She laughed, no; it was, *in fact*, the richest source of riboflavin in the *known universe*, which is bigger than the whole wide world. Uppity kids want to one-up on everything they do. Her girl-friend came out for the public display of affection, with a big wet kiss, right in the spirulina. And he'd only wanted a massage.

Let's see: Dr. Feelgood. Lotus Unfolding. Soothing Outcall— Wait! Rosa Massage. Outcall OK. Great hands. That's Rosa in Watsonville! Bingo!

So he punches the number and Rosa picks up. "Hello."

"Hi, Rosa. It's Michael, on the bicycle. Remember me?"

"I do. How can I help you?"

"I saw your ad in the Happy Daze."

"Yes. I have an opening at three. What's your address?"

"Oh. Well, I'll come to your place."

She hesitates. "You'll be more comfortable at your place."

"Nah. We have a showing this afternoon. I gotta be scarce."

"Well . . . I suppose . . ."

"If it's a problem I can . . ."

"No. Not a problem. I'd like to see your house sometime."

Does she want to case it for artwork? "Yes, well, I'd love to show you sometime. Three?"

"Sure."

"Luego."

"By-ee."

Why do they do that? Must they jump on every chance to sound stupid? What are the odds that she makes tiny hearts above every *i* and at the ends of sentences? At least the gold digging is transparent and up front, unlike the more civilized social segments, who have the couth and forbearance to get acquainted. So the day reveals its plan, with a ride and a rub foremost but beginning with a few unsavory tasks. Because an ugly fact of life and business is that anxiety desperation still requires paper pushing and phone calls. So he heads down to it, ready to plow the drift on his desk.

Which seems like a curse on a man with better things to do. Then again, how much more can he do? Not much is the short answer. He needs money in the short term in order to enable reasonable cash flow to float the show for the long term. And the question persists on each call and sheet of paper, whether this snippet or that blurb will affect meaningful change on the . . . er . . . uh . . . situation. The answer persists as well: Nah. Not likely. He could sell three cars from each lot daily and still need to weather a six-month low-pressure system.

Mulroney doesn't mind the tedium or the pressure. He hasn't minded for many years, when mechanical effort led to leverage in all things, and a man on paper could be a king in the market-place, where the greatest stuff can be had. Now the mechanical effort is reduced to mechanics and maintenance, a chore, but he's done it for so long and knows the moves so well, he just knocks it out. Takes what, an hour?

Johnny Lunchbox might grit his teeth when the alarm goes off an hour before sunrise for another goddamn shift with the two-hour commute and job politics—but there's none of that where Michael Mulroney lives. Business independents and self-starters understand retirement; it's not the end of work. It's the end of mandatory tasks. Take Allison: she works the garden and loves it. Mulroney works his way up hills on a bicycle and loves it. That's the true definition of retirement: not having to do what you don't want to do. Sure, the bullshit and melodrama never completely go away; they're part and parcel with sunrise. And the rant and rave to close a deal takes a bigger toll as the years stack up. But all told the world is good, and it promises more of the same, if only—

The critical attitude at this juncture is to perceive potential as a swing in the right direction—for the bleachers—on any one of several variable pitches. What are the odds of a strike out? Infinitesimally remote is the correct answer, which bodes well for a player who knows how to read the eyes. Scientific fact: Michael Mulroney is as good as it gets and still loves the game, so there's nothing else for it but to love the game and let it show. Attitude is everything, and winning begins in the heart and head, just before it goes up on the scoreboard and in the wallet. Mulroney remembers busting his hump for a dollar an hour and feeling great because he'd started out at sixty cents. Now he can squeeze the turnip just right, and what does he get? Oh, Count Dracula would envy that move. How many people can make a hundred grand by squeezing a cash and volume discount and pumping margins on a phone call? Count them on one finger is your short answer. Not that he can just grab a hundred large on one easy call at any time. But he's done it many times in the past, which will repeat itself if you can just buy the time, or finesse the time at any rate—and that's the critical component: at any rate. Debt doesn't matter—Dick Cheney had it dicked—and neither does the interest if you have faith in the roll. You still got to say yeah, fuck it, I'll take the fucking lot, meaning an entire lot of cars at the auction—at eighty-two cents on the dollar, no, make it seventy-two. Do you know what that means in real money? It's a different world than a dollar an hour—or three hundred dollars an hour, or a grand an hour—and Michael Mulroney is one of its card-carrying action figures.

Mulroney had this tax lawyer once on a state audit— Mulroney was clean, but the state bastards took him for the ride. The bureaucrats saw him making more dough than the entire State Tax Division payroll. That gets a bunch of GS-7s pissed off. Mulroney met his lawyer once because that's all it took. The lawyer got high marks for keeping the ride short and going toe-to-toe with the nimrod tax bullies. He was big money, but at his level what can you do, quibble? Three calls to check the guy out came up cherries: this lawyer was the go-to guy on state audits.

So Mulroney went. The guy was with one of those six-name law firms, and he wasn't one of the names. The firm had the entire nineteenth floor in a prime location, all paneled in endangered hardwoods for the spendiest show in town, chrome and steel outside, plush, cushy and heart-grain inside. Mulroney opened with the key question: why wouldn't an outfit like this want the go-to tax guy on the letterhead? The guy laughed—said the firm did want him there, but he declined. They insisted, and he threatened to leave. Sure, he was a bullshitter, but that was later. For openers, he said, "Twenty-six partners and associates in this firm all submit personal financials annually, and only one is solvent."

The lawyer was short on cash—said as much by way of concession to fun and extravagance as a lifestyle, including several wives and cars and a steady flow of top-drawer liquor. It happens, but the lawyer wasn't broke like the rest of the firm. He was only strapped for cash, on the edge of the abyss instead of down in it, clawing out. Eight bills an hour and coming up short? But that's kicking the horse. At the time Mulroney was way flush, and he chuckled at the calamities of some people.

Big M Mulroney never wanted wood paneling or a nineteenth floor, but some days he made eight bills an hour times ten. Or twenty. How can you not love days like that? You can't. How can you not know those days will come again? Just sitting back, rolling a controlled substance, inhaling deeply, and feeling the dough come at you in waves is lovely, lovely, lovely, a day of bliss and harmony. Some guys added the toot, and that was okay but not so much for Mulroney. It made him anxious. He made way too many phone calls on the toot, and a stoned reverie tended to mute him up and make him look much smarter. Like now, with things tidied up and responses in place, the M will be out-of-pocket, away from the office, in a meeting, attending to important business, which bolsters attitude no less than another latte and maybe one little inhale of the magical herb. What could make for greater success on a beautiful day than a full schedule with a great ride and a massage? Of course, a bridge to the financial future would enhance success with greater greatness, but not to worry, because that bridge appears to be, as they say, under construction.

With big-picture perspective, the path seems productive and perfectly suited to the skill set at hand.

Mulroney knows the way
to carry the sleigh
through the white and drifted snow . . .

So he ponders life and business, leaning back into the lumbar support only an executive office chair can provide, taming the dragons as only a Big M can do. With work dispatched and consciousness mildly altered, he moves out, via the bathroom for an executive dump of semi-massive magnitude that alters consciousness more significantly still, with consideration of yet another million dollar idea in the process: a toilet seat with lumbar support, a one-up on those Japanese units that squirt the anus free of fecal debris and then blow dry the tender membrane. Besides lumbar relief, The Mulroney Throne could also include a delicate applicator for the ChapStick. But surely they already thought of that.

Lightly stoned and a few pounds lighter, an executive could well justify a lie-down for a minute or two for equilibrium adjustment, but no. The massage will be restful soon enough, and besides, a quick shower will rejuvenate and remove the odd scent and/or dingleberry, because cleanliness is pivotal to first impressions on a masseuse. Which is no more nor less than brushing and flossing before a dental exam. It's merely polite.

Then it's the kitchen for the latte boost on the way to the beach for a mile or so walk to stretch things out and for perspective. Could the sky be bluer? Could blessings be greater? The house could slide into escrow easy as downhill on a mudslide, but again, all things in time.

A half-mile or so down the beach, a crowd gathers at the water-line to watch a big man reeling something in, his rod bent double, his muscles bulging. An eagle ray breaks the surface thirty yards out, a thick, sixty-pounder with a four-foot wingspan, flapping into the shallows and onto the sand. It breathes heavily, critically fatigued and hooked a few inches into the mouth.

Mulroney is saddened by the struggle that seems so unnatural, so void of benefit to anyone. He's had days like that.

The big fish and fisherman gasp in unison, the man apparently dumbfounded and fearful of the other—the eagle ray confused on what behavior could possibly alter the unfortunate situation, till Mulroney parts the crowd and asserts, "Cut the line. He'll slough the hook in a few days." The fisherman shrugs—he has no knife. Someone offers a fingernail clipper, and Mulroney cuts the line. The crowd watches the big ray flop weakly in the sand.

A woman mutters, "Stingray. Look out."

"Come on," Mulroney says to the big fisherman. "We'll ease him back in. You get one side; I'll get the other."

"He'll get you with his stinger," the fisherman says.

"No he won't. He's tired. He needs a break. You ever need a break? Besides, he's not a stingray. He's an eagle ray."

"He has a stinger. I can see it," states a woman in the crowd. The crowd murmurs warnings, reaching consensus on the ray's nasty intentions.

"That stinger can shoot out at you," says the big fisherman.

"That's the stupidest thing I've heard all day," Mulroney says. "It won't happen." He turns to the woman. "Did you see somebody get hurt by a ray on TV? Or dream it? Or make it up?" He stoops to liberate a fish out of water, to help a natural player return to his element, perhaps wiser, perhaps recognizing the true M as few fish have a chance to do. Or maybe Michael Mulroney feels a bond.

The fisherman follows Mulroney's lead with trepidation. They lift the wings into the next wave and move out, giving the ray some depth until it's underwater.

"Okay, and out to sea," Mulroney advises, as the ray swims gracefully out. The crowd applauds. In his moment of heroism and happy interface, he accepts group approval on a noncommercial behavior. In the limelight of a righteous act, Mulroney bows, smiling sadly inside, wishing for a helping hand that might ease him back to his depths as well. He bows to the crowd to keep it light, humorous, and subtle, achieving the imagery of a man on the beach, doing good in the world. The small but engaged audience chuckles. A few applaud. Someone gasps, "That's Mike Mulroney!" Those with cameras make the scene immortal.

Mulroney corrects, "Michael, if you will. Big M OK Cars, at your service." It sounds corny. But it can't hurt. Because when you get down to it, it's a nonstop campaign, running for office or selling cars. You work the stump where you find it. You don't shy from responsibility. You don't grandstand or blow your own horn, but you step up to do the right thing and take the credit when it's due. And let's face it: every candidate these days is striving for more than meets the eye, sooner or later.

Mulroney is further affirmed in his decision to forego the liedown, lest he and the fish would have missed an excellent opportunity. Isn't it grand, the way things work out for the best in the most stimulating weather in the world?

The route to Rosa's is mostly negative grade, which gets really negative on the way back. But a massage in seventeen miles will be sweet. Maybe Juan Valdez will throw Mulroney's bicycle in the back of the truck and offer a lift home. Maybe they'll bond and be asshole buddies.

XIV

Esteffeno y Phillippé
or
A Bastion of Liberal Thinking

At fifty-six, Steffen looks like, talks like, and is protégé to Phillip at sixty-seven. A perennial practitioner of the soft expression, Steffen tilts his head and juts his chin as a chronic mode of emphasis, doubt, wonder and the way it is among men of reflection on the California Coast. Ever so gently asserting the true context of the avant-hip local scene, he avoids the macho burden, shuns the macho concept. He could be gay, or not; the dramatic point being that either/or is A-OK, and if you have doubts, then society will deal with you in timely fashion. Steffen and Phillip are friends and riding companions who keep a more moderate pace than the bike shop elite. They call out to the more compulsive cycling set speeding casually past, "Oh, nice one!" Or, "You just passed a couple of dope-smoking geriatrics!" Or, "You're ready for the tour!" Steffen is known as Esteffeno on these outings, and he does the catcalling because it seems more suited to the younger set.

Phillip became Phillippé as part of Steffen's—Esteffeno's—fantasy, which he borrowed from that movie a few decades ago about the Hoosier who dreamed of bicycle racing in Italy. Further grist for Steffen's and Phillip's mill is their common past, including childhood constraints and traumas as inflicted by the Catholic church in the tender years, with intimations of attempted buggery and values run amok. The church's evil ways are the likely source of Phillip's sexual confusion, which serves him to advantage in the neighborhood, given the social capital granted to victims and the minority oppressed with a bonus payout for revelations of childhood abuse. Phillip and Steffen had both been altar boys, and they revel in the mother lode of priest jokes currently on the circuit. Do you know the difference between a full nelson and a Father Nelson?

The two friends also enjoy a running joke on their appetite for a little brown round now and then. So? What's it to you? And it is a joke, followed by laughter every time.

Steffen's rapier wit cuts most often like a butter knife, with soft poignancy and wicked humor, endearing him to many. As an effete dilettante for whom bicycling is an intellectual sport, he is proud of his legs, his annual mileage, and his riding regimen. He defends his medium-grade bicycle with a biblical passage: If an Acme bicycle was good enough for Jesus . . .

Steffen and Phillip's friendship is visible and could be intimate, but nobody cares. Two old guys who ride bicycles and may engage in anal sex are harmless. So what? The general assumption is that Steffan and Phillip get high and get it on, not so often, but whenever they want, leading suburban lives in the meantime. Some men would rather not admit being gay, especially those married to women. The local betting line would lay odds that Steffen wears his underpants backward—except that nobody would make a line because it doesn't matter or make a difference or change perception for anyone. Yet the duo compensate with a vigorous, public yen for firm young women. With murmuring speculation they ogle passing females, comparing notes in soft glances sideways. Could churchly culpability run so amok?

On any weekday, they might pedal a few miles, stop for a latte, and pedal on. So what? They are the eldest two riders around, besides Mulroney, and they live in the neighborhood, but they have yet to see if he'd like to join them for a ride. That's what.

Michael Mulroney is a car salesperson—*used* cars at that. Magnate, shmagnate, Mulroney came up to the sun deck after a long passage below the water line. Mulroney runs ads on TV and fills the air otherwise with visual pollution, with all those plastic flags and silly signs promising perfection in *used* cars. How utterly blue collar, and he doesn't read *The New Yorker*, so he can't very well join the road talk on the juicy tidbits therein.

Mulroney is not offended but is rather relieved that Phillip and Steffen offer no potential for friendship and stimulation. He doesn't mind their sexual preference or their antics. Their stares and pithy asides can be offensive, and that's a fine how-do-you-do for two egregiously liberal men in tights that emphasize the gonads.

Phillip and Steffen are content to go their separate way, and so is Mulroney. Phillip the elder rode professionally on a European race schedule with a paycheck, many decades ago. The aura lingers, because he harks back so often and still wears some of the old kit, like the droll knit socks and funky jerseys.

Steffen and Phillip jovially recall this week's cartoons in *The New Yorker* as Mulroney overtakes them. Riding politely behind,

Mulroney wonders how long they'll ignore him. And why would two dyed-in-the-wool Californians read *The New Yorker*, if not to compensate something or other?

"Hello, boys," Mulroney demurs, easing alongside.

Seeing Mulroney in riding togs, Phillip's brow scrunches as his eyes strain on Mulroney's new bicycle. "Olioglo?" Phillip rides a vintage Alligator frame in aluminum from twenty years ago and openly covets carbon, even in the mid-range, but cannot muster the initiative on fixed income.

"CX-61. I just . . . picked it up."

"Hm. Campy components. Super Record. Electronic shifting." Phillip looks straight ahead as if wearing blinders, because years of sizing up riders while showing no interest is a developed skill. Still, he has difficulty in constraining his regret, much less his envy and resentment, as if a used car salesperson should experience CX-61 glory and a committed road racer for decades cannot. Mulroney is not proud of the bicycle, yet he savors the exchange and visible ruffle. Phillip can't help himself either, effusing soft wit at Mulroney's expense: "I suppose it'll be a nice bike for you, especially if you're going to use it." The suggestion is that Mulroney is a wheelman-come-lately in the worst ways of the affluent suburbs, where chic pursuits are attacked with massive accessorizing, rather than the blood, sweat and tears that make a difference on long grinds up major hills and sweeping descents. The wanna-be will get bored and/or lazy often as not—or claim a lame injury or sorry circumstance—and the rig collects dust. Not that any grind or descent in the suburban foothills makes a difference in the world of cycling, but values and priorities remain pure.

Mulroney understands, himself a well-seasoned veteran of competitive dialogue. So he sees Phillip and raises: "Yeah. I might get tired of it. Who knows? So far, though, it's a breeze, especially with those Certification Eleven wheels on there. You know those, don't you, Phil?"

Mulroney understands timing, so he waits for the subtle side-glance that affirms Certitude 1111s front and rear for effort-less climbing in the four thousand dollar range, for rotational advantage only. Or, more succinctly in the range of exponentially greater value than Phillip's pile of Alligator junk. "I'll try it for a while. See if I like it. I'll let you know if I get ready to sell. Give you a shot at half price. Only ten grand or so. That would be a sweet deal for you, huh, Phillip?"

Mulroney can parry. Oh, how sweet it could be to tell peeping Phillip that he would have been pilloried with his eyes gouged out not so long ago. Now he might go to jail, where he might casually drop his soap, but he should be cautious in picking it up . . . or not.

But no. Mulroney stays calm, savoring the tart reality that Phillip knows that Mulroney knows, and between the two, Mulroney has the least to lose and is easily the tougher player. So he finds his cadence, easing into optimal averages that are stronger than on day one. He feels good, and the pace will now quicken. The three of them pick it up to eighty cadence, give or take. Each rider shifts subtly as the game picks up, as speed climbs from twelve through fourteen on its way to eighteen, as if men meeting on a casual ride accelerate as a matter of recognition and respect. Or a petty pissing contest. Because some men ride fast, and anyone is welcome to join in, given the balls to keep up, given the riding chops to turn forty-five miles at seventeen per, *average*—

If you got the juice, asshole. Let's get it on!

Oh, Phillip's challenge is unspoken but clear, fair compensation to all else he may show or fail to show. The guy was a pro, on the pro circuit, and even if that was decades ago, a pro does not forget the tricks and moves of the cutthroat game, where stealth and nuance are integral to creeping machismo overall. "Nice," he casually calls. "Wireless functions and cadence."

Mulroney presses the button to cadence, to show how easily he can keep an eye on things. "Yeah. Why the fuck not?" Mulroney strains a bit, talking at such a sustained speed, but he has a few tricks himself, primary among them the significant grade coming up in a quarter mile, which doesn't seem so far, but internal gauges verge on maximum for pressure, temperature, beat and flow. Can he make the grade? Because at only five percent, he can smoke a condescending blowhard easy as Certitudes can stomp an Alligator.

Mulroney makes the incline and pulls ahead, not so dramatic as Lance but with equal gratification. Phillip was a pro, after all, and nobody pays Mulroney. Steffen is less aggressive trailing by a few yards, as he calls in soft superiority and strained intellect that maybe they should turn around for something or other. Steffen learned the soft quirks from Phillip. They fall back, giggling again over pithy snippets, trying to remember where they were before Mulroney butted in. Mulroney eases the pace.

Phillip laughs out loud about one priceless cartoon showing a monk with a bulge in his robe over a caption about too much leavening in the rectory. That cartoon reminds him of the penance imposed on his own aging penis, though he pronounces it *pennis*, perhaps in deference to Steffen—please, not Steven.

So Mulroney lags till they catch up, and he asks, "Sounds like you guys aren't getting any pussy."

Steffen is aghast at such blatant disrespect for women.

Phillip says, "No, not like you. My wife is frigid. Her pussy is frozen. She wouldn't let you stick it in there if you paid her."

"How much did you offer, Phil?" Phillip will not respond, so Mulroney presses, "What's she look like?"

Steffen says, "She's beautiful." He glares at Mulroney, who pulls a hankie for a one-handed nose blow. "Lose the handkerchief," Steffen advises, offering a chic freebie to the used-car king.

Mulroney pokes a finger into each nose hole then wipes the hankie sideways to snag what's left. "Lose it? I didn't lose it. I got it right here, Steve."

Steffen and Phillip ignore the ignoramus; Mulroney won't lose his handkerchief or obnoxious habits, requiring others to suffer. The handkerchief flops from a jersey pocket, waving to anyone who sees it. Steffen accelerates, not a move but distancing in a soft statement of contempt. Phillip moves up with him, closing ranks and leaving Mulroney behind, where he came in. "Okay," Mulroney laughs. "These five homos, I mean gay guys, are relaxing in a hot tub."

Phillip moans.

Steffen turns around to stretch his face in displeasure—inadvertently touching tires with Phillip, causing both to veer into wobbles and a likely crash.

Phillip wrenches a foot free of his clip to break the fall, then wobbles the other way and wrenches the other foot free.

Steffen emits a tiny screech.

In unison, they save themselves by the hair of their chinny chin chins, laughing off the fall that would have made the circuit with excruciating amusement for the Big Boys.

Mulroney grins and proceeds to the punch line—"You know, just soaking away. And this big ole wad o' splooge pops to the surface. Like in a lava lamp. And one of the gay guys says, 'Oh, God. Who farted?'"

Holding cadence at seventy-eight, Mulroney expects no laugh but asks anyway, "What? You guys don't think that's funny?"

Phillip breaks into downhill devil-may-care, transcending ignorance and wheelman posturing, hitting it to forty, fifty and higher, showing his tiny top gear in back that wrenches him to speed and skill outpacing anyone in the near radius.

Mulroney falls away to the shortcut into town as Phillip and Steffen head for the bridge. He regrets losing a few of the sweetest miles, but he regains refreshing solitude. Besides, it's massage day. "Hey, you guys take it easy!" Mulroney calls out, no hard feelings, what the hell; it's why God put forks in roads.

"Slanjová!" Steffen calls back.

"Campai!" Phillip weakly adds.

Slanjová? Campai? What is it with that femme fatale and his dominatrix? Then again, they found each other at this stage of their lives and miserable marriages. Phillip's not a bad guy. He complains about no pussy but seems thoroughly gay. Maybe he's not. He likes watching through windows, but that wasn't pussy. Not really. It was a filthy rich woman entertaining herself, which is also grist for Phillip's mill. Oh, rich people do attract followers. Maybe Phillip wants to be gay but can't afford it and needs a sponsor. Steffen is easier to figure; he'd be a twit no matter where he stuck his dick.

But who cares? Rarely have two individuals engendered greater indifference in a third party. Those two would rather be with each other than alone or with their wives. So what? They're going down the road right now agreeing that Mulroney is an asshole, laughing and being happy. Mulroney cannot fathom any greater indifference no matter what, though in the big picture he wishes they didn't know him. That way they could all think of something else.

That's life in the proverbial small town, though in the rarified suburbs of the central coast, nothing proverbial survives. Originality rules to the point of tedium. The Mulroneys are moving soon, and it doesn't matter where to, because it will be far from the tyranny of tolerance. You want to be a whacked-out fuckwad tower-sniping shitball maniac pervert? Welcome home. And good riddance. Steffen and Phillip will stop for twenty bucks worth of latte frappe mocha macchiato grande two percent homo talls in medium cups just up the road, where one will be short a few bucks and the other will be short the balance. They'll stare at the nubile girls and teen boys and cool off, reviewing the rigors of Catholic school and the sick, sick, sick situation with the priests and altar boys and nuns and so on and so forth one more time. And that's the negative outlook Mulroney successfully avoided, until running into those two

He'll need to tolerate new people wherever. Some assholes are made for each other, and that's a good thing no matter where. They keep each other busy, canceling each other out. Alone, they're a bigger nuisance. Those two were made for each other. It's just like some goofy kid walking onto a lot loaded with fresh cars, and the kid wants one that's been there for months. It's got sixty thousand on it, a few dings, worn upholstery, no floor mats, iffy skins—he has to have it. Chemistry. Kid thinks he can fix it up. So? What's the harm? Keeps him busy.

But those superior fuckers get Mulroney pissed off. That's his character defect. So Flip and Steve are in love and like to ride together. They'll find some nice bushes for a lovely communion and the world will be right. Who cares? That's what Mulroney thinks.

He thinks . . . Oh, shit. He thinks he's not getting a massage . . .

For there on the corner of 129 and Lakeview in the dirt lot that would like to be a grassy yard but can't because of the wind and dust and trucks running over it stands Rosa Berry crying her little eyes out. Mulroney scans for bruises, contusions, abrasions, and/or breaks. He wheels in to find out how badly Juan Valdez beat her and why. He'll get no massage, and that's a tough one. Then again, maybe it's only allergies.

"Hey, Rosa. What's up?"

Rosa may want to say what's up, but she can't quite speak through the blubbering. Like a child who had her dolly decapitated, she laments her losses in broken sobs and syllables. She's lost it all, from love, happiness and those truths we hold self-evident, to the sofa, her desk, her chair and her artwork—*her* artwork, not his, but hers. That is, he took her original Gonzales and her toaster—her *toaster* for fuck's sake. On that note she achieves comprehensible speech: "Now why would that prick need my toaster? My toaster! Don't I eat toast? Aren't three dozen toasters enough for one greaseball? What? He needs three dozen and one?"

Juan Valdez could not leave a toaster for a lousy toasted bagel because opportunity knocks at forty cents on the dollar, and those toasters go ch-ching ch-ching at the fafa kitchen accessory emporium on the mall for a hundred sixty bucks—each—or they would have if that creep hadn't stolen them first!"

That is, Juan Valdez is a thief. Those toasters were *hot!* He didn't beat or rob her, really, but she feels mugged. Worse yet, a woman who doesn't ask so much out of life has had her world turned upside down *again*. "And every fucking thing is going wrong, and I can't stop it, and now I can't even toast a fucking bagel!" Rosa's emotion gears up to wobbly—to the level known as tantrum. She screeches and shakes her fists.

"Where's the kid? And the dog?"

"The dog is lost. Panchito is with his uncle, looking for the dog or something."

Mulroney won't ask if Juan Valdez took the massage table or the body oil. The betting line on a massage feels about seven to one against, a prohibitive long shot behind the swayback nag. No point in straining the issue, so he mumbles regret and his hope to see her soon as he turns his front wheel but stops.

"We . . . I . . . Come on . . ." She's still a tad choked up and tries to wave away the annoying emotions of the thing—but Mulroney is not part of all that mess; she waves him in and leads the way. Up the minimal wooden steps to the minimal wooden stoop they slog. They back down two steps so the screen door can open on a room or a hovel, depending on perspective. This whimpering woman in middle age with recent aspirations to Noe Valley Victoriana murmurs in hoarse sadness, "Welcome to my space."

Mulroney assesses practicality for fitting his bicycle into the adobe-come-lately, because he sure as shit won't leave it outside. He doesn't mean to sniff at the cheap new carpet but can't help the olfactory cringe on the cloying smells of plastic and glue. *The Little Window Unit That Could* chugs along as if aligned with that segment of Rosa's figurative ride, uphill. The space has no feeling, except for numbness and crowding, with two people, a table, some knickknacks, and a bicycle. She shrugs, allowing that he can't very well leave a bicycle outside if it's worth more than some people's . . . but she needn't finish the thought; her meaning is understood.

Her space provides shelter from the elements, the end, clarifying her preference for outcall. A massage table waits in the center, as the primary tenant. She turns on a boom box, and new age space music sets its dreamy mood of stellar relaxation.

Mulroney appreciates the effort and attention to detail and moreover nearly lusts for a massage; such is the need of a man with muscles and a bicycle and a happy convergence of the two. Wiping her nose on another whimper she says, "I told you."

"Listen." He removes his shoes and sox, demonstrating rare skill in standing up for the removal, at his age or any age. He peels off his shirt, subtly sucking it up. "I'm gonna close my eyes and feel the ropes unwind. I'm really tight." He hesitates, until she finally catches on and turns around. He peels off the shorts and skivvies and stretches under the sheet on the table.

"You want it deep?"

"Yeah. Deep. Make me groan."

"I'll try."

Mulroney knows the syndrome, in which a person surrounded by great weather, stimulating company and a cavalcade of color and style will default to personal failure as an excuse for depression. She's got a massage table and very low overhead, which would be grounds for stability and happiness in most of the world. But this is the land of success—make that fabulous success—with no plastic surgery or glamorous sex or expensive cars for underachievers. Failure is clearly the case for a woman from San Francisco, where chic, urban Zen costs an arm and two legs, not to mention lifestyle accoutrements and updated panache that are simply prerequisite to staying in the game. Depression is simply one of the few cheap pastimes remaining. Then again . . .

Mulroney judges a massage therapist by her hands. Rosa is no masseuse but another turkey baster slathering oil that might keep him from rusting but won't soothe his muscles. At this rate he'll slide off his seat on the ride home. But lying prone is relaxing, and soon she finds her stride. It's not great or even good, but it's not bad and way better than the next grind up Hazel Dell.

In no time the client lets go, to drift in the acrid chemistry of carpet polymers and bonding agents, scented oil, the humming window unit and the cosmic harmony of a tambourine and a didgeridoo, unless that's a bass kazoo. He relaxes into lithe and lean recollections of youth. She enables long-forgotten feelings, working the neck and shoulders, down the spine to the sacrum and hips, thighs, calves and feet.

When she says, "Turn over," Mulroney is mush. "How you doing?" she asks, more composed than thirty minutes ago.

"Mm. Good. You're great." He hears himself saying it and feels himself believing it. What a surprise.

"Thanks. I've always had the gift."

"You can make a living as long as I'm around."

"Yeah. If you call seventy-five bucks an hour a living, one massage at a time."

"I think a living is what a person makes of it, and you develop what's available to you."

"So you think this is it for me?"

"Do you mean giving massage is it for you? Or dealing original art is more your line of work? Because I think the one would return seventy-five an hour, and the other would be more of an investment, where you could add some zeroes on the return."

Rosa sighs. "That's what I thought. That's what Juan said. Do you know this area has three of the five highest-demographic precincts in America? That means rich. You knew that. Art might be dead everywhere else, but we got some tasty originals in this neighborhood. If that can't get your interest, signed prints by major artists are thick as fleas around here. I don't mean here. We don't have fleas here. You know what I mean."

"Yes. I know what you mean. I'd know it if you had fleas too. Little bastards love me." Mulroney is seasoned enough on flea-bit terrain, on which a woman feels necessitated to state that the place has no fleas. He closes his eyes again to drift again, into the second half. She may be a bona fide urban veteran and a gifted masseuse, but . . . He murmurs that she and her Mexican boyfriend are not typical art dealers. She strokes his shins in soothing release and moves to the kneecaps with subtle manipulation. She feels his pain and addresses it accordingly.

"I'm not sure what you mean by that. You must have original art in your house. You should know that you can't generalize on art dealers."

"What I mean is, neither you nor your associate in the truck are similar to the art-dealers I know."

"He's not just a dealer. He happens to be a very gifted painter."

"Ah, very gifted. That seems to be chronic around here."

"What? You have no artistic pursuit? Or real art in your house?"

"Only some finger paintings from my rosebud period."

"Oh. You don't collect."

Oh? "So the real money is in art dealing, but you're giving massage. How many massages did it take to buy a Gonzales?"

She moves north. He cracks an eyelid to see her blush. "None. It's not an original."

"You said it was original. It looks original. If I'm not mistaken, it's signed."

"No, I didn't say that it's signed. I said it's not a print. My associate painted it. It's a copy."

"He copied it?"

"Yes. I told you, he's very good."

"And he signed it? That's . . ."

"Illegal." She goes deep on the quadriceps. "I didn't know at first. It doesn't hurt anybody, but I'm not comfortable with it. Besides, it's only illegal if you try to sell them as originals."

"You and Juan would never deceive anybody. I just know it."

"Yeah, yeah. Toasters are one thing. But art forgery isn't just the next step."

"No, of course not. I would think blenders and Mixmasters were the next step. Then came art forgery."

"Like I said, the whole thing makes me uncomfortable."

"As it should. A toaster is petty. But a load of toasters is grand theft. Your instincts are correct."

"God, you're hard."

"Sorry."

"I mean your legs. You should stretch more."

"Yeah, I know. I keep planning to stretch, but then I forget."

"I guess I could make more. Money." Her dismissive laugh shows uncertainty, suggesting that personal disappointments have mounted to tragic levels, and a once-confident woman has been rendered tentative and anxious by sheer circumstance.

"Then you should make more," he murmurs.

"It's not that much, really, when you think about it. I mean it wouldn't be that much . . . for you. It wouldn't be anything for you, comparatively speaking. And it really wouldn't be that much for me, but things could add up, you know, if enough persons—people wanted it. That sounds disgusting, but it's not. Not really."

"Hmm. What are we talking about?"

"I was thinking, like, seventy-five. I mean another seventy-five. You know, seventy-five for the hour and then another seventy-five for the last few minutes, you know. The happy ending is such a . . . cliché, but I wouldn't mind calling it that. Because, it would make people happy. I think."

Mulroney takes a peak. She just proposed a chicken choking for seventy-five dollars. That seems bold and beyond, not to mention the other, whatchacallit . . . the morality thing. Sounds reasonable, considering relief on investment, but a gal down on her luck shouldn't have to give a massage *and* whack a guy off for a few bucks more. No big deal, but the massage should be enough. Mulroney was ready to cream over prospects for a massage, much less a flog o' the sausage. And it seems so . . . messy, what with the goo, even with a damp cloth. Then there's the other mess, with the claims and threats and dirty secrets. Who needs it? Well, anyone who needs a wank is who. What a world—in this part of it at any rate. But gee, she is good, and no Samaritan would begrudge her the extra few bucks. So she can have it. Why not? Besides, after last night and a furry glove with teeth on the fingertips . . .

So he drifts again on a tiny thought, that seventy-five bucks to a woman down on her luck is a good thing to give. From the semi-consciousness of the thoroughly relaxed, he murmurs, "You know, Rosa . . . It's like I tell my wife when she wants more dough. . ."

She works the iliotibial band, going deep to find the twitch. Up and down, side-to-side, she asks, "So? What do you tell your wife?"

"Nothing, really. I give her money. I'll give you seventy-five bucks. But you'll see: it's never enough. She likes to buy stuff. She buys stuff she likes and gives it to me as gifts. She loves the buying. Gives her those, uh . . . what the runners get. Makes them happy . . ."

"Endorphins."

"Yeah, end dolphins. So I tell her: I'll pay her two hundred dollars an hour, her choice—oh, yeah. Right there."

Rosa goes in. "What's the choice?"

"Car wash or blowjob, either one. Two bills an hour. Some lawyers don't make that. But it's a joke. You like jokes, don't you? I'll give you the seventy-five bucks. So don't bust my balls." -

"Gee. You are a sensitive guy. But neither one takes an hour."

"I don't pay for the . . .the task. I pay for the time. Two bills an hour is a hell of a rate, but it doesn't matter. I don't get either one."

"You're not joking. You're serious. You want your horn honked for eight bucks."

"Nah! I give her a hundred anyway."

"I hope it doesn't take a half hour."

"Takes longer with a hand wax, but only a few minutes."

"You're disgusting. You're self-centered and greedy and cheap. But you know that. I think you've known it for years but self-justify by dropping some chump change with your miserable load."

"Gee, Rosa. I wonder why you're down on your luck. You're so cheerful and service-oriented. You got a very shitty outlook, you know? Now you say I've been miserable all these years and didn't even know it."

"You knew it. You're telling me you'll settle for the eight-dollar fellatio and throw in a tip."

"The what?"

"You heard me. Don't tell me I'm wrong."

"You're wrong."

"So an ambitious gal can make four bills on a big gulp and a car wash if she takes two hours?"

"I doubt it. I expect attention on the rims and bumpers but not exactly a full detail. I try to be fair."

"You're too much. Who washes your bicycle?"

"Some days we run a special, same deal on a bicycle."

"So three hundred dollars for a car wash or a bicycle wash?"

"What?"

"Did you really come over here thinking you'd get creamed?"

"Creamed? You brought it up. Not me."

"I didn't bring it up. But I got a better idea. You give me three-seventy-five—that's seventy-five for the massage and three hundred to forget the sexual harassment."

"Sexual harassment?" He sits up. "I got a better idea—"

"Please. I had a long day already. Okay? Lie down." But the hand is shown—she's desperate. "Okay, you give me . . . uh, three hundred dollars and I'll . . ."

"You'll what? That's blackmail. What about the art forgery? That's federal! And a felony." She proceeds to the stomach, where she changes the subject to flowers, rutabagas, and chard.

Mulroney wants to get up and pay up—seventy-five bucks, full stop, thank you very much—and hit the road, where a guy on two wheels can think about things without someone hammering him for a handout. Man, gentrification can ruin a nice neighborhood. Next thing you know, the local rattlesnakes are a lesser hazard. But Rosa seems back in the groove, moving deftly, easing tension at will. "You really respond well," she says.

"Yeah, thanks. Try to keep me calm, huh."

"I admire a person who's successful in business."

Mulroney moans, "Do I know him?"

"It's you," she chortles, changing pace to country gal who slides sideways like butter down a flapjack to where resistance melts. And she murmurs, "All around the mulberry bush, the monkey chased the weasel . . ." Of course, it's a test, and failure will mean hazard and consequence in his life of days, make that month, until . . . waaiit . . . !

"Pop! Goes the weasel . . . My God. You must have needed that."

"I've been harassed."

"Yeah, right. Feel better?"

"Why did you do that?"

"Why did I do that? I did that for the same reason the kitchen crew slides a cheeseburger and fries out the window and yells, 'Order up!' It's what you wanted. That'll be three hundred seventy-five dollars, please. I'll be out here washing your bicycle while you . . . clean yourself and get dressed." And out she saunters, Miss High and Mighty, as if . . .

It is not a fine state of affairs. Twenty minutes left on the meter, and she walks out. Should Mulroney keep the sheet? But how can he carry a load of rooster cacka home in a sheet on his bicycle? He'll just hose it off. What's she going to do, take it up to a DNA lab in the city? Then again, these whacky women can fool you, especially if you show them a juicy target. God, life gets complicated.

And burdensome. Mulroney is living right and looking good, and a man so engaged in personal improvement and muscle definition must be irresistible to women. But he's been sexually objectified and financially exploited. He's not so much in the pink and magnetic to women as he's overwhelmed and abused. Bad luck runs in threes. He's been whipping boy to a lonely old woman and victim to a gold-digging desperado. Feeling used and exploited, he wipes massage oil and man yolk from the scene of the crime and thinks it's not just the women who ruin life's simple pleasures with need and greed and petty bullshit. It's the same with those talking magpies, Phillip and Steffen, who pull up outside, profiling like number three on the hit parade. Look at them, stopping to chat with Rosa like it's a beautiful day in the neighborhood. They're sociable to anyone willing to watch their highbrow superiority. They're asking Rosa why she's wiping down Mulroney's bicycle as he exits her shack carrying a sheet. "Hi, guys! How's it hanging?"

"In 'n out lube and bike wash?" Steffen yells.

"Kinda," Mulroney yells back. "I got a massage—you know, with the happy ending. I just want to rinse out this sheet to destroy the evidence." Unspoken but clearly comprehended is Mulroney's follow-up sentiment: Fuckers. Go ahead and wag. You don't shake your mugs when you're gumming the bratwurst, do you? See if you ever make it to cocktails at Casa Mulroney.

So the odd couple rolls away for the second good riddance in a single day. Avoiding those two might be best for all . . .

What the . . .

Rosa Berry pulls a digital recorder from her fanny pack—Fuck! A seasoned veteran of the closing room should have seen that. Playback makes the hills alive with a muffled voice in a steamer trunk; it's unmistakable Mulroney calling out: *I got a massage—you know, with the happy ending. I just want to rinse out this sheet to destroy the evidence.*

"Why did you do that?"

Rosa shrugs. "It kind of makes us even."

"Even? For what?"

She shrugs. "Whatever."

He tosses the sheet on the ground, walks over, and takes the hose from her to soak it down. "I'm with county vice, Ma'm. You're running a whorehouse here. You're under arrest."

"Right. And you're prepping this sheet as Exhibit A, your Honor?"

Mulroney hoses. "Why do we have to fight like this?"

"We're not fighting. We're jockeying."

"You mean for position?"

"Sure."

"No, we're not. We're done." Looking past her, he cries, "Oh, shit!" When she turns to see, he snatches the digital recorder from her hand and tosses it onto the sheet to hose it down and end its miserable life.

"You fucker!"

"Hey. My hose slipped. Okay? Don't worry. I'll buy you a new tape recorder. You want to play hardball; you're gonna get some fast pitches."

"I expect my money."

"You think I ride around with cash?"

"You think I work for free?"

"Here. Here's seventy-five."

"That's not what we agreed on."

"No? Tell me. What did we agree on?"

"Three seventy-five."

"For what?"

"Okay. Three hundred."

"For what?"

Rosa Berry, on the threshold of a man's world, defaults to tears. "You promised!"

"What did I promise, Rosa."

"You said you'd give me money if I . . ."

"Yes . . . ?"

"Oh, forget it. Just give me a hundred . . . seventy-five."

"Rosa. I'll give you a hundred seventy-five, because, in my humble opinion, you earned it. I'm fair. I won't even talk about poor service after the sale. What is it with you? Tape recorders, blackmail. Jesus. Are you that desperate to make a buck?"

"Yes."

"Well, you don't need to be. Here's seventy-five. It's all I brought. I'll swing by tomorrow or the next day and drop off another hun. Okay? Or maybe this afternoon, so we can get this over with."

"You didn't even plan on tipping me?"

"I had no idea you'd be so wonderful."

"You can come this afternoon?"

"No promises." He throws a leg over. She whimpers tentatively into a soft sob, marking the scene as where he came in, kind of.

When he smiles halfway, she asks, "Why don't I need to be desperate?"

"You got skills."

"Oh, great. I can really flog a donkey."

"Not that. Sales skills. You got it. Trust me. I'm in the business. I can tell."

"You mean . . . I could sell cars?"

"No, no, no, no, no . . . I'm not saying you can't sell cars. I thought you were asking for a job."

"I am."

"That wouldn't work out for me."

"Why not. I'll never give you hand jobs and never say a word about it. Or . . . I mean . . . I could . . . But I thought . . ."

"Let it rest. Okay?"

She sobs, and they part as they found each other an hour before, with Mulroney in spandex pedaling along and Rosa in tears in her barren front lot and woeful life, calling meekly, "What am I supposed to sell?"

The aftermath is laden with remorse, perhaps the greatest toll of the aging process and poorly judged stimulation. Time was, innocent fun was just that. Those were the days. But the cross was not Mulroney's to bear alone. Like many sorry situations, this one also boiled down to blame. Of course, it goes both ways, with a big lug humping it up the road on one hand—a rich guy who takes the needs and sensitivities of others as part and parcel in his own superior service. On the other hand: look at her, wiping her eyes like a little girl—a little girl with incredible hands, seething need and no inhibition. Mulroney would be a regular if she weren't such a whack job. No pun intended. At least Mulroney knows the score—knows the difference between denial and delusional. Sure, he's a misogynistic fuck—or they'd call him one in the editorial section of the Happy Daze—but he's not meanspirited. He only profiles affluent, and she grabbed his pecker. Full stop—well, after a few minutes. Maybe he could have stopped her sooner. He didn't. So what? He'll throw her a C-note and be done with her, because life is thick enough without a needy nutter standing by.

She could tear up a sales floor, but no way. Next thing you know Big M OK Motors might score a vintage Mark IV, a real plush guzzler worth about eleven cents on the dollar on account of the hundred dollar fill-ups and nine miles to the gallon, but a collector car, a car that'll go for eighteen to twenty-seven grand, depending on the buyer, and here comes the Big M vintage ace salesgirl, Rosa, whacking off some Arab to squeeze another three grand out of the deal—oh, he's seen it. No way. Then again, an open mind sets fear aside for a more accurate assessment of risk. Because risk is what the system rewards, any system. She looks pitiful, but isn't that how it goes with your rare bird who can work the front end *and* bring it home? So pathetically, tragically sad, and then they grow teeth down to their knees. Mulroney wishes the kid and dog would show up, because nothing would keep her mind off her miserable life like a kid and a dog. They could give her perspective on what's important. Then again, the kid and dog probably wised up and went home.

Feeling better, all told, back on the open road and sorting thoughts in the clean, rational air, Mulroney chuckles; a whack like that say two, three times a week would be nice, say between lunch and nappy poo. And no old lady up the road to worry about, with her animal torture and crazy social stuff—and no loans or grants.

It wouldn't work. Besides, old Betty Burnham will be scheduled as necessary until grant fulfillment. Betty's nice, but she gets so thick and syrupy. Things get weird when it's one-sided. She seems okay with that, but she won't be for long, same as any deal. And until it's closed, it ain't closed.

Allison wouldn't mind, in the practical sense. No need to drag her through the wallow, but if she knew the score and prospects for a remedy and how that might help her move to a warmer place, she'd be okay. Why not? You got to love her. Really.

Mulroney suspects that he could be a candidate for psychiatric care, but a self-made man knows he'll be better off with self-correction. And besides, what self-made man or woman ever fit the profile they call normal?

Ha! Show me that guy or gal, and I'll show you a real nut case.

Besides, a shrink would recommend a few hobbies or a social cause, like tending to sick kids or volunteering at the dog pound. Mulroney would be open to either, except for the financial problem still at hand . . .

Aw, shit. It's the good-time boys again. He should have waited a few more minutes. Looks like a flat tire and no spare. "What, no spare?" Phillip shakes his head like an old man punched in the gut, like he might pass out. Mulroney pulls over and digs into his seat pouch for his spare tube and offers it. "Don't worry about it. I got plenty." But they ignore him. What? Do they expect him to fix it?

"Wait a minute!" Steffen says. "Phillip fell." Sure enough, the old speed demon was showing his stuff down Nacho Grande, because downhill abandon is what the old guys can still show. Accelerated to forty-five as a seasoned wheelman can do, he could not stop for a sapling fallen across the road, and he went down.

Steffen holds his cell phone in the air and says his battery is dead. He can't leave Phillip alone, so Mulroney will have to go.

Mulroney nods. "Go where?"

"To a telephone!"

"Who should I call? The wife?"

"The hospital."

"You think so?" Mulroney moves in for a closer look. Phillip is shaken, but not too badly.

"No. I'm fine. Let me try to ride easy."

So the trio sets out for home, knowing that the route arrives first at Casa Mulroney, where ice packs and reefer might be shared among friends, or maybe ice packs and ibuprofen would fill the bill. "We can stop at my place," Mulroney offers. "Get some ice on the sore parts."

Steffen juts his chin sideways, as if to question stopping you-know-where for *any*thing. But Phillip trumps with old-guy wisdom. "Yeah. Ice would be good. I'm definitely swelling up."

"Best not call the wife," Mulroney says like a veteran straight man.

Steffen and Phillip share a coy smile, as if Mulroney can be subtle after all.

XV

Oops.

The odd trio plods homeward. Phillip groans on the ascents, moans downhill, and carries on like a child where a man would be mum. Mulroney could break away to prep the ice packs, the drinks, and reefer. But the slow pace feels right, and he's slow to service or cocktails with these two chipmunks—and he doubts they drink beer. They'd prefer a nice Gewürztraminer or something sweet and pink, what they won't get at Mulroney's. Best to ice the bruises and get them on their way.

Yet alas, in the hundred yards before the last curve into the homestretch is Betty Burnham's, where the front garden is enjoying a horticultural manicure at the hands of herself, in a bikini top, baggy Bermudas, and a floppy hat recycled from the original wagon train. Oh, God; Mulroney winces at the sizzling effect Betty Burnham's billion dollar celebrity has on the good-time boys.

"Oh, my!" she titters from thirty yards.

"Betty Burnham!" Steffen's hoarse whisper is rife with urgency, fulfilling his post as social administrator for Phillip, keeping Phillip *en scene*. Like now, providing thumbnail curriculum vitae for the elder's edification. "Burnham's. Highborough! Billions."

But of course, Phillip knows the coordinates, having visited only last night. He moans up the two-percent grade. "But does she have ibuprofen?"

"Michael! How are you? Staying fit, I see. Can I offer you and your friends something to drink? Iced tea or lemonade?"

"No, thanks, Betty. My elderly friend here took a fall and has to get some ice on his injuries."

"Oh, God. Did you say lemonade?" asks Phillip with slippery ingratiation.

"Yes!" Betty replies. "You men wait here. I'll be right back."

"You're an angel," calls Phillip.

"Hardly!" Betty insists.

"Friend of yours?" Steffen pries.

"No. Never met," Mulroney says, as Steffen and Phillip smirk. "Yes, we're friends. Nice lady."

"Does she know?" Steffen asks.

But Mulroney is fluent in bullshit. "Does she ever," Mulroney assures. "You guys would never guess what I come here for. Well, maybe you could."

"My God, Michael. What makes you that way?" Phillip asks sincerely, for the good of society.

"What way?"

"Forget it," Steffen says.

"Here we are," Betty announces with a tray, a pitcher, tumblers with ice, and a little bottle of pain pills.

Phillip takes them and says, "Thank you. You'll have to forgive our absent-minded friend here. I'm Phillip."

"*Enchanté*, I'm sure. I'm Betty."

"Oh, I didn't forget. They know who you are, Betty, and you'll find out soon enough about them. I mean who they are."

"It's so nice to meet you," Betty says, happy to gloss the apparently rough surface. "I'm new here, you know, and I do like to make friends."

"Too bad you got mixed up with the riff raff," Steffen says, jutting his chin sideways and forcing a laugh to show humorous intent. Mulroney makes bottoms up in a glug, glug, glug, down to the cube slurp and the grand finale sigh. And a belch.

"Pardon me. Ready, boys?" But they're not ready. They're sipping cool, delicious lemonade with genteel aplomb in the presence of a billionairess. They linger in the mists of heady numbers. They savor the growing potential for osmosis, after all, until interrupted by the Big M yet again. "See you, Betty. Thanks. You're a lifesaver." He clicks into one pedal and rolls, aware that the talking magpies might stay back for some high end, high level schmoozing. Who cares? Not him. In fact, this could get him off the hook from another tedious round.

"Uh, Michael," Betty calls. So he stops and waits for her to catch up. She speaks softly, in confidence. Stern as a God-fearing citizen she says, "It's really quite none of my business, but I was over at your house a short while ago . . ."

"Wha?"

"What wha? Don't give me wha. I wanted to say hello to your wife. It is a neighborhood, so I wanted to introduce myself and . . ."

"Isn't that pressing the issue a bit? I mean, how many other neighbors have you walked down the street to meet?"

"A few. But not your wife. Not yet. I saw her. She is quite pretty, but you know that. She seems painfully shy. Hardly a match for you, but then again she seems perfect. You're so . . . forward. At any rate, I thought it would be the nice thing to do."

"Thank you for that, Betty. You are very nice, I'm sure." Mulroney squints for the ulterior. Betty B feels the jaundiced eye.

"I was going to knock on the door and, I don't know, borrow a cup of sugar or a hand hoe or something . . . I didn't mean to interfere, meaning that I wouldn't want to change our special friendship. I mean, you know, what happened between you and me. I did enjoy that, and I hope we can do it again. Sometime. Maybe. Soon."

Mulroney does not go blindly where few men dare to go, nor does he fear risk, rather he goes boldly, after applying his gift of calculation. He weighs and measures then trusts his instincts to speak with reason—and forges ahead. This aging but game woman's revelation is blurred, nonspecific, and troublesome. A man who thought himself done with practical need might well be in for a life of resignation—a life reduced to base fulfillment and/ or consequence. That could be the case here, but what can a man do? Allison is charming and lovable, which was never in question, and the world is intriguing, with its demands and options where least expected. But the current path is off course. "And so?"

"So I knocked on the door and heard voices and laughter. I waited and knocked again. I could tell there was something social going on, and I didn't want to intrude, but it is afternoon, and I was on a social call, so I stepped around to the side, because that's where I heard the voices coming from, though it could have been from an open window, I suppose, but you know me; I don't stand on ceremony, and it wouldn't have been the first window I stuck my big nose in. People do want to be friendly. That's my experience. But it wasn't a window. It was your back deck. This young man with this huge . . . camera was filming your wife. Naked. Not just naked but . . . oh, dear. It's quite none of my business. But she . . . she was . . ." At this juncture Betty B can utter no more. Her breath comes short on the horrid truth, and every indication is that morality in the neighborhood may have been breached.

"What? She was boning the camera guy?"

"No. Oh, my, no. Nothing like that."

"Nothing like that? You said she was naked and worse. What could be worse?"

"She was . . . posed. Posing." Mulroney ruminates, sensing the Tweedle brothers, all eyes and ears straining for more.

Why would Allison take up with the camera guy on the back deck? That makes no sense. "When was this?"

"A while ago. Michael. I don't want you to be hurt. It was simply so . . . It's none of my business is what it is."

"But you made it your business. Don't get me wrong, but you're . . ." Whoa, buddy, thinks a more circumspect Mulroney; do not harm the baby when changing the bathwater. Talk about compartmentalizing; Ms. Highborough Billions Burnham can gulp a gob o' pecker paste and everything is doilies and lace, but let Allison get naked on her own back deck, and the neighborhood has a disturbing situation. Mulroney needs no reminder that Allison's ass would make Betty Burnham a good Sunday face, and the photo op potential on some behavior is far worse than on other behavior. "Keep an open mind, Betty. That's what I do. She gets up to . . . you know . . . her own thing. I have to tell you: that lemonade wasn't instant. It was fresh. I admire that in a woman. And word does get around. Thanks."

So he mounts again for the brief coast home and more pressing concerns. "Should I come along?" Betty Burnham verily croons to join the prosecution. Popping in on Allison and the camera guy might seem an intrusion elsewhere but seems natural here on the Coast with such a magnificent view of the biggest ocean in the world and luscious events unfolding.

But no. "No, thanks. I'll see you later," Mulroney calls back, accelerating with dispatch as a CX-61 can do.

In eighty more yards he turns up the drive to see a black van, side doors open on an array of photographic equipment. Leaning his bicycle against a wall, he removes his cleated shoes for better comfort and stealth. Padding around back, he slows near the end of the hedge and eases in for the close-up—small world; so does the camera guy. The scene blends seamlessly with the scene already simmering in Mulroney's mind's eye—hard to imagine, but there it is: spread eagle Mulroney—the Ms, that is. Allison in the buff on a chaise lounge squirms this way and that with no inhibition for the nether regions revealed. "Michael!" she calls as if glad to see him. "Look! I'm a model."

"I can see that. A naked model. With no discretion."

"How can you say that? There's plenty of stuff I wouldn't do. Scotty wanted me to go hands and knees, you know how they do, with a coy look back over my shoulder. That's like the guy who offered the little girl a cookie to stand on her head to see her underpants. But I'm really not wearing any. I wouldn't do that. That ought to make you feel good."

"It doesn't. But we can discuss that later. For now, why don't you put something on?"

"Because. We're not done. Are we, Scotty?"

"We're getting close," Scotty murmurs, clicking away on his camera, tripod mounted, then moving into video mode. "Okay, here's what I want. If you can arch your back, one knee up, legs slightly open . . . We're going for Lana Turner above the waist, maybe Rhonda Fleming below. Get the picture?"

"Like this?" Allison is a quick study. So is Mulroney, who moves gently to the table for a lens cover, which he installs forthwith, pre-empting objection with his own directorial debut.

"Not like that. What I think we'll go for is Lucille Ball above the waist and Doris Day below. Get it? Get the picture? Look, Scotty. Let's get something straight here. You're a young guy. You got your camera. You want to shoot my wife naked. Right? That's my wife. I'm her husband. She's naked. You're taking pictures. You may not realize the risk you run here."

"Is that a threat?"

"Threat? From me?" Mulroney takes the other lens cap and sails it like a Frisbee, then picks up the tripod and camera and swings it like he once saw Jimi Hendrix swing a guitar, with finality on impact. Sure, it would have been better with some lighter fluid and a Zippo, but as noted, a man must be practical. "Next time I'll aim for your head. Now. Does that sound like a threat?"

"Michael!" Allison calls, hardly coy, over her shoulder, hands, and knees.

"You'll hear from my lawyer," Scotty replies.

"Hell-oh-oh!" calls Judith Elizabeth Cranston Layne mere paces out from rounding the corner, her exuberance overflowing like a riverbank, a muddy one. "Did I tell you, or did I tell you? Is this the most fabulous view of the entire ocean, or what? Oh, wait! Watch this! Oh, hello! It's only me. Sorry to interrupt—oh, God. Oh, my!"

"Sorry. Please don't let us interrupt," says the woman in tow. "I'm Midla. Midla Danyte. I've admired your lovely home for the longest time. I've driven out of my way for years just to pass by, and every time I wondered who is lucky enough to live here. Every time I knew it would never be me because it would never be up for sale. Because, who could ever live here and even think of moving? Was I ever surprised to see it on the market!"

XVI

Party at Mulroney's

Everyone knows her parents didn't name her Midla, so there's no point in dwelling on her past or a given name that seemed so wrong. She's probably processed many issues in coming to terms with herself and what her name should be. Why focus on perilous, depressing youth, when we might witness the very real results of successful adaptation to success and feelings of well-being—and precisely whom this woman is processing, on her way to being?

Plain to see is originality in her hair, tummy, jaw line, laugh lines, crow's feet, lips, hips, breasts, nose, abs, high thighs, and hind side, for starters. Then it's on to the very most exquisitely tasteful tattoos and rings and pins and staples arranged just so to give the effect of . . . art. This crowd understands evolution. The intellectual/spiritual continuum thrives in the land of the open mind, where all ripples fade in progressive context, which is key to whom a person has become rather than whom a person no longer is, which may have been an old person the new person struggled for years to be away from, which might sound awkward but makes perfect sense among growing population segments of the new life in happier times. Maybe the new life is part and parcel of the bold economy because we can't very well scoff at money, which isn't to revere greenbacks per se but rather to recognize the mobility and accessories that money can buy. Materialistic? Perhaps, but fun, and that is the critical point we strive for: these new times want to be happier. Don't you?

Or are you stuck in the same old stodgy stuff?

Her name may have been Jane or Linda or Sally. So what? What harm to anyone if she calls herself Midla? No harm is what, not even in the extra effort required in remembering new names. Like when the gal who cuts Mulroney's hair, Bonnie, became Isis Rianan because of the power of the I, not to mention three of them, along with the power of Isis, Egyptian Goddess of Power, and Rianan from the old Fleetwood Mack song, which sold a powerful heap of albums for a powerful mountain of moolah. Bonnie swore she felt better the very minute she became Isis Rianan. She knew it was a good move, even as her friends struggled with it, forgetting it or mispronouncing it and then shrugging and calling her Bonnie. She estimated that the full conversion in usage from the old name to the new name would take a year or two and would be well worth the effort. Mulroney advised, "You're crazy. Fleetwood Mack. You want to sound old? Or passé? How about Isis Islii? I just made that up. Five fuckin i's. Two of 'um fucking capitals. You like i's, don't you?"

"I *like* it!" Bonnie cried, changing just that quick to Isis Islii, which was like transplanting a young tree soon after planting it, which should not be okay, with the roots reaching for life and getting traumatized again and stunted from too much transplanting. Shouldn't it?

"Hey, how about Isis Islii Isley? You could be the long lost sister of the Isley Brothers. They're old too, but man. They were the real deal, much better than Fleetwood Mack."

Alas, the wisdom of the ages and Mulroney prevailed again, and so the name adapted as nature intended to Islii Isley, avoiding terroristic association that had come onto the scene practically overnight, which seemed unfair at first, until factoring the natural happenstance of all things and spiritual corollaries stipulating no coincidence, and Magic Happens.

The new gal, Midla, looks interconnected and cosmically receptive to vibration, magical hooey, and moolah. The Universal question remains unanswered, however, whether these or any mysteries of the universe can be sorted in the sub-orbital context of two point seven five, specifically speaking. Naturally, the buy/sell plane in constant flux relative to the moment is where we truly live—and the moment is focused on a woman in the buff, generating surprise and awe in some quarters on her state of physical fitness—which quarters include the most recent quarter bringing up the rear, which is Mutt 'n Jeff behind Aunt Bee.

Phillip ogles.

Steffen glances back and forth, Phillip to Allison.

Scotty, apparently inured to loss where art is in the making, works his damaged video camera. Undeterred or compulsively stuck, he circles and pans, stepping carefully over low railings, potted plants, and ceramic bunnies—zooming in and out, kind of.

Most admirable among Allison's revelations is her free spirit. As if playing to her following at last, she entertains with less ceremony or encumbrance than if she were clothed, with a fluidity that most find endearing. "It's because of her breasts," Betty Burnham notes with humility.

Betty dropped in, after all, establishing a pattern: uninvited and unannounced. She didn't say hello because it's only been a minute, and it's a crux of nudity, society and art, hardly warranting a how-do-you-do. This is what great days are made of. Hello?

Witnesses to the creative process are given to analysis in such a zone of intellect that is naturally populated with persons of business, art, and monumental cash reserves. Betty Burnham's poignant perspective is soft but assertive: "They're really small. And lovely. Oh, how I would love such freedom."

The Burnham words linger, unchallenged.

In the neighborhood spirit, Betty says she just came on in when she saw Midla Danyte riding shotgun in Judy Liz Layne's tacky white Beemer. She doesn't say tacky aloud but rather plants the assessment precisely into an elliptical pause, as if white is the new shit. She followed the scent, as it were, down the street, as a friend in need will do, because that is who she is, which everyone who knows her comes to learn, bye and bye. She smiles serenely.

Phillip and Steffen accompany like remora alongside a shark, securely niched in the food chain, keen on the scent of some juicy flecks. Steffen whispers coarsely, "What a great ride." He giggles, treading gently with Phillip, crouching and whispering to avoid detection. Soon the predators will feed, leaving scraps for the scavengers.

Betty's presence is something, but not like Allison's. Betty concedes, "Women with small breasts are lucky. They don't sag. Allison's—may I call you Allison? I feel like I know you—Allison's are well shaped too. Don't you think? It's why she looks so . . . wonderful!"

"I think so," Phillip volunteers.

Allison looks down at her breasts, first left, then right. "They are small, aren't they?"

"They're perfect," Scotty murmurs, his eye in the viewfinder aiming at the perfect orbs.

"Everybody thinks my wife's breasts are wonderful. Isn't that nice?" Mulroney fetches a towel near the hot tub, seeking to end the exchange, the show, the intrusion, wrapping things up, as it were. "Sorry, you fellows have to leave so soon. Betty, I'll bring your cup of sugar up later. Miss Layne, this is not a good time for a showing. You should call before a showing. But you know that. Don't you?"

"I'm so sorry. But I did call. And Ms. Danyte is a serious buyer. And she's leaving—"

"Please, call me Midla."

"Yes, leaving. That's what I said," Mulroney says.

"Mr. Mulroney," Judith Elizabeth Cranston Layne persists. "I have a *cash client* looking for a house in *this* neighborhood, in *this* price range, standing *right here* with a pulse and a keen interest in your house, which happens to be for sale. Do you *really* want us to leave *right now*?"

"Tell me something, Miss Milda . . ."

"Midla. My name is Midla. And I'm not a Miss."

"Are you a player, Midla? Are you ready to ante up? Because, frankly, I'm tired of the nonstop parade of homes. We got too much traffic here. Are you a tire kicker or a player?"

"How much is it?" Steffen asks.

"I didn't know it was for sale," Phillip says.

"I may be," Midla says. "I haven't seen it, have I?

"Is there a Mister Dannit . . . ?"

"Danyte. Our last name is Danyte. And no, we have no Mister. My life partner is Earlyin."

"Don't tell me: you adopted a boy child and named him Couldbe. Yes?"

"That's so clever. Mind if we look around?"

"Hell-oh-oh!" calls Marylyn Moutard with four hot-flashing wives in tow and four resigned husbands behind, just stopping in to say how they luuuv a good joke as much as the next person—and they sure as heck still love the place, so can we please get down to reasonable negotiation? Because a buyer meeting a seller halfway is called reasonable where they come from. While single dollar increments are great fun, they'd rather cut to the chase in a more reasonable way.

"Maybe you should be shopping where you come from," Mulroney chides. "For reasonable prices. Because once you get to the top of the hill, you pay top-of-the-hill prices, where I come from. Where were we? As I recall, you're a little short on the money issue. Yes? No?"

"Two million something or other," the lead man says with forced good cheer, but he stops and turns to the sudden approach behind him and a request—make that a demand, or is that a threat?

"*Ciente*! One hunnerd dollars pay right now." Juan Valdez is seeking payment owed to his associate Ms. Rosa Berry for one monkey spanking, specifically ordered and professionally administered. His hungry eyes highlight his urgency, flitting from window locks to doorjambs to crawl spaces as if seeking a route of escape or, more likely, casing the joint. Squinting inside through the big back window, he turns to Mulroney. "You have art, Señor."

Is this a statement, or a prospect?

Allison is back at the door with refreshments, losing her towel but putting it back in place once she sets down the tray bearing the wine, glasses, and napkins. "This is fun," she says, heading back in for beer, in case anybody wants a beer, but stopping to ask the thin air between her husband and the apparent gardener, "A hundred dollars? For a massage? Must have been a good one."

"The hundred would be for the wank," Phillip explains.

Mulroney turns to the intruder; impugning character and degrading life's good work is slanderous and may well warrant litigation, which may be an idle threat leading to a stalemate in some cases, but in this case will likely lead to a few spendy laps around the block in the process. Make that wind sprints—oh, you do not want to tie up litigiously with the Big M.

But the parry freezes at Mulroney's hip joint, which twangs in pain down his leg like another accusation. He braces on a railing to keep from falling and with a grimace faces the collective perception of an aging man in bicycle tights and denial of the Big One. Mulroney appears to be frail from overuse, both physically and morally, and alas, evidence for the prosecution stacks up on one side while the defense gets bolstered on the other.

Easing over to a table till the pain subsides, Mulroney smiles sanguinely. "Wouldn't it be something if we were decrepit at middle age and grew stronger with each passing decade, till we grew old and could click our heels? I'd be trying out for the Olympics. Did you ever think about that? As it is, I need to sit down."

"It's already been done," Steffen says. "It was awful."

"Phillip, you and your boy can go now. You're not welcome here, with your tasteless humor and vulgar innuendo. This is my house! Okay?" Mulroney sits, hobbled but not humiliated, at least not willingly.

"Wait. Have some wine first," Allison titters, setting out crystal wine glasses and beer, going back in for the three light whites she's kept chilled these many months, in case friends might stop by. Chablis is casual enough to frill away a lovely afternoon in the serene, sweet tipsy doodle that matches the breeze and elegant wafers with Camembert sumptuously oozing, which is also on hand, just inside. She won't be a minute.

So the guests cease their endeavors at Mulroney's house—at Mulroney's expense. Scotty picks up camera parts, eyeing each for damage, sorting the evidence of assault and destruction of property.

Phillip and Steffen choose seats in reach of the wine and snacks, in *response, s'il vous plait*, to their new friend, Allison, who invited them to stay. "Frankly, I don't think Brad Pitt's done anything worth a hoot since *Legends*," Steffen says.

"That may be," Phillip concurs. "But he was so deliciously buff as *Achilles*; admit it: you couldn't help but think of Michael here."

Steffen covers his blush with a sip of wine and another, leaving no further option but a chin jut aimed at the thin air.

Judith Elizabeth Cranston Layne with Coldwell Banker Clifton Baines chatters to her client gaggle over this fabulous Chablis on this marvelous afternoon with such incredible views—and Camembert on the way! Perfectly ripe! "Oooozing!" she verily oozes in an onomatopoeic overlap of cheese and climax.

More notable to the more frugal segment of the gathering, however, is Judy Liz Layne's surreptitious yearning—westward at the fabulous view—as a practical ruse to cover her true yearning. She perks on Marylyn Moutard extolling the subtle yet significant value of an ethereal phenomenon that combines a house with the power of nature to an extent that investment analysis becomes incidental—except of course as it specifically relates to a market vortex slapping you smack in the fucking head!

Oh, if we can only wake up and smell the ambrosia . . .

Not really—Mulroney added the fucking part and the ambrosia, because he can't imagine anybody talking like these women do, non-fucking-stop with ablutions to the mist—or the smog—with a compulsory overdose of seasoning and unreality, neither of which will make a pinch o' shit's difference next to the signatures on the line and the money on the table. Most amusing is Marylyn Moutard's conflicted motivation. On the one hand is her forte, facilitating a sale for her client in a market thoroughly established as upward, with demand exceeding supply, in which Econ 101 stipulates rising prices and every seller's dream: the bidding war.

On the other hand is the hot, gristly bone shimmering in the quicksilver just out of reach, so to speak. What red-blooded, long-tooth, real-estate professional would accept a commission of eighty-two-five when a blink as good as a nod could turn it to a hundred sixty-five large? To put it succinctly: Marylyn Moutard fairly invented the double-ender in this county, and she sure as shit ain't settling for one big fat scoop when two should be hers by rights. You think developing common interests and trust with eight people is easy? Or fun? It's not, and the pain and suffering show, ever so slightly, like a twist in a thong that pinches her cootch but not so much that she can't emote morning glory for the wonderful world we live in—especially with these *views*!

So relax: if anyone can shuffle into the end zone for the whole six points, it's Marylyn "who cuts the" Moutard.

Mulroney is amused with Marylyn's dilemma, with potential on the one hand and greater potential on the other, leading on the one hand to a glorious commission—yet on the other hand hinting the happiest day in her life since her last double-ender.

Then again, with two ups on the same unit, the play is easy: let them duke it out. Does it get any better than a bidding war? Oh, these Californians can swing some dick when it comes to acquisition in the millions, and they don't need you or your measly, petty, penny-ante bullshit standing in the way once the decision is made to *buy*.

Well, the blood mist of acquisition carnage may yet descend. In the meantime, Mulroney faces a more difficult challenge. The apparent gardener, boyfriend, art fence and sweaty, muscular fellow is demanding a hundred bucks for a hand job he, Mulroney, had no say in and certainly did not request. Push come to shove, it was a great hand job, the little city gal understanding a man's needs and textures. Then again she was coldly professional and too fast for lasting love, or for any love, not that love was on the menu, but accuracy is still best. Truth be told, slower is better. Slower shows more affection—like Allison used to do, for fun.

Those were the days when a kiss was just a kiss, before the sauce took away her bones and much of her brain. It's hard not to love the woman you swore to love forever and meant it—which meant you didn't need an oath at the time because the love was real, before she morphed into something else with a clinical label, but the profile suggested was an autistic child in a tantrum. The guests don't see it, because she won't let anyone see it except her husband, which should be the case for her naked body, but it's not.

These nosy bastards wonder what's wrong with Mulroney. But they'll be at home when it's time to clean up the mess, and so will he. She used to pass out at the point of inebriation— what a relief. Now she becomes aggressive, verbally, and hostile over what's been missing in her life. Random observers find her demands reasonable in a laughable way. Mulroney does not comprehend what Allison wants, what Allison freely gave away in her every waking moment, what every soul gives away in exchange for something else. Maybe freedom isn't so free. Maybe the passive, subservient personality is where she's taken refuge these last five decades, for convenience or refuge. Mulroney doubts that anyone knows, though many will theorize for a fee. Why did Mulroney bargain for a normal woman and get an invalid, a wife in need of supervision when drinking?

Because life is fated, as if written and ordained. Because love can't stand a chance, but then the liquor changes everything. Because, this is what happened to him and his.

Could it have been avoided?

Maybe not.

Did he do anything to prevent it?

Probably not.

It's that simple. Situations result from small decisions, stacking up for loss on a dead-end journey. A fair assessment of Allison will require two columns; one headed *Drunken Allison* and the other headed *Admirable Allison*. With social and sexual skills, a sympathetic ear, and sundry other attributes, a life mate might be constant to the end of the road. But things change—breakdown prevails, which seems cynical and accurate. Mulroney also factors positive aspects in these difficult times, granting her the benefit of many doubts because her heart is unchanged from those fresh, young days and so is her mind, he thinks, when she's sober. Yet alas, the positive pales in the slosh.

That's the catch.

When she's sloshed, she has no heart, no mind, no give, no meaning, only the rankling demands of a severely handicapped woman reduced to childlike tantrum. The aging process is inevitable, requiring flexibility of spirit. She has that. Mulroney is a good provider, at least on paper, but he can't handle drunkenness, not anymore. The challenge approaches, in which patience and forbearance for one spouse may outpace that of the other spouse.

How do people stay married for twenty, thirty, fifty years and then divorce? Divorce after decades of marriage defies social expectation, which should disqualify social norm as a standard for any reasonable behavior. Marriage also suffers the burden of years and can often end at the intersection of Familiarity and Contempt. Loathing becomes cumulative, until quirk and idiosyncrasy tower above all else. Decades of marriage require an open mind, and that's what age should enhance. But it doesn't. And Mulroney needs no excuse to get away from his mate—he only needs refuge from self, as life comes down to reckoning, on paper.

Allison makes him tired. So does the reefer, but he only smokes it because he's tired of the situation, always thinking, planning, strategizing, repressing his alcoholic wife. And because he likes it.

Allison is supportive as often as not. Of course, Mulroney's persona as chauvinistic bore is a show, a building block on which a Big M empire resides. Allison is cute, free of body fat, and blessed with small, pert breasts, like in her teen years. She's eccentric, beyond the social norm, and that's good and should be good, but when she's drunk she's a cunt, which is burdensome and demoralizing. It's an imposition on life—one with apparently deliberate intent.

She's more than casually naked in front of strangers. She's showing off her female form in a phase of life she doesn't mind calling well preserved—make that a calling out, one she doesn't mind hearing from a murmuring crowd. Naked by design in public marks her as unstable, as compensatory, as a woman in need. Her splendid hip line, her still trim ass and above average muscle tone could make for a playful display—a woman posing nude for art, caught out, as it were, and dropping everything in deference to an entertainment for drop-in guests. Mulroney wouldn't mind so much because she is the hostess with the mostess, and everyone appreciates recognition. But the other motivation moves into the psyche, what's left of it, or an altered version of it, in which this woman, Mulroney's love, seeks revenge. Does she lay this straw knowingly upon the camel's heavily burdened back? Does she call his bluff, parading naked for a bonehead group of interlopers to prove their appreciation of her? Or does she merely work the master, though protector and provider he may be, calling him out on vanishing youth, on the best years gone, on the disjunction between paper and reality?

But Mulroney took nothing from her, unless you want to count fundamental stability. But that shouldn't count, because shit does happen, and in this case the paper appearance will soon be reality once again—this is a short-term glitch, an event in nature no less random or certain than clouds in the sky. This is real life, not Mulroney, but life. It demands adaptation and shifting to find the comfortable position, to remove the lumps as necessary. What is Mulroney's role in a romance decomposing? For starters, decomposition happens. Mulroney has never served as facilitator but rather has pissed on the drunkenness parade at every opportunity. All of which begs the starting question: Did you ever come home to a drunk?

He will always love her, always care, not by choice but by bond, by that overlap on which the heart is not a lonely hunter but is rather bound to another soul. Yet he cannot maintain the demon. Just look: she glows in audience appreciation. She has their admiration—and their sympathy. She'll serve fresh fruit, gooey cheese, and discount wine with the towel tucked loosely under her arms, and thereby ensures their continuing support. She'll let the towel slip in the act of giving. She'll giggle. She'll pull it back up like a child, but she's not a child. She's a woman with no basis in rational thought, and Mulroney is her husband.

A man reaches the age of confidence and thinks he's past wondering how things got so bad, how he ended up here, where he doesn't want to be. Yet it happens. She steals his energy, sticking the emotional air hose up his ass and inflating him with malaise, just when he needs his wits to fend off vulnerability, to avoid the loss of what he's taken a lifetime to build, which is nothing short of security. Maybe they're not so secure, or maybe they're secure like inmates in a federal slammer. They seem hardly happier.

Like now, with the macho Mexican field hand drifting on the fringe, discreet as a cat burglar, backing off from his ridiculous demand for cash. He grasps the crystal stemware with his thick mitts like it was a plastic tumbler, pouring cheap Chablis down his gob like lemon water at high noon. Juan Valdez squints again through the windows, seeking art and Allison, ever hopeful that the masters live here in the upwardly mobile, ever-reaching hills.

But that's a generalization. Betty Burnham won't need to reach again, except for sympathy and company, which she can find easily with the service her late husband assured was of excellent quality.

Where can such an ill-conceived afternoon lead? To new friends, shared insights, common ground, good offers? Mulroney represses, because a born salesperson approaches the final third of life at a disadvantage, with every potential squirting adrenaline into his already twitchy system. It's the combustion ratio of the ultimate piston that enables the true closer to close the mother-fucking deal beyond mortal skill levels, even when the mother-fucker doesn't want to close. And the off-road action is smooth as a baby's bottom, with a true closer at the wheel. The action feels good. It lingers with tingly vibration because nobody wants a rough ride anymore. Mulroney knows the way. The adrena-line may enable a tomorrow that's worth a good goddamn, if it doesn't kill him first. Oh, he'll pay on the back end. The idea is to defer painment—make that payment.

Look at Marylyn, counting an imaginary stack of money in her head as if nobody can see what she's thinking and then counting another stack twice as tall. She'll get to have and to hold one stack or the other. Is she really worth another squirt of heart juice?

Then again, does a man want to spend one more day than necessary here in Screwtown?

Wait a minute! Get a grip! Can a man afford to forget the rudi-ments now? It's a devilish brutal scrum, but every one of these bums is as bruised as the home team. Any progress to date was built on the fundamentals. So?

Now get back in there!

Then again, Mulroney may be one more figment of an over-worked fantasy, another personal sophistry or worse. So he fades to past tense, which isn't the same as has been, but then again . . . Maybe Big M is all that remains of an old man—a hormonal aberration with outdated sales skills and comparatively low cycling cadence on average. Maybe denial is done today. Maybe escape on a bicycle is a multi-faceted mode for former men and active pussies. Maybe his quiver is empty—but wait!

Attitude is everything.

There it is, proof that the warrior attacks!

The true raconteur will show abject indifference at this juncture of the transaction, where the game is won or lost. The right tools for Mulroney are solitude and silence, which may seem as unavailable as the exit of a mall department store. Still, the exit exists. Hmm. Is that like Dennis Hopper in *Apocalypse*, when he said, *If, man. It's the middle word in life?*

Is, man, it's the middle word in *exist*. Or maybe it's the missing word in exit. Fuck it. Whatever. The first step is to fetch a dress, a simple number from Allison's closet. Back to the bedroom and out to the kitchen in less than a minute, he hands it over with concise instructions: "Put this on and don't interfere when I tell everyone to leave. If you don't obey me, I'll put you out this afternoon." It works, to the surprise and relief of both parties of the first part, since it doesn't work too often. Because knowing each other too well most often leads to bluffs called with growing frequency. Old spouses trade challenges like adversaries in the mirror, which is more or less to the perfect opponent, which is what a spouse of many decades becomes. The most frequent result is stalemate. Then again, she does fear growing old alone.

She slips it on, and with a semi-huff she slinks back to the kitchen, perchance to peel some grapes.

Mulroney repeats that it's been swell, but we think we're going to take it easy now. He pauses ever so briefly to allow the proper response, so leave-taking can begin. But the collective response is less than audible.

Judy the obsequious Layne knows full well the meaning and reward of dominance—what she calls *controlling the room*—so she steps boldly forward to say, "We're working on an offer here."

Mulroney knows with equal fervor the guiding hand of the sales manager. "Take it somewhere else. Call it urgency." This gentle but firm directive may actually be a great ploy for the seller, not exactly conforming to the tenets of the technique known as *The Take Away*, in which the product is suddenly pulled from the market, no longer for sale, compounding desirability and value, especially in Asian capitals with regard to those edible species on the verge of extinction and in California, where unavailability is to image what lumens are to luminosity. *And*, in this case, the process of driving prospects off the property may benefit that segment of the transaction referred to contractually as: *and the buyer wants to buy.*

That is, the cunt's glare sears the balmy air with icicles.

Marylyn Moutard senses only icing on cake. She can't draw a line over who should leave first and which position will offer the greatest advantage in the offer-tendering phase, because Judy the you-know-what Lane could go desperate at any moment, namely the moment she sees goose eggs chalked up to her commission column. This is some tricky tundra, rife with sinkholes and snares. But it seems very obvious to any woman with her eyes open that now is the time to make an offer—a full offer at the very least! And Judy Cranston has her eyes open!

Marylyn begs to disagree. She does not trust the situation to play out best on its own. Rather she sees the deal as done, thanks to her, with the question remaining on rightful commission or half that amount. Or, in a win-win situation, she can do what a gal in the driver's seat can do best: step on it. She must continue in stealth toward the double-end on one hand but prevent losing the entire deal on the other, which can happen with a nutter like Mulroney. What can she do? Only what a Moutard would do, smile sweetly and take action—*and control*—back to the buyer's side, *her* buyer: "We're just leaving. We have two more places to see. We may want something a bit more dramatic in the views. And we're way over budget here."

Marylyn smiles sweetly all around, saving the last lump for Judith Elizabeth Cranston Layne, leaving Judy EDLtheC no recourse, but extra sweetness returned until sugary one-ups verge on the gag reflex. So the sales sisters affirm that we're all in this together, that sharing is good, that we can make this happen, and commissions are best for everyone. Right? They affirm their love with a peck on each cheek, one each for the other and again for the other side in perfect synchronicity. Right? After all, we can only do what's best for our clients. Right?

Marylyn adds a dash of secret seasoning with a pregnant pause meant to let Judy know where the advantage lies and that this is what she came for.

Mulroney sorts strategies in a heartbeat; Marylyn has played a great lead, a truly impressive move seen only at the consummate-pro level, but it's a smoke screen, obviously so to an observer at the consummate-pro-with-more-than-half-a-wit level. What, you want more view for less money? It's a veritable give to arch-nemesis Judy Layne, but hardly a concession, since everyone knows that Marylyn can work these bumpkins if she hones in—that she can be back by sundown with an offer no less blazing than Carol Doda's twin forty-fours.

Fatigue and tedium ooze over the sorting and strategizing, reminding every pro present that she who tires first loses. Disadvantage Mulroney, who must also shoulder the burden of Allison's petty but endless challenge.

Mulroney itches to remind the Moutard party that the piece o' shit toothpick construction they want to call a house, the one leaning over the cliff on untreated two-by-fours, has much better views—views that will likely hold up all the way down, when the motherfucker breaks off and falls into the ravine on a common, everyday, run o' the mill magnitude 4.5 tremor, because the Richter Scale defers to gravity with complete disregard to demographics. The panoramic vista will be especially dramatic for those who remember to wear a base-jumping parachute—but he doesn't say squat because he doesn't know that the timbers aren't treated for termites; he just made that up. And they may be two-by-six. And even if they're not treated, him saying so won't help matters. He could offer more delicate imagery of a house collapsing into the gulch on an earthquake of relatively pussy magnitude, but . . . nah.

Make no mistake, cynicism is fun and good for a laugh, and it's the laughter, however dark, that kept the inveterate pro fit for so many years—kept him in the game and still a triple threat where many others had retired long ago. It's the laughter that was, is, and shall be a cornerstone of Mulroney OK Cars. Used; pre-owned; fuck it; whatever. It's fucking cars.

Point taken, and then it's time to let go, to smile sweetly like the rest of the vultures gathered here together and to murmur, "Thanks, Marylyn. Good luck."

So the toothsome women lead their beloved clients away in a slow, segregated drift down the steps to the walkway and out, cautiously exchanging pleasantries on loveliness, from the flowers to the intricately arranged flagstones on the walkway, and to the curiously strong-looking retaining wall and the view relative to fabulous. Value is indicated at every turn, but avoided at all cost is specific value, lest the other side attack boldly in every buyer's nightmare: the bidding war. Oh, lightning arcs with growing frequency among the eyes above the lovely, toothsome smiles. A wink and a nod never hinted so many dollars as the market adjustment shaping up in the thickening atmosphere of the flower-studded walkway among lavishly blossoming trees on this very personal stairway to heaven with views to die for.

Judy Layne out-graces Marylyn Moutard with the double-edged farewell: "It's so good to see you, Marylyn. You look terrific. I'll talk to you later about that other. Okay?"

"Oh, anytime," Marylyn says. "Later or tomorrow. No rush."

The good-time boys are next, as if waiting their turn in the taking-of-leave ceremony, as if challenging Mulroney to give them the boot. But of course that challenge is also imagined, also Mulroney's cross to bear. He steps toward Phillip and Steffen with his own tired smile, squares off, and shoots a hand to his eyebrow, as if to smooth it down. The smaller man flinches and ducks. "Sorry," Mulroney says. "Now I'd appreciate it if you boys would scram."

The elder turns the other cheek and then his body for an exit with maximum elegance in obvious disdain for such ill-mannered something or other. The smaller man looks around and follows. Mulroney turns to Juan Valdez, though Juan Valdez is turned away, literally pressing his face against a window, hooding his eyes for a better look, leaving a smudge of nose grease.

"Leave now or I'll call the police."

Juan Valdez takes his time, turning slowly at last with his own challenge. So Mulroney picks up the patio phone and dials 911. "Yes. I have an intruder on the property. Yes. He's peeking in the windows like he's about to break in. Yes." As Mulroney gives his full name and address and repeats each one twice, Juan Valdez eases out with methodical slowness, like a garden slug baring fang, who might ooze on over and engulf you—or engulf the flower-studded walkway and all these fucking trees and views and shit. He saunters out with assurance that he, like the old governor who fucked the maid, will be back.

Which leaves Mulroney in another tête-à-tête with the ineffable Betty Burnham, so warm, comforting and service-oriented, though a man can't help but wonder what fortune awaits, since oral intimacy in series must surely lead to something else. Or could life become so simple on simple needs met with a resource he can only call fortuitous and, at least for now, renewable? A potentially pesky problem rises and delineates, which is Ms. Betty's compulsion to oversee Mulroney's best interests. At least she's not gold-digging, which might sound like small potatoes at first blush, but a man of uncertain means can tell you it's a first order of concern, with modern women ready to seize the jackpot. But not Betty Burnham and her billions. She could do much better.

She takes his hands into hers and squeezes just so with her own sweet smile; it arcs no electricity and is sincerely loving. She appears to be realized at a level reserved for the truly evolved, where caring and helping are equal to great wealth, or at least they're made possible by great wealth. "I do love your place," she says.

"Make me an offer, baby."

"Oh, you . . ." she giggles, and there you are: love, what every sentient being longs for, once the money thing is all worked out.

"I guess this turned into one of those days. Man, oh, man."

"Yes, I can see that it has. Well, you know what these kids today are saying: shit happens." She giggles. "I have to tell you, I love talking like that. I didn't use to. I think I was repressed. It's like . . . like the other . . . with you. Do you take my meaning?"

"I think I do. You don't seem at all repressed. You seem natural. You're spontaneous and in the world. No hiding away for you. You're comfortable in your own skin, as they also say. Are you telling me that your joie d'vivre is a compensation?"

"Maybe. In part. Happiness is always part of a balance. Isn't it? We have a choice, I think, most of the time. Besides that, whatever you think is possible is already partially true. You know? Well, you remember what I told you about my husband?" Mulroney bunches his brow quizzically. "You know, about being so good at . . . something?"

Mulroney feels suddenly like a failure there on the patio, with the wife forcibly dressed and disciplined in the kitchen, and an old lady from just up the road teasing him on another lip lock.

She titters with anticipation and says, "He only asked for it twice. Can you believe that?"

"You made him ask?"

"Not formally. But I thought he should at least indicate an interest."

"An interest? I can't think of a man on the face of the earth who wouldn't demand Betty's delights daily—if he thought it would do him any good. I mean the demanding part."

She caresses his arm and laughs elegantly, as a woman of leisure can do when she's amused. "You do know how to make a girl feel good."

Careful, Mulroney thinks, sensing the perfect opening to ease through on a grant, or maybe a loan, unsecured, to keep

Mulroney World moving along. But no, not now. Not with ovations that sound like teen romance and a dash of acid flashback thrown in. And not in a direction that feels hazardous, make that perilous, like the cliff under the house with the untreated two-by-fours.

Simply receiving by virtue of asking could define heaven on earth in some quarters, but simplicity fades on prospects of retiring to her house for ten minutes of fundamental need fulfilled and a personal check. It would not be simple. It would be thick. "Thanks for stopping by, Betty. You may have saved the day."

"You're welcome, Michael. You owe me one. Don't you?"

"You know I do."

She squeezes his hands again and turns, coy as a deb, as she likely turned fifty years ago, though now she glances back with fewer inhibitions than a deb, with the carefree abandon of a downsized heiress to billions, as she hints at the lovely, unshackled times ahead. She too saunters down the flower-studded walkway with—Could it be?—a swing in her ass? A suggestion? A tease? A practiced resuscitation? An invitation to drive the Chevy home? An aging woman's attempt at rebellious behavior redux? A debutante at sixty-something, come home to the old playing field? Of course, it's all that and more of the same. She compensates her ample hindside with a pucker and quiver recalling the subtext on the Big M OK Cars sign: *Satisfaction Guaranteed.*

But Betty B has soothed a savage beast, which is the restless stirring of life unlived—her own life, that is. She is a walking, talking demonstration of sense, or what she makes of it, and she has a point—"Hey!" Mulroney calls. "See you on the corner, huh?" And he smiles at a first thought of affection all day—or in many days—for a game gal and a happy woman besides.

Well, except for the affection he feels for Allison, really.

Betty B sees and also feels. "By-ee!" she warbles, killing the warmth with that thing they do. Then again, a guy could cut a gal some slack, especially a game, happy gal, especially when she's not going jugular at the first scent of commissions. Oh, but she has the teeth, as necessary.

Betty Burnham's point may be well made, though taking her point just now may be unwise, with the camera guy sneaking inside to press Allison on re-scheduling. Allison wants their session postponed, or a vigorous discussion prolonged. The camera guy is still in pursuit, outstaying his welcome or stated purpose, though some purpose is painfully evident. He's got his camera gear put away, his cords rewound and cases stacked, awaiting only the humping of all that gear to his dented van.

Mulroney could cut him a deal on a newer model to enhance his image and increase his rates and pump his bottom line, but why should Mulroney help a guy who's inside trying to score with the wife? Why was he here in the first place? He wants to inspect the contents of Mulroney's wife's underpants, which some men might find flattering and reassuring, but Mulroney does not. She freely admitted that she's not wearing any, and besides, this shenanigan has no relation to Mulroney's exploits. The camera guy looks to be about thirty-five going on nineteen, like most of the guys around here, maximum horny but too lame to come out and say what he wants, and broke. He's not so shy with Allison because she told him he's cute as a puppy. So what, he thinks he can move on in with no reprisal? Puppy hell, he's like most of the boys around here: pussies in flannel shirts, tattered jeans, and soft-spoken fear of women. Christ, she's got him by two decades. He looks confident, which is her doing, but still, in Mulroney's house?

"Hey, camera guy."

The camera guy looks up, surprised but impressively nonplussed. "Yes, sir?"

"What the fuck?"

"Pardon me?"

"What are you doing?"

"I'm . . . talking. To Allison."

"Yeah. I got eyes. The question was more . . . whatchacallit. . . figurative."

"Oh. Then I'm . . . uh . . . I'm recruiting a beautiful model."

"Oh. Yeah. For a minute there I thought you were recruiting relations of a sexual nature with my wife."

So the camera guy blushes, conceding the truth. "No. I'm not. I'm not that at all. I'm not sexist, if that's what you mean. Not like some people."

"Not sexist? So it's okay to be pressing an issue with my naked wife in my home if you're not a sexist? How come you never asked me for some up close and personal shots on my nut sack, if you're not a sexist? You're not only a sexist; you're a sexist with gall."

"It's not *a* sexist. It's sexist. It doesn't take an article. And I'm not pressing anything. I love her—natural modeling aptitude. She's the best a man—a photographer could hope for. She is beautiful. I see it, even if you don't."

"Yeah, yeah. You're a champ all right. Now go."

Which is the perfect directive, allowing the camera guy to morph from embarrassment to indignation and the clean exit, with a harrumph that could have been scripted.

"Yeah, yeah," Mulroney says. "How dare me!" He calls down the walkway, watching the ruffled camera guy carrying the whole load in one trip to the dinged and dented van. When Allison steps past, apparently on her way to lend a hand, he says calmly, with effect, "Think it over very carefully, dearest. One step farther and it's over."

To his amazement, she stops. She stands beside him in a faint fidget, as if waiting for the rest of his threat. "What's over?"

She knows good and well what *what* is. Yet she presses for clarification. "You and me? We've been over. Haven't we?"

He shrugs. "You tell me. It ain't the honeymoon anymore. That's for sure. We get along. I guess the question is whether that's enough."

"Why don't *you* tell *me*."

He shrugs again. He nods. He turns to her. "I love you."

"You do? Why?"

"Familiarity, I suppose. So many days together. The routine. The little things I know about you, how you think and feel. The usual stuff."

"You don't act like you love me."

"I stopped trying. You get drunk, and I don't love you. It's like when we were kids we had these snails in the garden with long eyes, and if you touched the tip, the eye would shrink to nothing, then in a few seconds it would grow back out. But if you kept touching it, it wouldn't grow out all the way. Then it wouldn't grow out at all."

"So you don't love me."

"I still grow out part way, but it's getting shorter."

"Looks to me like you grow out every chance you get. Two can play that game, Honey. Mine's young and cute."

Ouch. How could she know? "Congratulations. I'm sure you'll be very happy together."

A tear rolls down her cheek. "I doubt we'll be together. He's really dull. I just want to get even."

"Even for what?" Mulroney is no politician, but he could be.

"Do you think I'm blind? Everyone knows you slept with Betty Burnham."

"I did not. Sleep. With that woman."

As if scripted by a higher power, the camera guy fumbles the bundle on cue. Cases, tripods, cord, and stuff clatter to the asphalt mere paces from his dented van.

"These kids," Mulroney murmurs. "All theory and no common sense. My mother would have called that a lazy man's load."

"He's a nice boy," Allison says. "I don't know why you have to be so hard on him."

"Did you say hard on him? Did him have a hard on?"

Now Allison blushes, conceding something or other, including the hard on or at least its imagined presence. "How would I know?"

"How would you know? The same way you've always known the difference between medium and large. Besides, you said as much."

"Yeah, yeah. Michael, give it a rest for once, would you, please?"

"Give it a rest? While you're out on the deck buck naked with a young man in full sexual pursuit?"

"Sexual pursuit. That's your game, not mine. He's an artist. You've heard of art before, I'm sure. They've had paintings of naked women for a long time now. I'm sure they were your favorites back in school."

"But you just said . . ."

"That's if I want it. I think you can see what's possible here."

"Yeah, well. I'm not sure what you see. Betty Burnham is a very nice lady I'm friendly with. But sexual relations? What do you think ever happened to my taste?"

"I can't vouch for that. I only know availability and satisfaction when I see it."

"She's fat! You know how I feel about fat women."

"Are you saying you'd leave me if I got fat?"

What would she expect him to do? "I'm not saying anything. I just wonder what you would expect me to do."

"No more than I ever expected—what you told the guy when we got married, that you'd love, honor and obey me forever."

It was not forever. It was until the first one croaks. "Enough. I'm tired."

"I'll bet you are."

"Yeah, what's that supposed to mean?"

"Do I have to spell it out? You're an old man who still rides a bicycle for dozens of miles and then has sexual relations with the old lady down the road."

So the blush comes full circle, though Mulroney pleads innocence, since he had no sexual relations with anyone, Your Honor, since his last bicycle ride. Honest. "I did not."

Just beyond the bottom steps and out on the drive, the camera guy swings open his back doors and hurls stuff inside.

"Then why are you blushing?"

"Same reason you blushed when I asked if the camera dude had a hard on. No reason at all, right? Betty Burnham has a warm personality. She makes everyone feel welcome. She's open and friendly. And smart, with some interesting comments on her old life. So we're friends. I find her easy to chat with. But sexual relations would be the product of a troubled mind."

"Finally, we agree. The way you stare at her chest is troubling too."

"So what? She's showing nine inches of cleavage. It begs to be stared at. So? I'm guilty of looking at her cleavage. So what? How does that compare to what the camera guy was staring at?"

"Fine, Michael. You're tired. Go to bed."

"Let me share something with you, Allison. I'd hoped to spare you the anxiety—call me old fashioned. We're insolvent. I show assets on paper around twenty million dollars. That used to be some real money, you know. You're my wife, so those assets go to you when I croak. Okay?"

"Or maybe I'll get half before you croak. Okay?" She lets that sink in, sharing Mulroney's regret on the sentiment. "You've done well for yourself, Michael. You've done well for us. It's impressive. Okay? Why have you never shared with me, but you share now?"

"Because I'm stroking three million in debt, which sounds serviceable on twenty in assets, except that the assets don't cover the monthly stroke. We're ninety days late, Allison. Ninety days and then some. We're at the mercy of the bank, Allison, and the bank is not merciful. They're losing money, and they're ready to foreclose. I can get relief from creditors, but bankruptcy won't keep the roof over our heads, and once we lose the house, we won't get another one. So I hesitate. Oh. Kay? So I find myself thinking up the wildest, craziest schemes, like, say, befriending a lonely old lady up the road and perhaps, maybe, just maybe requesting a bit of support for a neighbor in a time of need. Okay? And your contribution to the effort is a daytime drunk and porno session with a guy in heat."

"That's not fair."

"No, it's not fair. I'm sorry I put it that way, but there's hardly any subtler way to put it. It doesn't even matter because my little plan wouldn't have worked anyway."

Allison stares in the direction of the most fabulous view of the biggest ocean in the world, trying to sort one view from another. She shrugs, her demeanor a mix of resentment and encouragement. "It looked to me like it's working."

Mulroney agrees: on the one hand, few impromptu defenses have ever worked so well, and on the other hand, he senses growing support for his grant application to Betty Burnham's Fund for Developing Californians. Yet the indictments stand, coming and going. Allison is no fool and neither is Mulroney. The silence deafens—till a tired engine wheezes and sputters, and the dented, tired van blows smoke in great billows until gears jam in a sickening clatter, tires squeal and alas comes the impact of a bumper crunching into a tastefully low retaining wall lining the drive. The bumper falls off, so the camera guy gets out, flings his back doors open once more with a vengeance. The back doors do not fall off but spring back on the recoil in an apparent assault and battery attempt. The camera guy weaves well and avoids the strike, then hoists his bumper inside with a grunt and slams the doors that won't close. His repair costs will be minimal—some baling wire to hold things in place and some Bondo to minimize rattling. Mulroney's repair costs will come in under ten grand, or, as they say in the neighborhood, also minimal. Come on. What's ten grand to Big M Mulroney? On his way back to the driver's seat, the camera guy presents the one-finger salute and calls out, "So sue me!"

Of singular value is the dilution of the prior impact; material damages are more convenient to dwell on than character impugnment, infidelity, or insolvency.

But the material echo fades, leaving Mulroney live and on the air. He ponders the age-old response of men caught red-handed:

an offer—nay, an insistence—that he and the wife walk down the road to affirm innocence, to ask Betty Burnham whether the relations at hand were actually, shall we say, inappropriate. It feels weak, like a bluff that may be gratuitous if she believes the insolvency part, and he believes she does. The gratuitous bluff feels convenient but transparent, with a risk-benefit ratio that may taunt the gods of random chance. Betty B has only to blush at such an affront to good taste and discretion, not to mention morality, community standards, and the family values we hold dear, on absolution of all parties. But Betty B seems hazardously primed for romance, suburban style, with mad dashes to divorce court and the altar, or some whacko shit.

So accusations remain unresolved, with guilt presumed until proven otherwise. Allison looks sad—as sad as he's seen her in years. While any person looks best with a smile, Allison's sadness endears her. Her robe falls open. She cries.

Some days.

Mulroney shags a beer, because the situation is grim, and he flat doesn't care about the health hazards of re-hydrating with beer, which is both carbonated and high calorie. Because he needs a beer to buff the views most fabulously available to him and his one and only.

The phone rings. It's J. Cuntworth Layne III announcing that her clients, Ms. and Ms. Danyte, have decided not to pursue a purchase of the Mulroney property based on their deeply feminine intuition that Michael Mulroney is criminally chauvinistic and abusive to women.

Mulroney takes the few seconds to guzzle what's left of his first beer and reach for another. "You called to tell me you don't have an offer? The fuck is that? And you call yourself a salesperson? I mean salesbitch? You think you can score some political points and put those points in your pocket and take those points down to the supermarket and spend them on groceries? You stink, lady. Don't come back. And tell those two crackpots to stay outta the neighborhood. Do you hear me?"

Alas, Judith Elizabeth Cranston Layne with Coldwell Banker Clifton Baines did not hear, because you can't hear once you've hung up, which she did somewhere between *the fuck* and *salesbitch*, but Mulroney is reasonably confident that she caught his drift. And he feels better, telling himself how good that felt, maybe.

Good riddance is what he feels. Though a man reaches a cumulative point of negative reaction to his no-frills sense of right and wrong, where he begins to doubt. Would he be way ahead of the game if he could bend a little, in adaptation to local needs? After all, it is their market. Maybe he should take a lesson from George Bush Junior, who got to be "President," who said, *When in Rome, do like the Romanians*. After all, did he want to sell this dump and split to Sanityville or fuck around with political points of his own?

Fuck. Maybe he should call her back. After all, a slice of humble pie goes down well with a tumbler of full-pop offer.

Of course, he should call her back, especially when one little thumb press gets him a dial back to the last caller. "Hello. This is Judith Elizabeth Cranston Layne . . ."

Yadda yadda, Mulroney thinks; she goes through that whole schpiel for each caller, killing the chance that anyone with half a wit would wait around to leave a message. But Mulroney will because he's turning over a new leaf, as they say in the rest of the world. So he waits for the name and genealogy and professional history to run their course and nearly says, *Look, Judith*, but then he thinks best to kiss her ass in the grandest style, in undiluted deference to her tastes with flourish—with, *Look, Judith Elizabeth* (*Cramden*?) . . . But the message comes to life in real time with a voice asking, "How may I help you?"

"Look, Judith. I . . . Tell your clients that I regret any bad impressions. I'm in therapy, and I need their help too. I'm trying to change. In the meantime, let's not allow our petty differences—my petty deficiencies to get in the way here."

"Mr. Mulroney. My clients hardly view your deficiencies as petty. They think you're pathological. They think you need far more than therapy. I'm sure they're being facetious when they suggest forty thousand volts for starters, but they—"

"I'm afraid I have to ask for an extra ounce of forgiveness while I get rid of this other call. I'll be right back. Hold that thought."

And with modern technology's relentless wonders, another little button gets Marylyn Moutard, out of breath to the point of climax, proclaiming, "We have an offer!" Which proves that the Brady Bunch wanted the place all along and was not only willing to budge but had the dough and could spend it, given ample guidance. The heavy breathing suggests an image of Marylyn extracting the Moutard. But this is hardly the place or time. But maybe . . . later . . . on principle, once the moolah is in the Moutard's mitts . . .

"Yeah, yeah. We had an offer. We had several offers. Do we have a number with a pulse?"

"How does two point seven sound?"

It sounds like we have a deal, though a man has to wonder, especially a professional in sales, if the fifty large below asking could come back to the table with a little calmness in this, the moment of crunch, where millions are made or lost every hour of every day of man's existence on earth. And now women too. "It sounds like a place to start. Marylyn, if you could excuse me for just a minute. I got a . . . uh . . . some business on the other line. Can I call you back in a few?"

"Business on the other line? What do you call this? Michael, I had to browbeat these poor people till they cried. The wives cried anyway. They're emotionally distraught, but they really, really, really want that place. Now tell me we have a deal. I know who's on the other line, Michael, and I know what she's got."

Really, really, really want. That's what's wrong with America. Isn't it? Is Mulroney reasonable here? And practical? Wrong and sick is what they've made themselves, and for what, a vacation house? Or maybe the emotional stuff is a ruse, so they can beat him out of fifty grand at the finish line—so they can throw a Cracker Jack and soda pop party and harmonize in a great yodel that it's on the Big M? Yeah, the used car guy with all those plastic flags . . .

"Yeah, tell your needy clients to take a few barbiturates and have some drinks. I'll get right back at you. Frankly, Marylyn, I think if they're emotionally distraught, you're to be congratulated. It's a milestone. It's where your better salespersons relax and bring it on in with a soft touch. Call me in twenty minutes."

Which brings Mulroney to the hairpin, where one press disengages the second call and reengages the first call, but if it's done wrong, out of synch or with imperfect timing, all calls end, leaving the caller with the burden—make that the psychological disadvantage—of calling back. But it works. "Um. Okay, Judith Layne. Where were we?"

"We were nowhere, Mr. Mulroney. We were merely eschewing your evil temperament."

Mulroney waits for more, but there is no more. The rub is in the interface, where Judith Layne also waits and will continue waiting till lifestyles freeze over. She's a modern woman in day heels who drives a luxury SUV in Ivory Coast Chiffon *and* in a sundress to match. The lifestyle ensemble is obviously in the buck and a quarter range plus, plus for fabulous accessories to die for, like the solid gold gossamer chain and diamond teardrop earrings, the Lady Montague watch and the double diamond ring that proves her hubby's love. And she will still subvert the stylish lifestyle standard as necessary to get more moolah, like in the very moment, as fiduciary dominatrix with a whip and a chair: she will curb the beast onto its tiny perch, as she curbs the eighty-two five commish into her pocket. Mulroney realizes some itches cannot be scratched, and Judy Layne the bane of sane men may be one of those itches. Oh, he could scratch to his heart's content and draw blood and leave a scar. He could advise Judy Lame to . . . to . . . tell those carpet munchers to . . .

But what the hell; they're just a couple of dull, nervous women who didn't hurt anybody, except for their offensive waste of space and time. And oxygen. Make that their offensive essence, beginning and ending with their no-punches-pulled indictment of a hardworking man trying to provide for his family. But he merely wants away from them and does not hate them, so maybe things are looking up. Maybe Judith Vagina Baines will close them on this deal when the Brady Bunch falls out. "Well, Judy. I can't do more than apologize and try to change. I hope they'll make an offer if they like the place. Tell them to please remember: Allison is a woman too, and she's a seller. If it would make you and them more comfortable, you can deal directly with her."

Judith Oliver Cromwell Baines with Coldwell Inquisition Brimstone Lane is still mum, but this can hardly be called waiting. Dumbstruck at the magnitude of the new leaf—make that fig leaf, which is all Michael Mulroney needs to cover his little bitty gonads and pencil thin peepee—she finally concedes, "I must say, Mr. Mulroney, I find your comments conciliatory. I'm surprised, pleasantly so, and I will pass these things on to my clients."

"Why, thank you, Judith."

Next come two presses, which seem excessive at this point, though the message could not be more concise. "Hi, Marylyn. Here's the deal: You snooze, you lose. We got another offer coming in. I already told them they'd need to beat two point seven fifty."

"You mean two point seven, don't you?"

"Yeah. That's what I mean. And I mean they have to beat it. Not you. You win either way. Am I right? I mean, a steak tartar gal like yourself won't walk away casual from a double-ender, but three points beats a kick in the ass, doesn't it?"

"I'll get back to you."

"Yeah. Whatever, like they say here in Box o' Screws."

"I think you mean Canna Screws."

"Yeah. Like I said. What. Ever."

XVII

Back Down the Road

A man may wake up knowing the end is nigh, or he might ease into the clubhouse turn on a casual lope one sunny afternoon, leaning to the inside, rounding to the stretch. He may finish in the lead or back by a nose or back in the pack, and it won't matter. So why worry in the meantime? He'll give what he's got and be done, tired and relieved. Or maybe just done.

Mulroney can't pinpoint the beginning of old age, but some days are better than others, and better days aren't as frequent as they used to be. At least a bicycle ride is a great excuse for feeling tired. It's a better workout than showing the house, where all a guy gets is a great excuse for feeling miserable, no extra charge for the tedium and niggling bullshit. But a day beginning with a thirty-five miler and ending on tragi-comedy at sundown and still no sale could be a toxic combo. Who knew? Mulroney didn't know.

But he learns, shuffling down a dim hallway to the sunroom as shadows lengthen, and the fabulous view of the biggest ocean in the world fades to black. Mulroney suspects he's in better condition than ninety-five percent of his peers, but distinction feels pitiful, like a turd who knows he doesn't stink so bad. He plops down for a TV and beer soak, sinking in with a vengeance before circumstance and considerations thereof can sink into him.

By chance and timing, as if he's due, he tunes in to two hail-fellows sincerely beating snot out of each other on whatever-the-night fights. Boxers and punchers, bangers and bleeders; they seem a right compensation for the head-butting, nose-banging, jaw-clubbing, bloodletting carnage at Casa Mulroney on that woeful afternoon. The knockout punch comes somewhere in the later rounds, as Mulroney drifts from ringside into the ether and out. His corner man throws in the towel, and they drift . . .

Until the bell rings to end the round—and rings and rings. Wait! That's the phone! Groveling in response to human operant conditioning, Mulroney struggles up from the depths and the sofa to reach the phone. Why? Might this be the Voice of Redemption, calling with good news and money? No, it won't be that, because it never has, never will. Yet he lunges, because hope springs eternal no matter what we know is true, because humanity fears that something might be missed. Well, humanity except for Michael Mulroney, who is apart from that song and dance most of the time. So maybe this lunge is another wasted effort. But he's there, so he picks up with a groan.

A man on the line speaks with a Vuh-ginia-affectation that Mulroney takes for a prank—it's probably one of his goofy friends. But scanning the file in mere seconds, he can't put a name on the caller . . . because he has no friends, not real friends, not old, trusted, adventure-sharing friends. Whatever, the affected fellow goes on about Big M Mulroney's reputation up and down the coast and to the far side of Nevada too. Maybe the guy is from LA and couldn't quite get traction on the English accent. But he knows the score: that Big M is the OK car specialist who won't bullshit you with pre-owned, or worse yet, certified pre-owned, as if a guy in a white robe with a clipboard and a stethoscope can look up a car's tailpipe and call it something other than a used car.

"Ha! Am I right?" It's a used car no matter how many miles or who sat behind the wheel or the make—"Am I right?" The guy asks and pauses, like he expects the Big M, himself, to say yes, you are correct. But Mulroney says nothing and comfortably so, awakened as he was from the deep sleep of the deeply depressed. "I take it this is the Big M, Mr. Michael Mulroney?"

"Himself." Mulroney waits for the pitch, ready to set the phone back in the cradle.

"Right on, man. Precisely. Good. Yes. Now . . ." And so in the vein of the severely-over-compensating-for-failure-to-be-hip, tediously-superior class, the caller from Vuh-ginia via LA proceeds, "A few of us were talking, you know, and we all share acquaintance with our particular friend Mister Lombard Cienega. Perhaps you've heard of Mr. Cienega. It just so happens that our great good friend Lombard will be celebrating his eightieth birthday next week, and we do so want to pitch in on a little something. We thought it might be fun to surprise him with a toy—that is, a real toy with maximum wow, if you get my drift. We want to make a big impression. What do you think?"

The fuck? Mulroney doesn't think in the middle of the night, well, at nearly midnight anyway, and he wouldn't share if he did. Yes, he's heard of Lombard Cienega, just like he'd heard of Betty Burnham; peas in a pod—that's what the society page called them, profiling them as forces of nature, which doesn't sound like peas but has a certain satisfactory ring, since few things are more forceful than nature. Peas may lead to carrots and onward, to rhubarb, rhubarb, mumbo jumbo. The guy prattles over greatness and reverence, as if Betty B and Lombard Cienega are any different than the Big fricken' M. Some people have more moolah than most, and some are a tad short. That's all. Mulroney gives it a moment because he doesn't know his top-drawer inventory or availability by heart. He'll need to check the inventory files, and that won't happen till tomorrow morning, not tonight, up and out of a deep sleep. The man on the line waits for a reasonable answer, after all, as if midnight is just after brunch. Maybe he derives further superiority by staying mum, waiting a direct response. Mulroney enjoys the silence, wondering how long the whole wide world could stay so mum. But then a little buzz drifts between his ears, as he recalls an amusing item that made an impression in recent weeks, and he demonstrates a move—a cool move made to look easy but a move nonetheless reserved for the seasoned pro of global caliber. "I . . . have a . . . Let's see here. It's a 1937 Duesenberg Model J cabriolet in canary yellow in a condition we call Concours d'Elegance. Perhaps you've heard of Concours d'Elegance."

The '37 Doozy came on a month ago and was likely still on the blocks at three point eight, factoring about a third over as premium for actual mileage of a hundred ten—that would be one hundred ten miles. Priced a tad high, the car would be more desirable for being more expensive. The higher the price, the smaller the market and the greater the exclusivity, desirability and envy factor, all of which strove for perfection. As an ultimate car it could be seen as a toy and perfectly so by the rare owner who would not store it hermetically as "an investment." Ugh. How utterly bourgeois. The rare owner would in fact call it a driver, as the car was designed and built to be, albeit eons ago. The rare driver would treat it like his father's Oldsmobile, even though his father would be a hundred forty and long dead, like Oldsmobile, or Duesenberg. The profile seemed ideal for local tastes and values and right in the crosshairs for the likes of Lombard Cienega. And to have it known as a gift, as appreciation for the wise application of the elder gentleman's money and power would make the transaction flow with magnanimity, generosity, love, and reverence. Now there was service after the sale and another force of nature.

"Yes, I believe I have heard of that rating as it relates to the condition of a car. My understanding is that Concours d'Elegance is showroom perfect, or maybe a bit better."

"I can't vouch for that. I can vouch for its condition, which is Concours d'Elegance. And I can vouch for actual mileage of a hundred ten."

"Thousand."

"Miles."

"A hundred ten miles?"

"Vouchsafed."

"And the price?"

"What is the budget?" Touché; no man of a superior nature wants to freely express his limitation.

"Precisely. Can you please tell me the number of dollars that should appear on the bank draft?"

"I have to see. The market does change and can change quickly on these vintage classics of extreme rarity and extreme excellence, and this car will not likely come along again in our lifetime. It will be somewhere in the mid-four range."

So ensues another silence, as if to see which stature might rise to stratospheric indifference on the price of a thing. Straining the line is the question the fellow wants to ask but can't: does the mid-fours refer to hundreds of thousands, or millions? Well, it really should make no difference, considering the magnitude of respect, regard, and spiritual debt owing to Mister Cienega, a social, cultural debt that could never be repaid in a simple . . .

"That would be four point three to four point seven."

"Yes. Of course . . ."

"Let me see what I can do. Can I call you back in a few?"

"Of course. I'll stand by."

Only Mulroney is often sung to the tune of *Only the Lonely*, and Mulroney sings it, noting improved pitch on a sleep-deepened voice with less effort than, say, in the shower or rolling down the road. Still drowsy, he carries on like a crooner. He can't actually carry a tune, but he scores again, dialing direct to the Doozy dealer's home phone to learn that the car is still available, and yes, three point eight can take it. "What? Whaddaya got? Talk to me."

A call back to the original inquiry opens on unctuous cordiality, including the weather and prospects for more. They agree wholeheartedly on the blessed relief of the weekend approaching and review a few activities we're all so fond of, like, for example, walking along under sunny, blue skies. Or viewing fabulous views. And the great blessings of lasting friendship and decent family values. But somewhere this doily shuffle must find a point. Each party is determined to postpone the meat until the hors d'oeuvres are thoroughly picked over, with a few flies buzzing around. Another ring in Mulroney's head reverberates like a familiar bell, going into Round Ten. These are the championship rounds. He feels intact, all systems stable, and he knows how to wait for the opening on the knockout punch, because it will come, surely as pride cometh before the fall. With ring wisdom Michael Mulroney can be a Heavyweight Champion in the World and cure life's niggling shortfall on one fell stroke of a used car on an incoming call. He could call this a laydown or a bend over, but in these times of life and death as they relate to reputation for service and product knowledge, he can only call it providential. A half-million dollar margin is sitting on the table. It not only glows, it flashes like a lightening bolt, if only a closer of stellar caliber can harness the power—can raise Thor's hammer and strike! And bring this motherfucker home.

Of course, the devil is in the doubt, and questions buzz like stray static in the clouds: who in the world keeps a half-million dollar margin a secret on a deal that feels damn near public? Will this gouge come back to haunt? Could a very sweet deal make all parties happy parties on, say, four point oh, or even three point nine? Minus federal, state, local, and out-the-ass taxes, rendering a net of chickenshit point one. Why bother? Why pussy-foot around with a Band-Aid on a compound fracture, when a splint and a transfusion are indicated? A half mil could loosen the screws like no tomorrow, could turn this slow descent on a Judas cradle into a waterslide to Paradise. But then . . .

Even chickenshit point one could warrant a price drop on the house to get that lump o' coal off dead center and get the Brady Bunch or the harpies or anyfuckingbody in here to get the show out of hock and on the road. The obvious truth of the numbers on the table flashing in effervescent reality is that a man must make a living, be it honest or otherwise, and these are corporates on the buying end—or else they're family fortunes or otherwise capital conglomerates feeding much as a lamprey or other blood-sucker on the body collective, doing what comes naturally to balance the system. So what? What will it be? A hun? Three hun? Or half a unit? This is action, on the fly.

Mulroney describes the Duesenberg as the most delectable entrée a person could possibly imagine, as beyond fantasy and perhaps the perfect iota for the man who has everything and then some—buying time, he carries that tune, as he was trained to do and could do blindfolded, formulating the perfect pitch on a soft drop all the while, until a stray arc jolts him into saying, ". . . it came on last month at four point three, and I'm told a few offers are in process as we speak. It's rare, and it's new. A hundred ten miles. I offered three point eight. Do you want it?"

Into the silence that can only be called preggers, the two men measure each other in terms of magnitude, fortitude, verisimilitude. In Mulroney's corner, unspoken terms are harsh: *What, this bonehead thinks I'm bluffing?* But a man of extreme skill will often overlook his extreme efficacy in the clutch. The affected fellow on the far end sizes up the Big M, the situation, and the numbers, and he finally speaks. He does not say yes, we'll take it.

He says, "I beg your pardon. It's so late, and I do get excited, you know, until I forgot to introduce myself. I'm Runnymeade Runyan."

Perhaps you've heard of me? At least he has the good taste and forbearance to avoid verbalizing the question. Moreover, he demonstrates non-specifically that the vintage classic automobile suggested may indeed have extreme wow and will be acceptable under the terms offered. His warmth and carefully chosen language also indicate acceptance, such as it is or can be in such a rarified class of person, of whom Michael Mulroney may be blended into the fold, as it were.

The half-million dollar price drop becomes a donation fit for the gossip wire by sunrise. As casually cavalier as a caviar canapé on toast, hold the crust, Big M becomes ensconced with the values we believe in—while he sleeps. As a new player on the block with brilliant potential, Mulroney gets another phone call early the next morning, at an hour Mulroney would find distasteful, which distaste he would demonstrate by answering the phone, *The fuck you know what time it is?* But luck holds, even up from the depths at hazardous speed, as he fumbles the phone to the point of moaning, "Hullo."

"Oh, hello. Runny Runyan here." And that's how it is in the top drawer, neat and orderly but snug and snuggly too. Runnymeade "call me Runny" Runyan describes Mulroney's loyalty as most effective at a level rarely seen in America since the halcyon days of our President, Ronald Reagan. "And I must say . . ." He must say that the home crowd is tickled fucking pink with prospects for such a wonderful toy for our great friend Lombard Cienega—that a couple of the fellows actually heard about this car, they thought, but couldn't believe it to be real, yet alas, it is! Mister Runyan did not say *fucking*, but Mulroney could hear it, given the masterful nuance and silky inflection and perfectly ambient ooze, like soft-boiled eggs at room temp. "We can't *wait* to see the *look* on his *face*! But the reason I'm calling is, well, yes, I know it's early for some of us, but actually a tad late for others, if you get my meaning. But at any rate some of us were chatting, you know, and your name, Mulroney, is bouncing off the walls at State Party Headquarters. I mean, not actually at HQ per se but off the walls figuratively speaking, of course, of those of us in a position of, shall we say, interest." So ensued the next silence in a series of silent interludes, these silences sparing any iota of one-up. Rather—oh, brave new world—they sizzle in searing excellence.

For starters, Mulroney is speechless. Runny Runyan thrusts the baton further out front, proclaiming as if to a crowded auditorium, "We need men of your caliber in the legislature. I'm talking Federal, of course. That would be the U.S. Senate. We see you, and you're up, which should not be to suggest an automatic in, but then again, you know. That is, your name is in the hopper. We'll be in touch."

Yet again, Mulroney hasn't a syllable to say. He has distinct thoughts: that it isn't his place to say that he doesn't feel like a Democrat, what with the lefty whining and spending, but he can't be a Republican either, given the slime. And he can't see running for the U.S. Senate from California if he's moving to Hawaii. But then a U.S. senator mostly lives in Washington, which could be worse than California in many ways and is certainly not tropical. Then again, he could be Senator M from the great state of California and hang out on the beach on Maui and work shit out from there and just skip the voting on the Senate floor. One vote; how big a difference could it make? And surely nobody would wonder why he'd rather be in the tropics instead of Lodi or Sacramento or D.C. So, maybe he'd give it a go.

On the serious side, he wonders why he left a half million dollars on the table when he could have solved his problem posthaste, at least for a few more months. Fending off regret, he knows why: because of the far greater return with this bunch, maybe. This talk of the U.S. Senate is smoke up the wazoo—Runnymeade Runyan knows it but may not yet realize that Michael Mulroney knows it too.

As if amused at the dazed comprehension of a man thrust into greatness by the select steering committee, Runnymeade Runyan breaks this silence with a warm chuckle and comfortable phrasing, "Yes, well. We'll be in touch."

As if Runny Runyan will be delivering the vintage classic to Mulroney. Ah, well. It's all pie in the sky till the moolah clears. And the beauty of making no money on the deal is that the ultimate closer doesn't give a flat flying fuck if it closes or not. Gee, how did Mulroney get so Big?

Repressing the big question of dollars left on the table and why, Mulroney rises to another question with a far better range of answers. Why does he feel so good? Or good at all? California is miraculous and so is the healing process.

He stands up, hardly taking the full count.

He flexes his legs and hands, toes and fingers, and feels that pain has taken a holiday on a morning of azure clarity, on which potential seems fabulous all over again. He literally assures the ref, "I'm okay. I'm good." Rarely have sunbeams converged so poignantly on a man so recently grappling with life, self and the circumstance therein. He wakens in a balm of color and light, as if God is his cut man. He dreamt vividly, something about boxing, but can't remember what, except for snot and spit flinging over the top rope on a roundhouse right.

He shuffles to the bathroom robotically to take a whiz and wonder: What, the California Republican Party is thinking of running the ultimate used car salesperson for the U.S. Senate? That sounds like an eleven to one shot in Vegas. Then again, it is a '37 Doozy ragtop with a hundred ten miles. You could eat off those heads. You could slide in behind the wheel and feel like 1937 all over again, which may be the year Ms. Betty Burnham and Lombard Shenanigan and Runny Nose Onion have in mind right now, harking back to a time BEW, Before Extreme Wealth. Shaking the dew, he laughs: *rich, old fuckers*. Laughter is a symptom of something new, but he doesn't test it.

The morning miracle continues through a brief span of minutes, in which the man grinds the beans and fills the hopper and tamps it down and twists it into place and pushes the buttons to make the espresso and steams the milk to make it a latte. It's a quiet time, delicately delineated by morning sounds: birds chirping, a car passing, Allison up and about. She's happiest in the morning, fresh and energetic and most of all optimistic. She'd rather be happy and usually is. Mulroney maneuvers the parts into the process for the little cup o' joy that will bring him up to his own potential for happiness. The body is too stiff and sore for another ride, no matter how clear the blue, blue sky or how great the potential for personal improvement. Allison never gets exercise, but then she never rests either. Lithe and limber as a pussy willow, she'll come around soon, so they can share the same happiness again, perhaps, once things get moving out of the rut they've come to—out of the rut he's driven them into. It's temporary, or should be. Big M Mulroney is not a fool or foolhardy. He knows his safety nets, and though he's fallen through one or two or three, he has a few left to break the fall, including the big one. That would be liquidation. Even at pennies on the dollar for goodwill and auction prices on inventory, he could still keep his shirt on—and maybe her shirt too—with enough left over for a couple tickets to Hawaii, first month, last month and damage deposit. He pours the slightly foamy milk over the magic elixir for the taste of renewal. Maybe it's psychological, but the eyes open wider on that first sip, as if to see more. Are you kidding? Mulroney without resources? Do you happen to know of a used car lot, say, in a hundred mile radius? *Aloha, I'm Mikale, and I'd like to show you the sweetest ride this side of the Pacific High.* How often over the years has a true blue double threat representing the front end and the close wished for one more play on the sales field, to show these kids how to open the hearts, minds, and wallets of a lovely couple in need of basic transportation?

Setbacks happen, and then they're done. Or not. What can a man do, stress out?

The Chambers Brothers said it best on action relative to indecision: *Time Has Come Today*. Mulroney has a hunch that Betty B is on elbow-rubbing terms with the Cienega/Runnymeade bunch and may have an inkling of potential magnitude on peripheral return—or any return greater than zero. Damn! What was he thinking? So close, and now it's done. Then again, with a niggling questionable move shrinking in his wake on each step, Mulroney trods onward. Ahead lies resolution with emphasis on clarity.

Walking up the road overlooking the ocean, he thinks the view from the top too casual and convenient for a man to stroll, as if this path at this height in this rarified neighborhood is not in the world but is removed, isolated, detached, immaterial. No, scratch immaterial. It's way material. Just so: any man or woman could walk this stretch without four-wheel drive or Sherpa guides, but they don't. What, they'll park at the corner, get out and walk up the road and then walk back? No. A man in his own neighborhood—this neighborhood—is financially secure, or he has the paper stacked just so, to reflect security till the end of the month. He lives in a bubble. What do bubbles do? Theoretically, a man at the top needs to meet no challenge, except by choice, to soothe a challenged ego. In reality he could walk up this road and back forever, viewing the fabulous panorama with endless sighing. But this isn't reality; it's the unreality of the exclusively affluent, and as clear blue as the sunny skies might be, the bubble has popped.

Mulroney wants to shuffle down to the flats, where the world turns by manual control, where winning and losing are uncertain instead of prearranged or calculated for optimal control of dollars as they may influence the future and its beneficiaries. Is it any accident that the rich get richer? No, it's not. Does that source of irritation make Mulroney a lefty? Perhaps, but he feels confident that the grovelers and whiners down in the flats will irritate the bejesus out of him as well, likely by the third beer. Now there's a challenge, and the outing shapes up. He wants to descend back into the real nitty gritty, where the burgeoning Big M cut his teeth and dug in on initial ascent. Who was it? Yes, the rabbit, Br'er Rabbit, who said it best: *Why, I was born and raised in the briar patch!* And so he was, and Mulroney was too, and together they'll walk down to the flats whistling *Zippity Do Da*. That walk will require a climb back up unless a ride comes along. The downhill mile won't be too bad, but the mile back up will be a grunt. And he might miss the Brady Bunch or the harpies cruising by for another look. Or, he could be unavailable when a correct offer comes in. That's okay and would perhaps be the cornerstone of a takeaway, that maneuver close to the heart of the global-sales-elite who best understand desire and how to work it for fair advantage. Beyond that, prospective buyers might see Mulroney out for a stroll without a care and imagine themselves in that role—they'll see him on brief respite from the Life of Riley at the top of ridge overlooking the bay on the central coast. Who wouldn't think it fabulous, to possess the eagle's roost at the tippy top? Envy, as well, might precipitate an offer as yet unseen. Mulroney can't help a self-satisfied smile, imagining an observer with a thought bubble that reads: *Gee, I'd like to be that guy.* Then he frowns to better fend off the vanities. Then he waves to an SUV full of people who may well be house hunting, and he calls, "Hello!"

Yes, down to the flats, which descent will begin just up and around, once past Betty B's place, where a milestone will mark a momentous journey on what should be a memorable day.

A great benefit of cycling is the efficient decoction of life down to fundamentals. Exercise is a known antidote for anxiety. A rider is inured to negativity and distraction when he's gasping, looking up at another half mile of the steeps. What can he do but relax and maintain, muscle and bone, push and pull, ebb and flow, down to oxygen, blood, flex, release and guidance through the aerobic target heart range? *Nada* is the short answer.

And here it is, hardly by coincidence in this most recent inventory of riding and life fundamentals: Betty Burnham's house. Is that fresh brewed coffee on the breeze? That will be delightful and a certain boost on this special morning, on which Mulroney will ask for a loan.

Feeling so chipper is nice but disconcerting to a man who understands averages. Then again, luck and good cheer favor the receptive mind. On the bright side, a financially challenged man depending on his friendship with a uniquely wealthy woman has hope, which is all a salesperson ever has, really.

With logic secure, kind of, Mulroney ambles through the storybook gate at Pooh's cottage and follows the adorable stone walkway to the gingerbread entrance of the sprightly Ms. B's place. She's just inside awaiting a friend in need, maybe. Mulroney tap, tap, taps on the door. God, she would have been fun thirty years ago. Not that she's not fun now, and you never know; she could have been stiff-necked and dull back then, by design.

Mulroney listens for the pitter-patter of flat feet.

Give an old gal a chance. They move slower at that age. She could be primping or having a bowel movement—a certain bonus for an elderly person that could assuredly ease her into the spirit of giving. He feels good about Betty Burnham and their blossoming friendship, which is what it comes down to; so honest and open. He can even imagine bodily function in a person of her maturity.

He knocks again. Still nothing. Mulroney steps back before sidling around to the narrow path between the hedge and wall that runs to the back, where she must be tinkering in the herbs, probably stringing beans or filling her hummingbird feeders or fooling around frivolously. Maybe she dropped dead in the chrysanthemums—he'd hate to be the guy who finds her, but croaking in the garden would be better than indoors, and she's probably trussed up in a bikini and Ma Kettle's sun bonnet, so she checked out happily . . .

Then again, he should not be the person who discovers the body. Dots could connect unfortunately on that scenario, what with incidents and observations of the recent past. The Tweedle brothers could gnaw on that bone for a mile or two.

She's not here. Seems like old Betty must be out at the grocery or the Lawn 'n Garden, getting a jump on early tomatoes or late shade plants. Older people enjoy that sort of thing, and they do tend to rise early because they can't sleep anymore. Maybe they're scared. Maybe they think they'll beat the reaper if they get up early and keep moving. Maybe they're amazed at waking up at all. Mulroney can only imagine, but it won't be long. She's a great gal, but he doesn't want to see her at the grocery or the garden place, resolution notwithstanding. She'd glom on with the feelies, pressing her bosom and big hips into him so everyone could see how chummy neighbors can be. Why would she do that? Maybe she wouldn't, and even if she did, Mulroney can handle the bubbly bullshit in small doses, like by-ee, but public displays are foolish. It's embarrassing and, he assumes, intentional. Is she not Breaking News already?

She's not here. Let's see. Hey . . . What's this?

Better judgment would send Mulroney back around the way he came and back up the road or farther down and into the real world because a door ajar sends two possible messages. One possibility is that the door was left open carelessly. The second is more foreboding. Will a tiptoe inside find Betty Burnham *in flagrante delicto*, flailing away with the mailman, the meter man or, what the hell, the meter woman, after all? Or murdered, her elegantly humble bungalow a scene of mayhem? Maybe the little minks rebelled and ganged up and chewed her to pieces. Get a grip.

The police and media will storm the ramparts on this one, polluting the stain samples, walking all over the clues, smearing the blood and/or odd fluids. Betty B's dough should get the Feds in too—this woman is a ripple on the national economy . . .

Mulroney steps in to see what there is to see. Initial shock hits like a Louisville slugger on a line shot to the jaw.

Correctamundo on theory three: it's a Murder One that looks written for a low budget. The gore and gristle are beyond the scope of a wizened closer. Bleach blonde Betty Burnham with platinum highlights is belly up on the sofa, blotches purpling across her face. Faint twitches in her thoracic region can't hide the fact that she's racing down the white highway to Deadville. What can he do? Cardiopulmonary resuscitation? Mouth to mouth? He knew the drill years ago but forgot it. But how tough could it be? He's seen it on TV. You blow down the throat twice and then pump the chest double time. He could do it wrong, but how wrong could he be? That's what they taught—that you can't very well fuck up CPR on somebody going dead anyway. It must be coming back!

Okay, one step at a time. You take it easy to get it right. Okay, she's sprawled on the sofa, but it's not right. She's too twisted and curved, so he pulls her ankles to stretch and align her legs. He straightens her head and sticks a throw pillow under her neck to give it a small arch. He finds a suitable position to climb Hazel Dell one more time because this could take a while. With palms overlapping on her sternum, he presses, but the harness clasp is up front these days, so he unbuttons the blouse and removes it. The chest looks different, bluing, veining, slagging—never mind. He rises to near vertical and pumps. What was it? Sixty pumps to the minute? That's too slow. One twenty sounds too fast but feels right. Fuck it. He hangs around ninety cadence and counts a minute.

Then comes mouth-to-mouth in the clutch, which will be their first kiss, kind of, and an act of love. He pries the jaw downward, clasping the tongue with a handkerchief and clearing the airway—what the?

Oh, fuck. Somebody dropped a load in here, unless she was snacking on a dollop o' Smetna when she keeled over. It's translucent, maybe like spinal fluid—he checks the neck for breaks, knowing they'll call it Mulroney fluid at the inquest, which will be a drag, but he can beat the rap easy on a DNA, and that may be what it'll come to because spinal fluid doesn't leak internally from a broken neck, and this stuff smells like jizz . . .

Mulroney speaks internal: *You gotta get outta here . . .*

Okay, wait a minute. This is Betty Burnham, never mind the billions; she's a game gal who kills furry little creatures, but only because she doesn't understand. What can he do? Let her die? Give her mouth-to-mouth on a load? Wait a minute . . .

No! A minute may well be a luxury even Betty Burnham can't afford!

Wait, if he cups his fingers over her lips and holds her nose with the other hand, he can . . . Fuck. It's leaking . . .

Air.

Man, mayo . . .

Wait . . .

Okay, that's better, but not enough. We're not getting enough in there. The chest has to rise, but not too far, but more than that. Oh! He remembers! Get a plastic bag and make an air hole!

So Mulroney races to the kitchen where everyone saves their plastic bags and finds billionaire Betty Burnham's plastic bags under the sink. He snatches a handful and pokes a finger through one on his way back to the living room sofa and lines up the bag hole with the mouth hole and covers that with his own mouth and blows—that's it! The chest rises.

It falls in exhalation, which reeks of pecker nectar, telling the emergency medical stand-in that he has yet to clear the airway, that resuscitation requires free flow. He sets the plastic bag aside and grabs the tongue again and pokes around with the hanky, trying to soak up the throat yogurt, but it's not happening. Fuck it. You can't stop CPR like this. So he pumps the chest another minute and feels a twitch, unless that was himself. But he gives her the benefit of the doubt and dives onto another blow—oh, fuck.

He forgot the bag. Worse yet, Betty B convulses and hurls the load—oh, fuuuck—Mulroney moves aside but not far enough, not quite clear, and while most of the blown flecks graze his cheek, several find their way into the air passage—his air passage—as the most perseverant spermatozoa will do to be first across the line—any line—in their eternal race to fertilize.

Nothing will be fertilized here but Mulroney's past, present, and future. Not a minute will pass again, ever, without recalling the first hot moist contact of pecker juice on the soft membrane of Mulroney's mouth.

The scene lurches back to normality, or in that general direction, as he spits, hocks and spits while pumping the chest again. Fervor is fueled by Betty B's struggle to rejoin the living. Purple recedes to blue, navy to sky and then gray, like first light, easing to pink, like sunrise.

She's coming to, and her eyes open on shock and solitude—and on curiosity; who could possibly be in the kitchen gargling and hocking? And why?

It's only Mulroney, not singing but gargling disinfectant, because the perpetrator who overpowered this elderly woman and dropped a load down her blowhole could be an extreme risk for sexual contact. He could have been a former inmate of a federal penitentiary where anal and oral penetration with no prophylactic or discretion whatever go hand in glove. It would be a fifty-to-one shot 24/7 in Vegas that the perp is a carrier of diseases known to deform cells and shorten life, and that he's disgusting to boot.

Back in the living room, wincing from 409 aftertaste, Mulroney welcomes his hostess back to the world of the living. Wait a minute—409 disinfects, doesn't it? Or does it just clean? Fuck it; it's got to kill something. It feels like it's killing Mulroney. Man oh man, to think what some people would do to a nice lady who isn't hurting anybody but only trying to make a life for herself in the upper-middle-class suburbs.

Dazed and confused, she takes a moment to sort the scene and the players, and soon she squints into thin air, seeing again the events of the hour just past. Soon she says yes, that man was here, that muscular, handsome man who looks so rough and hostile but seems familiar—"You know, that man at your house. That Juan Valdez . . . I walked in the back door, which I never do, really. I don't know why I did—oh, it was because I stepped in some, you know, dog doodoo and needed to wipe my shoes. Anyway, I can't remember coming in, except that he was in the gallery. You haven't seen the gallery. It's where I keep the . . . Oh, dear! You have spunk on your chin!"

Mulroney thrusts both paws chinward as if to grasp the blood-thirsty beast attacking him and remove it forcefully, two-handed by the neck. "God, that's disgusting!"

"Really, Michael. I could say the same thing. But it's not, once you relax. It's full of amino acids, you know."

"Yeah. I heard that before. You don't mind if I think it's disgusting, do you?"

"You're such a kid . . . You know, I'm not feeling so well myself."

"I think I should call the police."

"Yes. Why don't you."

XVIII

The Facts, Ma'am, Just the Facts

Detective Sergeant Ryan has not seen it all before, but he's seen most of it. His years on the investigative end of law enforcement have inured him to the shock and outrage commonly affecting your inexperienced detective. That is, a 513 break-and-enter with a 429 grand-theft-intent, leading to a 111 assault-with-deadly-intent, compounded by a 110 rape-including-but-not-limited-to-forced-oral copulation with a woman of grandmotherly stature, vast personal wealth and a household word for a name, could not raise an eyebrow on said Detective Sergeant Ryan. Which isn't to call it a ho-hum situation but rather to underscore Detective Ryan's commitment to procedure, by the book. Does he sense more than meets the eye?

Indicators point to yes. He is not prone to camaraderie, Hibernian kinship or exchange of the blarney when he asks, "So you're Big M?"

Mulroney grants the half nod, what an international celebrity and candidate for the United States Senate musters for the well intentioned at appropriate times.

Jotting details such as full name, address, phone, social, date of birth, place of employ and so on, Detective Sergeant Ryan rechecks the list and then turns to Mulroney. "What happened?" Mulroney successfully constrains the mirthless smile often afflicting those in the chagrined phase of life. He further represses his honest answer: *Fuck if I know.* As if gathering his thoughts, Mulroney delivers his chronological account, beginning with a blue-sky morning and excellent conditions for a walk down to the flats, moving right out to a stop at Betty Burnham's on the way.

"Why did you stop?"

"Why did I stop?"

Detective Sargent Ryan waits, pen poised over paper.

"She's my friend. I stopped to say hello." She blew me a few days ago, making said friendship well established, and I stopped to see if she'd loan me a few bucks, less than a million or maybe three million but not more than that, really.

Detective Ryan takes note, as if a friend stopping to say hello is noteworthy—or possibly potentially a suspect behavior.

Never mind. Mulroney proceeds with the approach, the easy pass through the gate, leaving the perfect picket fence behind on the way to the knock, knock, the brief wait and call out: *Hello! Betty! Are you home!* Mulroney waited a tad longer, wondering what, thinking her gone to the Lawn & Garden or the farmers' market, but then he rounded the corner and headed along the path between the house and side hedge to the back door for another knock, knock but saw the door ajar. He entered, to where he shrugs, because Detective Sargent Ryan, knows the rest of the story—beyond the point of Mulroney's involvement, if you can actually call it that.

Detective Ryan jots and murmurs, and into that quiet industry Mulroney then relates what Betty shared verbally, including Juan Valdez' in flagrante apprehension in a heist—make that a mega-heist of obscenely valuable art. She walked in on him— walked in on Juan Valdez, that is. And now poor Betty is in shock with possible traumatic residuals, as she already debriefed to her friend, Mulroney, when the action was still fresh in her mind. Mulroney cannot speculate on the dollar values of a Monet, a Manet, a Titian, a Holbein—"Or that other guy. What's his name, Betty, does the Spanish towns that look like they're on acid and downers . . ."

"El Greco," Betty whimpers tearfully.

"Yeah, that guy. El Greco." Mulroney nods to affirm his grasp of Spanish art, and he proceeds: Betty B had Juan V red-handed when the painting fell from his grasp, already cut from the frame and rolled up. Or maybe he dropped the frame to better take her to the mat. "You know, like to whack her in the head with it, maybe. I'm not clear on that." Nor was Mulroney clear on the part where Juan Valdez, that son of a gun, forced his schwantz— make that his peepee or his dingdong or whatever you want to call it, you know, into her gob and flooded the pie hole with iffy lemon custard, such as it was, which was entirely too much, interfering with epiglottal function. "She choked. It ain't rocket science. You must see it all the time, in your gay community and so on."

"I thought you didn't get here till he was gone."

"That's right."

"So how do you know?"

"Betty told me. How else could I know? Give Betty a few minutes to gather her wits, and she'll tell you too."

Lying on the couch, Betty breathes deep, holding the oxygen mask over her nose and mouth. The medics wait outside. Detective Sergeant Ryan takes a step toward her. "Ms. Burnham?"

She lifts the mask, "Please. Call me Betty." As the informality settles, she underscores it with a sigh and a resigned smile. "What I can tell you is that Michael is correct. All that 'lemon custard,' as he calls it, can indeed interfere with normal breathing function. I suppose it can kill you. Anything clogging your throat passage can. Unfortunately for Michael's theory is that the only spermatozoa in my throat since Alfred passed has been Michael's own. Some people might find that disgusting. They don't love him like I do. They don't know him like I do, for that matter." She laughs with the sanguine insight of one who has gained perspective on life and love at last. "To say the least, and I really have no choice but to express my love. He's such a caring man, really."

At long last an eyebrow rises on the hitherto bored visage of the detective sergeant. Then up comes the other. "Are you saying . . . ?"

"I can't say it any more clearly," she says, just as a clatter and clamber come along the path between the side of the house and the hedge, announcing the arrival of the media, beginning with the local newshounds from the Sentinel, the Chronicle, *and* the Happy Daze.

"He's such a man. Anybody can see that. But he's unhappy in his current situation, and that's where I come in, a friend in need and in love I might add, offering support and facilitation so that—what is it they say? So that these two people may be joined together."

The trio in the parlor pause for a moment as a voice outside the window says in passing. "I think she said she blew Big M."

"I thought she said they're getting married."

"He's already married."

In unison: "Oh, God . . ."

So in hardly half a turn of the great wide world on its axis, a second long story is made short—or shorter at any rate. The headlines say it best, or bray it most succinctly. The local daily adheres to tradition, stating the situation with no prejudice but with objective ambivalence. Vague meaning may motivate potential readers to drop quarters into the slot and buy the damn paper, to see what happened after:

PERV SAVES HEIRESS—NOT!
—Can You Hear Wedding Bells?

Also consistent with historical pattern, the Chronicle spices facts with gossip, which is more fun and entertaining, so why not:

ART HEIST GOES AWRY ON FORCED ORAL!
—Used Car Intrigue, Patrimony Not Likely, Yet!

The Happy Daze, supporting and reflecting its name, achieves bliss with minimal inhibition and journalistic aplomb:

BETTY B BLOWS BIG M BEFORE BURGLE BUNGLE!
—Who's Your Daddy?

Not that anyone in modern California gives a snit who's blowing whom, though this match is most amusing, given the snooty neighborhood/corporate/big-dough overlay. Most ironic is that all three print media reporters on the scene miss their deadlines, causing a two-day lag in the breaking story, which palliates personal pain on the one hand but re-opens wounds on the other.

In the meantime, the day after Betty B's art/asphyxiation challenge, buried on Page 12, Section C, is a two-paragraph political bellwether, announcing the formation of an exploratory committee to examine candidacy viability on Michael "Big M" Mulroney relative to the United States Senate from California. Sure it would be a goof in the best of times—the M might be phoning in from Hawaii—but who wouldn't love the action and fun?

Well, it's a perfect example of *easy come, easy go*. No, wait. How about *you win some, you lose some*.

Things turn out as they usually do—however they need to. Despite Mulroney's best effort at defending his personal life from public scrutiny, he has won an admirer—make that a devotee. As a consummate sales professional of stellar caliber, he does not lose sight of value relative to the many components of a complex sale.

Betty B is a goner, surrendering better judgment to the fall, head over heels, into love. She has lost her wits to that great big lug from whom she would buy any number of used cars, if only he would close each deal himself as only he can do.

She can plainly see that Mulroney's rough and tumble relationship to society isn't vulgar at all but simply masculine—the kind of masculinity the world misses these days. Compared to the men she's known, he's cock o' the walk, and if he walks up to her place for any little thing in the world, it'll be all right by her because a woman knows when it's love and not another pantywaist money grubber looking for a handout. Michael Mulroney is a man—all man and what a man, and he doesn't pussyfoot around. Betty Burnham has all the respect in the world for Allison and hopes they can work things out amicably and isn't afraid to say as much because this is, after all, California.

Meanwhile, back at the CSI, Ms. Burnham nearly blushes a blue streak on having to review events in detail, orally, as it were. Yes, she walked right in on Juan Valdez with a Manet rolled up and tucked under his arm, and another Manet in his grasp, the second one framed in 24-karat gilt scrollwork that sold forty years ago for half a million dollars—that was for the frame! "And I can promise you: forty years ago a half mil was some real money."

Anyway, she walked in on him. He spooked, dropped the gilt frame and lunged for the exit, knocking her down in passing, but only inadvertently, she thinks; she's thinks herself a fair judge of character and senses a caring man, deep down inside, once she can feel his presence.

Later, but only by an hour or two, the perp—make that person of interest—swears he wouldn't hurt a flea, much less an old lady. This oath occurs down at the station, where the balance of the interview reveals that the rolled Manet canvas was actually painted by Juan Valdez, who happens to be John Waldon, former Avon-Award-winning thespian of critical acclaim but paltry income. John Waldon is also a forgery swashbuckler known in the curator underground as the *Artful Pimpernel*, an art restoration expert of global renown whose skill and lust for forgery have kept him on the lam. And for what, with poverty an uninvited guest who won't take a hint.

Alas, thirty grand or fifty might seem like a big ticket on a single project, but artistic integrity requires six months on a single restoration, and that's working solo. And what kind of studio backup are you going to find in a one-tractor burg like

Watsonville? You call a hundred grand big dough? You ever try to live on a hundred grand a year? Go fish.

Viewing the daily paper for leads on wealthy people collecting valuable art for purposes of prideful possession and social position, John Waldon came upon billionairess Betty Burnham's bio and sidebars, telling all, on the life and times of the reluctant mink and dry goods magnate. Recently migrated to the suburban south, Betty Burnham had joined that richest of regional traditions, the downsize flight of fancy, except of course for her art collection. It could only be called fabulous—make that amazingly fabulous, and what could she do? Leave it behind? Sell it? For what, more money? Betty Burnham, herself, responded to that rhetorical affront: "Do you mind?" Such news felt like fertile fields for a billionairess seeking growth. Just add simplicity.

Prospects improved on the third jump in the story, where the lengthy narrative got bumped to Section E by a last-minute double-truck special from none other than Burnham's, for every woman's needs.

The exhaustive tale of mind-numbing wealth with a syrupy overflow of humility was past the point of nodding off, by the time it got to Section E. Saving the sordid detail of a woman with neck-snapping skills was perhaps an effort to bury the harsh truth, yet that final leg of the long journey got crowded with iota that could hardly be called sundry. That is, rather than bury the lead, the journalist penning the narrative had participated in covering up the difficulties, some of which remained unresolved. To whit: deep in Section E came a brief reference to "youthful indiscretion" and a "blessed event" demurring obscurely on fading tracks to a bastard child.

We have germination and growth.

Sleuthing is naturally akin to acting and artistic replication, with overlapping intuition on cryptic data. Though this supposition may seem presumptive, any deductive arts practitioner will know the correlation is real. John Waldon ruminates reflectively, and Detective Sergeant Ryan comprehends with a nod.

Indeed deductive skills will overlap from one arena to the next. But how did John Waldon discover Betty Burnham's long, lost daughter, Rose Berry? It wasn't easy, till it was.

Step by step, John Waldon narrowed the range on the year of birth to a three-year period, then honed the place of birth to a regional radius and honed it finer on sheer logic and went to work. Birth records were converted to data files long ago in most places, except for those records still decomposing as microfiche—such as those in the basement archives of St. Chris Deaconess Hospital in South San Francisco, where, alas, a girl child was born unto one Elizabeth Smith in 1972—Bingo!

Maybe. Now what? For starters came the annotation that crumbled in his hands as he viewed it, near the lower edge reading: *A@B*. It could have meant anything. Adopted at Birth? Well, maybe. Who knew? The reference number following the notation could have been more than eight digits, but only eight remained. Nobody at St. Chris could ascertain the reference of the digits, but one Sarah Livingston, an elderly nurse and third generation St. Chris staffer, in the tradition of her mother and grandmother, called Waldon back. Over dinner with her nonagenarian mother, Sarah Livingston, had shared the story of the fellow looking for his long lost sister. Sarah Livingston's mother filled in the blanks: "The first three numbers are St. Chris. The second three are the adoption agency. And the third three are the parental file," old Mom said.

"Gosh," the Pimpernel rhapsodizes in the tenuous space between Detective Sergeant Ryan and himself. "Wouldn't it be nice to have an heir to whom the very essence of your soul might be passed along?" He didn't wait for Detective Sergeant Ryan's response but felt confident that he'd successfully planted another seed. Then again, he couldn't be too confident, and so he spelled it out, "I saw potential for personal gain in re-uniting a very wealthy woman with her daughter. Don't ask me how. My *spécialité* is improv. It worked out. Who could have scripted it better? But I . . . digress . . ." The Pimpernel seeks comprehension in the detective sergeant's eyes, but here again, faith is required.

The adoption agency refused disclosure of identity on adoptive parents unless the claimant could prove kinship. That was easy enough: John Waldon proved sibling status with a birth certificate showing that the Rose Berry in question and he shared the same mother. Documentation is a perfunctory challenge, after all, after replicating the Masters. The adoption agency accepted the proof and gave meaning as well to the final digit, leading to the Berry file, Harry and Betty. "Harry and Betty Berry?" the Pimpernel asked.

"We've seen worse," replied the adoption officer. "Apparently, rather than change the kid's name to Smith, like some parents giving babies up at birth want to do, Betty changed her own name from Berry to Smith. While preserving the baby's last name, it also preserved the path by which biological parentage could be traced. What Betty Berry-Smith did after that, we don't know."

Not to worry; John Waldon knew.

The rest was cake, except for working the stakeout and pickup on the long lost daughter. That was delicate and demanding. Rose's entry on the scene and into the truck was not planned or necessary. It was serendipitous and beyond that, a pain in the neck. The kid and his dog were a nuisance, but they could entertain each other, and what could Waldon do with them otherwise, leave them on the curb? No, he could not, even though the curb would have been the best launching pad to the ins and outs of life on the street, which is what every man and dog need to learn sooner or later. But leaving kids on the street can come back in all manner of criminal violations. So the kid and dog had to tag along.

The long lost daughter climbing into the truck felt like an omen, a good one. Dramatic conveyance was building, and a true thespian senses denouement in the making. The very best tension leads to a point. Rose's introduction to the scene felt like pure gravy till about forty miles out when it turned to shit.

Where did the kid and dog come from? Never mind, they squirmed and whined as a kid and dog will do—and barked. But they also turned, deftly as a plot point, from nuisance to linchpin players.

That is, John Waldon's sister, a three-time rehab dropout, needed help. Any kid is trouble. At least this kid—her kid—could keep his mouth shut at regular intervals, and he had a dog to keep him company. Besides, a man in a leading role chiefly characterized as swarthy and macho needs a dog or a kid. A dog craps outside, and that's tough to beat. But the kid was available, then he was a good match for the capricious daughter, who seemed receptive to a stint as a surrogate mother figure. It could round out her experiential resume if nothing else. So the extended family went down to Mexico North, California style. Unloading at Uncle John's new place—make that Uncle Juan's new place—felt crazy with the paintings and toasters and blenders and junk furniture. And the kid. Call him, uh . . . what was it? Panchito?

Fine, some kids and dogs can work into a scene, if they're smart, playing in the trees and dirt and ditches—like kids and dogs used to do in the used-to-be world, which appeared to be the mise-en-scène. The setup was good, except for getting her to shut up. She droned like an oscillating fan on love and life and money and money and life and love and loss, loss, loss, oh, my darling. Her script needed editing. Meanwhile, the paintings moved through the process steady as widgets on an assembly line, or maybe more like so-called art in your less sophisticated galleries, where the curators/experts got their degrees online.

But the real beauty of art replication is not so much selling fakes but in selling fakes as originals at a fraction of real value—how many hillbilly art galleries are willing to buy hot art? None is your short answer; and why sell them originals anyway when they'll buy fakes represented as legally acquired and the real McCoy? The discount is commonly called HUUUGE, so it's another win-win all the way around.

Your hot original market is a fraction thereof, comprised of very few galleries in the world—that would be gallery operators who know what they're getting and what the market will bear—and for that matter, who the market might be. Never mind which galleries are responsive to the live market; let's just say ninety percent of them are more than three thousand miles away from the source—any source. But hillbillies abound; movie stars, swimming pools.

The real payout is in originals taken from residential use and easily replaced by replicas. Maybe the change-out does not come easily, but the task fits into a dynamic cost-benefit paradigm, once labor and risk are factored against return. A seasoned marketeer then has original art to sell far closer to value with no theft report and more dough on one sale than a dozen fakes. At least that's the theory. Scoping takes time.

"Wait a minute." Detective Sergeant Ryan hates to interrupt, especially when a person of extreme interest is flowing forth. But it doesn't add up, so he has to ask, "You know this art game. So why would you take on a potential kidnapping and sexual assault rap on top of grand theft? Who needs the baggage, if you get my drift?"

"Please, Detective. Be careful. My lawyer is sitting right here, as you can see. If you want to charge me with kidnapping and sexual assault, that's your decision, but you must charge me first if you want to suggest such a thing. She got in the car. She came on to me. I knew her background. The end. Except for living happily ever after, on which we will soon raise the curtain. Surely you've heard. We're engaged to be married. Meanwhile, I also plan to be out of here in a few minutes, willing to forgive your confusion. I paid my future mother-in-law a surprise visit. Once again I'll remind you: the end. Do you think Betty will say otherwise and jeopardize her daughter's matrimonial prospects? Hasn't she caused enough damage already? Isn't it time for some support and understanding?

"Besides, the art rap would carry twenty to fifty. The other would carry life, but sometimes you need to take on a little risk to gain some insurance. *Capiche*? Reuniting mother and daughter was my plan and not for the money. I would have done it for love."

Detective Sergeant Ryan's face screws to the center at this juncture. He will not play into such a lame premise, so John Waldon explains that anyone who doesn't believe in purity and its motivational power might call him a gigolo, or a fortune hunter, or an opportunist, which behaviors, as far as he knows, are not addressed by the revised statutes of any legal code.

Then John Waldon sits back, hardly smug; he's merely finished, move to you.

Detective Sergeant Ryan suspects that John Waldon planned to ransom the artwork back to the old lady, but he can't quite form the question without incriminating the witness, which would preclude an answer. So he merely asks, "How did you plan to get the money from the old lady, so the grand reunion could begin?"

John Waldon asks back with a smirk, "How do you link irreplaceable value with mere money? Do you think a million dollars could replace a daughter given up for adoption? Maybe it could, but then a billion is a thousand million, and a loving daughter is once in a lifetime, so maybe two million would be a better exchange rate. Don't you think? Two million sounds better. It feels better. But that's between you and me. I'm sure Mrs. Burnham is already feeling very happy to have found her daughter, and now there's a wedding to plan."

Detective Sergeant Ryan looks down at his file, a tell that only the seasoned person of interest can read, indicating that the detective thinks the suspect is good, very, very good. You can't blame a detective for not wanting to compliment the slippery skills of the suspect before him, or not wanting to show admiration in any way. So he only murmurs, "Don't leave town. We'll be in touch."

So begins that most awkward social transition, in which one suspect/lawyer pair trades places with the next suspect/lawyer pair, and so face off, in transit between the waiting room and the interrogation room in the middle of a lazy afternoon. Again, with timing and panache the seasoned thespian among them lifts the scene from humdrum dregs to dramatic heights, where human emotion is succinctly tapped. John Waldon takes Rose Berry by the shoulders and murmurs at the perfect range of audience comprehension, *I love you. From the first minute I saw you, I knew . . .*

She chokes back sobs that may be tears of joy; in any event, John Waldon offers parting grist for the investigative mill, turning, profile left, with a parting line. "You know, Detective, a hundred dollars buys a couple bags of groceries and is nothing to sneeze at for poor people who work the earth. Your Big M is the real culprit here, trying to cheat a woman out of the hundred dollars he owes her for a massage."

"Thank you, Mr. Waldon. We'll look into that."

Rose sputters that it's true, wailing that he—the old guy on the bicycle—beat her and stole her money. She means beat her in business, but she said beat her. John Waldon rolls his eyes. She takes the gesture for support on the woman-beating issue as she hugs her multi-faceted fiancé around the torso, inhaling his essence deeply, just like when what's-her-name hugged Sal Mineo in *Exodus* when the bad guys wanted to separate them forever, no matter how deep their love.

Wait. That was Paul Newman.

Fuck it—John Waldon explains that a man who beats a woman in business is no different than a man who beats a woman up. Rose Berry takes it on cue, underscoring the debilitating nature of her suffering, babbling that "*hee-ee mm-mm-mmaadde mm-mme jj-jjj- jjjjjack him off and th-th-thennn he wou-wou-wouldn't pp-p-ppay me.* A hundred bucks."

The balance of Rose Berry's interview is blessedly brief, and though she's been apprised of her maternal linkage to millions that she's somehow always known were hers by rights, she is having a hard time making the leap—to *billions.* But a girl from the hardscrabble streets is no less compelled to collect her hundred bucks. She's been there—without the C-note. She won't pursue this to the bitter end, unless she does.

All of which gives the detective sergeant a splitter, nearly driving him to ask for a brief rub on the temples; it hurts so bad. He won't ask. He'll stew over grand larceny, kidnapping, and sexual assault, also briefly, and he'll wonder what's left, which appears to be very little, except perhaps for the load o' love honey in Betty Burnham's airway that she claims was not Michael Mulroney's but could have been, which compounds the headache and raises further questions.

Michael Mulroney concedes that he's only human, and yes, he did squirt pecker juice down Betty Burnham's gullet, because a guy at his age still riding long miles and also suffering fan fatigue and showbiz burnout knows he'll be found out sooner or later, especially with news dogs on the prowl and the odd couple ever willing to spew gossip. "They peeped through the window of a private residence, I might add."

But it wasn't yesterday that she blew him, and they both consented as adults when it did occur, and it wasn't a crime, and he hasn't done anything wrong, and in fact, he's being considered for candidacy to the United States Senate. As they speak.

Detective Sergeant Ryan is so stuck at this juncture that he stares off, envisioning four-wheel drive, compound low, some mongo fuckin knobbies all punching through on ten cylinders of turbo-diesel power. Now let's see who takes any shit from a motherfucking mud bog in a State motherfucking park—"What? Oh, no. Just thinking."

The detective sergeant is just thinking that he has few options remaining if he hopes to collar a perp on this one, and he's not looking forward to the damning testimony of Ms. Burnham, who happens to be in the waiting room. Herself is getting to know her daughter and her daughter's beau—and the beau's nephew and the nephew's dog, who will be like a son and a son's dog to them and, in the best possible world, a grandson and dog to her, someone to whom she can pass on the values and tenets held dear by this great country we love so much. Hearts and flowers never opened so brightly. The kid appears eager to learn.

Meanwhile, Betty takes a lead from Juan, make that John, and presses her front side affectionately against Michael Mulroney's on passing, assuring him that, "I love you. Since the first time I saw you on your bicycle and thought you were Billy Bob. But more than that: Michael, you saved my ass. Pardon me, but that's how I feel, and nothing will ever change it."

Mulroney returns a polite smile, wondering where life might have led if he hadn't walked around the corner and up the road bent on grant funding. The actual grant application was what, about one minute all told? And for what? So far it's for nothing but a heaping baggage cart, teetering precipitously with a steamer trunk full of guilt and a double duffle of poor Allison, not to mention an oversized bag bulging with Allison's revenge. That doesn't count the sheer peace of mind that went out the window on some brief flexing and wincing, followed by a messy aftermath any man would hope to avoid. The fuck. Mulroney is depressed, which shapes up as the moment, bloody and bowed, when a true player at the pro global level squints at his corner man's mug and gets the message: "These are the championship rounds."

In a mere matter of minutes, the incident is over—not exactly over, but resolved on criminal charges. Case closed. Detective Sergeant Ryan nearly bangs the gavel on this one; so urgent is his need for dismissal. And so it is, hardly a moment after Betty B says, "Oh, no! I didn't mean that Michael, you know, emitted his seed down my throat *this morning*! That was last week! I mean it seems like yesterday, but it wasn't. I was choking on yogurt. I always have a yogurt in the morning for my regularity, you know. I carry it in the car if I go out early. I have a little cooler for it, in case I'm going to be out past eight. So I was having my yogurt on the way home, like I sometimes do, and I walked in on John and . . . we were both frightened, and I choked. Michael guessed correctly; it *was* lemon yogurt. Some people don't like lemon, but I do. I like meringue too, in case you'd like to know. Michael thought it was the other, you know, spermatozoa, because I'd cleaned my shoes out back. Remember, I had dog dukey on them. Well, the only thing out there was a bottle of Clorox bleach, which I would never use, because it eats away the fabric. But the Lysol is under the sink, and I didn't want to take my shoes off, but I would have, but then I heard the commotion inside and ended up tracking dog poop inside anyway. And I already had the bleach soaked into a rag and on my fingers, and I must have touched my neck, which is what Michael smelled. You do know, Officer, that Clorox smells like splooge? Oh, dear," she titters. "That word makes me laugh. It's Michael's word, you know. He is *so* funny."

Leaving Detective Sergeant Ryan to repress his own assessment, eyes down yet again, not to hide his admiration for a slick witness but to rub his temples and summarize, "Oy vey."

XIX

Betty Burnham Gets Benevolent

Michael Mulroney consoles himself as only a world-class closer can do, that his utter indifference to Marylyn Moutard and the Brady Bunch as well as Judy the Snoot Layne can only make the property look better, as if he might just change his mind and take it off the market and live in it forever, maybe even happily ever after, though he has yet to sort the details on that scenario. And he suffers the short-termer syndrome; once out in the head and heart, he's out for good, let the dollars fall where they may. He'd sooner hang himself with slit wrists and a plastic bag over his head than live there forever, truth be told, or worse yet, go bankrupt there forever or until foreclosure, whichever comes first. The steep cliff looms perilously near, as if real life is accelerating down Hazel Dell lickety split.

But potential buyers don't know that; buyers in California want more than anything what is clearly just out of reach—so much more with a dramatic back story to share with friends over the great good times and cocktails daily and the views, views, views. Oh, God.

Consolation is marginal in a reality that seems altered. A night and a day have warped perception like a front-door peephole.

Traffic past the house is not only bumper-to-bumper nonstop; people slow down while passing so they can point and laugh over Big M, billions, blowjobs, and the United States Senate. He's not laughing, though he finds the shambles laughable. Worse yet, he's ahead in the polls.

Allison is not home. Who knows? Maybe she's off with an artistically minded photographer, seeking the perfect pose.

So sits a forlorn small business magnate in what his wife blithely calls the Blue Sky Room. Assaying the damage, Mulroney knows he's done but can't quite tell where to go or what to do. Or what he's lost. On the bright side, his fame is growing and sure to trigger a bump in sales—why buy a used car just anywhere when you can go to Big M for a great used car with a juicy story?

He has a personal stake in the California Republican Party and the exploratory committee looking into his viability. And he has much, much more, which is most often deemed desirable in the neighborhood. Then again, on the dark side . . .

At this shadowy, foreboding juncture, happy as a meadowlark on a fence at sunrise, up from her sanctuary flaps Betty Burnham, chirping a love song of her own, "Oh, Michael. It was a terrible misunderstanding. On the lemon yogurt, I mean. I mean it was lemon yogurt, not jizzbang—not yours or anyone's really. You're free. Free to go. We're free. What was it that colored man said, 'Free at last?' That's how I feel. It's been so awful. At least our love is known. That's something."

"Yeah, that's terrific."

"Oh, you. I can tell when you're joshing. I know how you feel. I can't blame you. I never meant to cause any harm. It's just that the heart falls when you least expect it."

"It's not your fault, Betty. What happened down there? With the detective."

"I told him. I was choking on yogurt. You're the one who said it was sperm. Sperm doesn't taste like yogurt. It doesn't even look like yogurt, really. Not even lemon yogurt. You really should try it sometime. Might save yourself a little grief."

Mulroney chews on developments, agonizing with a surge of regret that this entire chaos turned on his wrong presumption of bratwurst remoulade, when it was only lemon yogurt with a whiff of Clorox.

"Couldn't you taste the sugar?"

"Well, I wasn't exactly tapping the taste buds for analysis, if you don't mind. Okay, okay. It was an honest mistake, maybe, but it was bush league to say the least and still a mistake. Yogurt. Fuck."

"Come on, Michael." She pulls him up by the arm. "I know a wonderful little bistro in the neighborhood where they won't bother us. It's why I go there. Oh, don't you worry. We have ways to deal with celebrity. It's awful, but we can get by."

Mulroney is easily led. He's hungry, tired, and tired of it, wanting nothing more than to be told where to go and what to do.

In the months to come he'll look back in admiration on that brief interlude of an hour or two, what Betty calls "luncheon with just the two of us." And he honestly can't believe that Betty Burnham and Big M can take a tasteful table for two in a lovely corner of the terrace with nary a gaze or even a single head turning.

Maybe things are changing. Maybe things are only aging. Mulroney can no longer tell, though he does note that the bib salad is extraordinarily good, a flavor sensation he finds pleasantly confounding in its simplicity: a few parsed leaves, a faint sprinkle of . . . thyme? Some oil and vinegar—that was it! No balsamic! Hallefuckinlujah! Christ on a crutch; the asshole who ever thought that shit tastes good ought to be drawn and quartered—"What?"

"Oh, nothing. I just like to watch you thinking." Her bliss verges on bilious, but he cannot deny her happiness. "Don't you just love this place?"

Then comes the cream of squash bisque, which sounds revolting but isn't. It hits the spot and assuages the distraction preempting their lives. Betty B can't help it; she's a homespun gal at heart, so she pays homage to reality by plainly stating her feelings for Michael Mulroney. The "Big M" will always be welcome in her house—maybe forever, if that's what he wants because, you know, she does have some formidable means that most men would find compelling. That and their apparently mutual affection could lead to years of fun! And no matter how he feels about this proposition in the long run, she surely hopes he can find about fifteen minutes after lunch for another go on what she, for one, would consider the perfect desert.

Michael tries not to slurp, but damn that stuff is good. He savors it, allowing Betty the sanguine smile of a man who must defer to practicality. "You know I had a few million of my own, Betty. But I didn't manage so well on that one either. Frankly I like the soulful connection of living closer to the ground, like you do. But I owe so much to Allison, and I don't say this to hurt you, but I love her."

Betty touches his hand and then pats it; nothing further needs saying, so she calls for the waiter to ask if he has any of that fabulously decadent chocolate split layer cake today. He does, which works so well in palliating the moment with sweetness.

Yet dessert must wait for an interim course, a surprise perhaps, one that Betty prepared a few days ago and wanted to share, but then events got so wild in their little neighborhood. Which, by the way, has truly become home for this aging filly, and so she delivers her surprise sweetness in a soft murmur: yes, she wants to buy Mulroney's house—make that intends to buy Mulroney's house—for three point five or five point three. "Or whatever the fuck it is." She giggles. "You're so bad, and now look how you've made me talk. Like you!"

Mulroney's heart soars as his head shakes. "I can't take your charity, Betty."

"Not! Now hush!" She says the extra dough will be as a down payment on a half interest in Big M OK Cars. "But I might want to change the name to Big M & B OK Cars. I have to tell you: what you did for Lombard was a real hit. Never have I heard such resonance on a party donation."

"You knew about that?"

"I'm a Republican!"

Moreover, the package deal on the house and used car business will work perfectly for the new family she'll want ensconced just down the road and around the corner, meaning Rose and John and, of course, little Panchito and the dog. "The kid's name is actually Steven, but he likes Panchito and wants to keep it. And I suppose John can sell used cars as well as anybody."

"Do you mind?"

But Mulroney eases into the warmth of the moment, loving Betty B on a level far greater than any blowjob could achieve. Then comes chocolate split layer cake, which he loves far more than the squash bisque, and he wouldn't have thought that possible. For gallantry, chivalry, and the Republican standard, he attempts resistance once more. "You don't have to do this, Betty. It's a great house, if you want it. But don't buy it to help me. It's nearly sold. The business I can sell in a wink. Maybe."

"Oh, pshaw," she says, pulling out her checkbook and filling in the blanks. "What is it?" She looks up for guidance. "Fuck it. I'll make this for six. Have escrow credit me whatever's left. You fill in the blanks."

Mulroney wonders what Big M OK would bring in a healthy market at, say, seven times earnings—no, no, okay: six times earnings. He thinks she's about got it nailed. He doesn't know why, but tears well up, as he reaches over the table softly—make that lovingly—to whisk away a pesky crumb of split layer from the corner of her mouth.

She whimpers. The tear rolls.

"Oh, you," she chortles. "I certainly don't want to be a pushy mother-in-law, but they'll have that little place in the city as well, the one Rose is all excited about. I still can't figure out how she put that one together, but the mortgage wasn't too bad so we got rid of it, and now they can have a place in Noe Valley for, you know, that kind of fun." She makes the check for an even six, complaining that nobody ever yet invented a check with enough room for the zeroes, or maybe came up with an abbreviation for six zeroes. "You know?" Mulroney ponders the market on a bold new check with enough room for six zeros, as he asserts a C-note under a crystal goblet to cover a lunch well served. She looks up and asks, "Payable to you?"

"That would be great. But actually, you should make it payable to the escrow company."

"Oh, right. How dumb of me. I knew that. But I do trust you. You'd do the right thing. I know you would."

"Yes, I would do my best. But we need to keep the others happy."

"Yes, we do. Marylyn Moutard and Judy Layne. What a couple of cunts—I'm telling you. I think I've been around you too long." She blots the check and hands it across the table. "But I saw what those bitches were putting you through."

"Well, they can't blame everything on me."

"Don't worry. That's why I like hanging out with you, so I can watch you slaying Philistines. Tell me something, Michael. Do you think we can ever, you know, visit again? I mean, I think we could use the little Victorian place in the city."

Mulroney smiles sadly. He takes her hand to tell her he must think of getting his wife back. His wife of many years. So they sit in communion, reflecting on years and love, till he asks the poignant question that may extricate him at last while preserving everyone's best interests in escrow: "Do you remember when the Hump told Ingrid Bergman, that of all the barfly dumps in the whole motherfucking world he had to pick the dump she was hanging in? Then he said he wanted to bang her forever but couldn't because of love and all that?"

"Well, yes. I do."

"That's how it is, doll. You know what I want. You know what we can't have, on account of life and the feelings of others."

She squeezes. Then she swallows, so to speak, hook, line and sinker. Mulroney feels a huge weight rising from his shoulders and his heart—gone is the guilt of doing his wife wrong, gone is the burden of a Betty B blowjob, gone is the anxiety over being caught. And begun today is the first step toward resolution for a wandering, lonely man on an affluent ridge.

"I'm in your debt, Betty. Don't ever forget that."

"I won't forget it, Buster Brown. Just don't you forget it too. Okay?"

"Don't you worry," Mulroney assures, seeing the profound wisdom of a direct departure to a remote archipelago way yonder, over the horizon, out in the middle of the biggest ocean in the world.

Sorting and settling should be matter-of-fact but, in fact, are not. Michael M takes small comfort in the Brady Bunch's full pop offer, along with their claim that the listing contract requires the seller to sell to any party offering the listed price.

He wants to tell them to blow it out their ass or to buy something they can better afford, but he merely says, "Too little, too late. We have a full price offer that precedes yours." He does not remind them that the prevailing offer will as well avoid a sales commission paid by the seller. Nor does he remind either agent in the scrum, because he doesn't need to.

The Brady Bunch ask for a price to beat, but Big M Mulroney knows fickle markets, knows that the seasoned veteran shuts down the boiler room at the first opportunity and gets out of Dodge. What, they're going to outbid the Burnham billions? Not. Besides, he feels good, doing the right thing by his friend, she who supported him through thick and thin. He ponders a delay in the action to accommodate and savor—nay, to wallow in a bare-knuckle bidding war. He thinks Betty B wouldn't mind and would likely enjoy the sport of the thing, would likely call out, "Fuck it! Whatever!" But what could be gained, other than Betty B forking over a few more hundred thousand? Okay, another million or two, as these things sometimes go. She wouldn't care about that either, but then would come exposure to phantoms and variables, because that's what happens when a process is prolonged. Anything could unravel or turn against him. Besides, the effective operator follows the corollaries, chief among them: take the money and go.

Judith Elizabeth Cranston Layne with Coldwell Banker Clifton Baines takes the news harder than her clients and harder than the Brady Bunch and much harder than Marylyn Moutard, who insists that she will still get a hefty commish based on a claim that she first showed Betty B the house. Mulroney resists, but Betty Burnham pre-empts resistance to better keep peace in the neighborhood. "Fuck it. It's chump change for a chump. Let her get a new Beemer in chartreuse. It doesn't matter."

Judy Layne comes to Mulroney practically downtrodden to say that the truth of the matter is that Ms. Burnham first saw the house because of her, Judy Layne of Cornforth Baines. Mulroney reads the play and shuts it down. Game over. He assures Judy Layne that her accessories are as well suited as ever he's seen. He'll remember her for that, but he can't go back on the truth as it's already been established, so he must decline her offer of prior representation. Any further discourse on the subject should be between herself and Ms. Burnham's legal staff.

"Fuck," says Judith Elizabeth Cranston Layne with Coldwell Banker Clifton Baines. "We both know what she'll say."

"Only because she's already said it. You're late." At that moment, on a serendipitous phrase, Allison arrives home looking radiantly pleased that the deal will soon close; next stop hula skirts, coconut bras, mai tais, and tropical splendor.

"I'm sorry. I didn't mean mai tais. I'm going to try to stop. I know I'll need your support. Is that okay?"

He meets her sweet embrace. "Okay? It's the best news I've had in years. You stop. I'll stop. I'd trade liquor for you in a heartbeat. I think God invented reefer so I could help my best girl."

Mulroney knows by instinct that the day will come when she'll bemoan tourist traffic, centipedes, over-development, and oppressive heat. But seeing his wife at home and happy and looking forward to the next leg together, as it were, he feels good. Which is not to say that good is great, but it's easier to trust, and it's been a long time coming. So he offers humbly and honestly, "Allison, you're the greatest."

He is gratified as a global caliber closer can be, having stood his ground with lively feet and smiling eyes to bring this sumbitch home! He sees himself cycling around the bend and back to his bungalow in the tropics, whether it's a grass shack or a modest mansion, where a lovely luncheon with the little lady awaits.

Now let's pack this crap and get out of here. Okay?